THE
BECKONING

JOSH WEBSTER

A DELL BOOK

Published by
Dell Publishing Co., Inc.
1 Dag Hammarskjold Plaza
New York, New York 10017

Dell ® TM 681510, Dell Publishing Co., Inc.

ISBN: 0-440-10943-4

Printed in the United States of America

First printing—December 1980

SARAH FELT HER HEART CRINGE.
THE HORROR SHE HAD FELT
OUTSIDE, LOOKING UP AT THE
HOSPITAL, NOW LOOMED AROUND
HER IN THAT ROOM . . .

"We're glad you finally came back," the boy said, watching how that terrified her.

"We? What do you mean *we*?"

The boy burst out laughing. It was a deep, terrible, teasing laugh and suddenly Sarah knew where she had heard it before.

"No!" she cried. "Get away!"

She stood up weakly, feeling dizzy as she backed away from the bed.

"You know you had to come back," the voice told her. "You and the doctor."

"No!" she screamed. She shook her head and forced herself to walk back up to the boy. She grabbed him by the shoulders and shook him. "Peter? What are you doing? Is this a game? Peter? Peter!"

PROLOGUE

I hate them, the old man thought, as he rocked himself on the wooden cot, his hands held tight together between his thighs. I hate them. I hate them. The old man's head and face were shaven and his huge, hollow eyes sunk deep into his wrinkled skull. They wear uniforms and they're trying to hurt me just like . . . like . . . His mind went blank again and there was only the fear left. And then he remembered.

Like the bastard Union guards.

He closed his eyes and could see the prisoner-of-war camp again. It was dirty, and the stench of the near-dead clung to him like a drizzling fog in the mountains. Then he heard the sweat-box door creak open and four guards pushed the dozen near-blind, skeletonlike prisoners out with their rifle butts. The condemned were forced to stand at attention above the shallow mass grave he had helped dig, and everyone in the hospital shack who was able to walk was made to watch from the windows. He felt the sweating bodies push tight against his back.

The quick shots of the Gatling gun broke the silence like laughter from hell, lifting the prisoners off their feet, their bodies exploding red, the flesh bursting as they flopped back in their grave.

"Mr. Jackson? Mr. Jackson?"

The old man looked up at the barred window in the door. It was dark in his cell and he could only see the long blond hair reflecting the light in the hall like a halo around the shadowed oval face of the woman.

"Are you all right?"

She was thin and pretty, but he could not see that. And he could not see her small nervously clenched fists either. All the old man saw was an angel outside his cell, and he relaxed. He was hoping the angel would fling open the door and take him away from his horror forever.

He was hoping he was dead.

Then the angel was gone and he heard deep, rumbling laughter and the jangle of keys, and he was terrified again. He waited, gathering strength, then hobbled across the cell to the small barred window. He watched the young woman walk away down the hall. She had long legs and they pulled tight under her coarse gray hospital gown. She swayed in a rhythm he had almost forgotten. He pressed his cheek against the cold bars to see it longer and remember, but then the visions crept inside again and his legs would no longer hold him up. He slid down against the bolted door and cried. He cried for all the things he felt, things that were still inside, that screamed to him in his dreams, but that he could not remember.

Sarah combed her blond hair back with her fingers and obediently followed the doctor out of the locked wing of the insane asylum. She had heard his laughter first, then the keys sliding into the thick oak door at the end of the hall. He had stood, cold and black-eyed and waiting, and she had walked to him silently, her head bent, the way she had walked so many times before.

Sarah had been in the asylum for three months before he had come to her cell. She fought him then, but he beat her until she did what he wanted. Now she walked toward him like a zombie, her body no longer her own, her soul buried months ago, buried with the blood and the disgust and the terrible helplessness.

But now she had a weapon. Her body had given her that and she was hoping it would end the nightmare.

"You look tired tonight," Dr. Loman said. His voice was dark and distant to her, like an echo in a cave. It sent damp chills over her skin. She ran her fingers lightly over her stomach as he unlocked the door to his private room. It did not show yet, her weapon, but she felt it and hoped it would be enough.

The room was suddenly bright and it startled her. Dr. Loman turned and reached out to her. She stepped back.

"Now, now. Come to your doctor. You know what happens if you don't."

The woman remembered the heavy leather strap and the way he laughed and sweated when she screamed. But still, she did not walk in.

"Come along. I don't have all night," he barked.

Slowly her head lifted up until their eyes met. Sarah had never really looked at him before and now that she saw him it made her sick, but she did not bow her head. Her staring made him fidget. Suddenly she felt her pride return, something she thought she had lost forever.

"I'm pregnant," she said, still staring up at him.

"What?"

Dr. Loman's head snapped back and his face changed. He turned away.

"I'm pregnant. You did it. Please, leave me alone.

I'm pregnant. You'll hurt the baby, and it's your baby too."

The doctor paced up and down the room, then stopped. His hands were no longer moving. He grinned.

"It doesn't matter. I can fix that."

Sarah felt herself collapse. She leaned against the doorway until her legs regained their strength. She should have known it wouldn't matter.

"Come here," he ordered. He began to take off his jacket and tie.

"No," she whispered.

The doctor froze.

"What did you say?"

She stood up straight and took a fast breath.

"No," she repeated firmly.

"The hell," he laughed. He laid his jacket and tie on the desk, then began unbuttoning his shirt.

The woman stepped back out of the doorway.

"You still haven't learned," he said as he yanked his belt out from around his pants and curled it once over his big hand. Sarah felt her strength spill down out of her legs. She was not sure she could move. He approached her slowly.

"I think you need a little therapy."

"No!" she screamed. She grabbed the door, swung it shut behind her as she ran. She could hear him cursing as he fumbled with the door. Suddenly the full horror of what she had just done exploded inside her and she realized, to her despair, the futility of it all. The asylum was locked as securely as a prison.

There was no place to run.

The old man still lay crumbled against the door on the floor, but he was not crying now. He had heard shuffled footsteps again in the hall. He was too horrified to make a noise.

They're out there, he thought. Trying to get me. He took a quick gulp of air. They won't. I won't let them. Then he cocked his head. No, he cried to himself. Please, no. He heard the footsteps pass quickly by his door. Then he heard the jangle of keys and the big door at the end of the hall creaked open and boomed shut and heavier footsteps ran by.

The man slid his hand over his shaved head and shivered. He was soaked with sweat. They didn't see me. He smiled to himself and did not move a muscle. He just sat, leaning against the door with one arm bent over his head, holding his breath and listening. The hall was silent.

His smile grew into a toothless grin. He reached over his head and, grabbing the bars on the window, pulled himself up until his eyes peaked over the bottom of the small, open square. As he pulled himself up, he felt the dirty straw he had stolen from the stable to soften his wooden cot still in his fingers, and heard the barking of orders in the distance past the hospital shack. He saw the Union guards march what was left of his original platoon across the camp. Then there was the shouting of orders and a burst of shots and, looking out across the night, he saw the row of bodies heaped up over each other, their eyes huge and white and staring.

Jackson felt it all again, then he blinked and he was looking down along the empty hall with ceiling lights that made shadows in the doorways. They're still out there, he thought. In the shadows, waiting. The old man began to tremble uncontrollably. Then he smelled something, something burning. The stench of charred flesh? They're burning them again, he thought.

Then he saw the smoke bellowing thick, like a black fog, across the ceiling of the hall outside, and he realized where he was. Jesus, it's burning! He pushed at the door. It didn't budge. He started pacing back and forth across his small cell, watching the smoke filter in through the barred window. The man knew now that he was in hell. He began to laugh. He thought about the shadows in the hall and the camp and the haunting shadows of his dreams. They're all going to burn in hell. Then they can't hurt me anymore.

And his laughter grew hysterical.

Sarah dashed around the corner of the hall past her cell. The door to the other corridor, where the offices were, was locked. She held her breath and listened for the faint clanging of the keys. The sound was getting louder, closer. Her head snapped to each side looking for an escape.

Then she smelled it too. Smoke. It was curling out of the crack in the floor by her feet.

The stairs, she remembered suddenly. The heavy oak door at the end of the corridor banged open, and the woman heard the deep, hateful laughter. She inched along the wall and peeked around the corner. Dr. Loman was halfway up the hall. She sprinted across to the stair's door.

"There you are," he called in a taunting voice. The jangling of the keys grew louder and his footsteps echoed quick and hard.

She yanked open the door and dashed up the stairs. She tried the second-story hall door. It was locked. She hurried up to the third story. It was locked too.

Sarah felt her chest heaving and it was difficult to breathe. She forced herself to stand motionless so she could listen.

The sound of the keys echoed up the stairs, followed by the laughter, and she felt her heart almost stop. Her legs buckled and she fell onto the stairs to the roof. Slowly, pushing with all her might, she stood up and took a deep breath. She leaned back in the shadows against the wall.

Then she noticed there was no longer any sound of keys. Silently she stepped across the stairs and leaned around the corner to peer down at the flights below.

Dr. Loman was standing there, the belt dangling black and heavy from his hand, staring up at her. When he saw her, he laughed, and she began to back away up the stairs, her eyes locked to his, waiting to see if he would follow.

The jangle of keys began again, sending Sarah up against the door to the roof. She screamed, startled. Laughter echoed up the stairs. Then she saw smoke bellowing from under the door to the third story and she heard the muted cries. As she watched, the door exploded and a wave of heat and smoke rushed up at her.

Sarah reached frantically behind herself and yanked the latch. It was not locked. She fell out onto the roof as the door swung open. Desperately, she inched away from the stairway. She rolled over, away from the door, and lay still for a moment, trying to regain what strength she had left.

For her, the fire was a relief. She felt no fear of it yet. It had saved her from him. Minutes passed before she began to understand. She pulled herself back up on her feet and stumbled to the edge of the roof. Flames were shooting out almost half the windows of the asylum. The tortured, hysterical screaming of the patients locked in their cells began to pound in her head. Then another explosion rippled under her and a section of the roof collapsed, sending a huge tongue of flame up out of the hole. The roof was hot and her bare feet blistered as she made her way to the other end of the building.

The old man, hunched tight under his cot, felt the first explosion shake through him. He crawled out as the black smoke pushed into his room, only a foot above the floor.

Got to get out, he thought. They're going to kill us all now. No evidence. They don't want any evidence. Then there was the second explosion, and the barred window on the outside wall of his cell was blasted in across the floor. He began to crawl on his belly toward his escape. The smoke curled out the hole in the wall and he felt the hot wind behind him. Then the wooden door burst into flames and his pants were on fire and he screamed.

The crying below was terrible and Sarah could picture the other patients gasping, choking, burning in their locked cells. Only she and the three others in her wing considered harmless weren't locked up at night, but even they had no chance of escape with the hall doors locked. The horror of their fate overwhelmed her. Then she saw the iron loops over the corner of the roof. The fire escape. She ran toward it and climbed over the small ledge down the stairs to the third floor. Another explosion blew out a section of the building behind her. Bricks and glass careened out across the lawn. She spun and stared, horrified.

Slowly a white hand reached out between the bars

of the window above her head. She could hear the person crying, pleading. Then the hand pushed out as far as it could, the fingers stretched to their extremes. A flame burst out over it and the hand slipped limply back into the window.

Sarah felt her stomach wrench, and she doubled over and vomited. The iron grating burned her palms. Suddenly another hand reached out and grabbed her arm. Her head snapped up and her eyes met Dr. Loman's.

She screamed, a piercing, terrified wail, and tried to pull away. He was leaning out the hall window just above the fire escape stairs. Sarah yanked, still screaming, trying to break away. But she couldn't. In desperation, she pressed his arm against the hot iron railing with her body. He yelled and suddenly she was free. She crawled back to the iron stairs and stumbled down to the first floor. Then she put her full weight on the iron ladder and it swung down to the ground. As she climbed down, she saw the old man, Jackson, staring out at her through the open hole in the wall. His clothes were burning but he didn't move. She could swear he was smiling.

She stepped back across the lawn, watching the fire surround him. Her hands moved to cover her stomach as if she were trying to shield the unborn baby from the horrible sight.

Then she heard the creaking of the iron fire escape and, looking up, saw Loman weakly easing himself down. Flames, like huge hands, curled above him, reaching for him, but he escaped their grasp.

Suddenly the whole asylum seemed to scream, like a great wounded beast. Then the fire consumed it in one massive explosion.

It was the last thing Sarah saw before she fainted.

CHAPTER I

"They call themselves professionals, but they're hypocrites if they go through with it," Eric Loman said. He was standing in back of the crowd looking toward the new hospital.

"I don't find it so absurd," she said, edging back when a heavyset woman elbowed her way into the front of the swarm of people.

The sun stood high above the red-brick hospital, cutting a jagged shadow out over the crowd. There was a makeshift wood podium built on the stairs going into the main lobby. The mayor was there and the director of the hospital, as well as two prominent citizens who were on the board of directors. They were having a ribbon-cutting ceremony to mark the completion of the new hospital. It was a day of great pride for the town of Hapsburg and most of the residents were there. But the ceremony had not yet begun.

"I'm a psychiatrist, Lisa. I just don't believe a young girl could be possessed by a demon. It's ridiculous. She's very sick, her subconscious is in turmoil—but possessed? The hell with that crap," he said, shaking his head.

Lisa Mitchell glanced up at Eric. He was tall and thin, with thick black hair and a long black mustache. His eyes were deepset and dark and always seemed to be questioning her when she looked up into them. It was as if he had a secret only he understood, something that was not for others to know. Lisa liked to draw strength from that. She knew she would always trust his eyes. They did not lie.

"I don't think it's just superstition," she said. They were holding each other with their eyes now and they were no longer a part of the crowd. "There have been recorded cases. I know it's a religious phenomenon, but there are records to verify at least the possibility. Even if it is ridiculous, maybe the exorcism will help her. Who knows?"

"It could destroy her too. If they bring in a Jesuit priest and perform an exorcism it will admit to exactly what she wants to believe, that part of her *does* believe. It could take her over the edge. She might never come back. It could even kill her in her weakened condition."

"Or it could help."

Eric sighed as he thought back to yesterday's session.

Eric Loman looked through the one-way window, then unlocked the door to Security Room 513 of the psychiatric ward in St. Mary's hospital in downtown Philadelphia. The room was small and gray and sterile. There were no cords or sharp objects, and there was no handle on the inside of the door.

"Hello, Carol," he said, walking in. He looked at the ten-year-old girl and felt the sadness again crawling down through his throat. She was small, with thick yellow hair that was matted now and uncombably tangled. Her face and arms were covered with festering boils, and there was no longer any brightness in her eyes. The room stank of urine and vomit. No matter how much they cleaned, the stench would not go away.

Bob Thompson, Eric's immediate superior, followed him in, then stepped sideways next to the bed. The small girl jerked her head off the pillow. Her eyes were swollen and black and they burned as she stared. Bob felt the burning in his guts. She would not take her eyes off him.

"So how is Carol today?" Eric asked, forcing a smile and an easy tone.

"Fuckers," a rasping old woman's voice said out of Carol's mouth. Her voice reminded Eric of a child trying to imitate a witch, but it was deeper than that, more real.

"Nice language for a child," Bob said.

Carol sprang up and hissed through her teeth. Her breath was overpowering and Bob coughed. Then Carol cackled. It was a horrible deep cackle. Bob stepped back away from the bed.

"There is no Carol," the rasping voice said. "Only me."

"And who are you?" Eric asked calmly.

Carol flipped off her covers. Her chest began to heave and she gasped for air. Suddenly she hunched over, hugging herself tightly with her arms as she choked, trying to inhale. Bob reached out to her, frightened, and she sprang. Her small, bony hands curled like claws and flared out to scratch his face. It startled Bob, and he moved to grab her wrists. He was not quick enough. Her fingers uncurled and cut two lines of blood on both of his cheeks before he could pull them away.

"Damn," Bob muttered. He was trying desperately to control her, she was unbelievably strong. Eric stepped in, took one of her arms, and together they held her down on the bed.

"Do you want restraints again?" Eric asked sternly.

"You can't hold me," the voice threatened. "Just try. I'll get you. I'll get you!"

The voice made Eric tremble. He felt a shiver run through his chest but he steeled himself so she would not feel it in his hands.

"I hate you," the voice yelled. Then Carol turned her head toward Bob and spit in his face. The spit was bloodstreaked and oozed down under his eye.

"I hate you," the voice cried again, "you cock-sucker!"

"Maybe you should wait outside," Eric said to Bob.

"Can you hold her?" Bob asked, trying his best not to lose his temper. He could feel the saliva hot and wet, sliding down his cheek, but was holding Carol's wrist with both hands and couldn't wipe it off. It was making him queasy.

"Sure," Eric said.

"You got her then." Bob released her arm and pulled back quickly. Carol did not jump up. That surprised him. She lay quietly with one arm free, staring at him through her black-rimmed eyes. He stepped away from the bed, never turning his back to her until he was at the door.

"Jesus Christ," he mumbled to himself as he wiped off her bloody saliva. Then he left.

Eric slowly let go of the child's wrists. He waited, then sat softly on the corner of the bed. Carol watched him without moving her head.

"You shouldn't have clawed him," Eric said. "Or spit."

The little girl hissed through her teeth.

"I should have ripped out his balls and stuffed them down his fucking throat."

Eric had heard all of it before. She always tried to shock him with new and foul words, but now there was no shock left. Eric let the last comment slide.

"Little girls have pretty curls," he sang to himself, remembering the commercial. "But I love Oreos."

Frustrated by her inability to shock him, Carol screamed. Still Eric did not react. She looked at him and growled but his face remained impassive. Finally Eric leaned toward her and let out a scream of his own. It was a terrifying howl.

Carol jumped back against the wall behind the bed, and her eyes widened in fear. Then the fear faded and he could see the tears in her eyes, and the pain.

"Carol?" Eric asked softly.

The little girl nodded. Then she began to cry. Eric wondered if it was a trick—but if it wasn't, it meant that she needed something, someone, and it was up to him to help her. Eric reached out to her and brought her skeletonlike body up close against his chest. She was shaking and sweating, and she stank, but Eric held her and ran his hand over her matted hair until she stopped crying. Then he laid her in the bed and pulled the covers up over her chest.

"How do you feel?" he asked, wiping the sweat from her forehead. And how do I feel? he asked himself, watching his hands shake.

A tear grew in the little girl's eye and slowly rolled down her festered cheek. Eric nodded to her reassuringly.

"I'm scared." Her voice was soft now, warm and trembling.

"With me here?"

Carol smiled up at him.

"I like you," she said, still smiling. "You aren't sick when you look at me."

"Why should I be? You're a very pretty little girl." He reached out and took her hand in his.

Suddenly Carol pulled in her hand and doubled over in pain. The pain grew, and Eric could see it in the slow twisting that contorted her face. A feeling of helplessness burned inside him.

"Oh. Oh, it hurts," Carol groaned. She was holding herself with her knees pressed tight against her chest. "Make it go away. Please! Oh, no . . . Please!" Then she screamed. It was a little girl's scream, and it pierced through Eric like a sword.

"Kill me," Carol cried. She reached toward him frantically. "Please. It hurts too much. Oh, please. Please kill me!"

Eric felt his chest tighten. He couldn't stand it anymore. He grabbed her by the shoulders and shook her.

"I can't kill you. And *it* can't kill you either," he yelled. "It's nothing. It's just your imagination. It's not real. It has no control over you."

Carol stared up at him. There were tears rolling down his cheeks. Slowly she reached up with one hand and touched his tears. Then she tried to smile.

"It's gone now," she said.

"What's gone?"

"The pain. It stopped hurting me because it wants me to remember what it's like without the pain."

"Why does it do that?" Eric asked. He dreaded the answer because he knew it already.

"Because when I know what it's like without the pain, it makes the pain even worse when it comes."

Eric decided to talk as if the demon were real for a moment, so he could understand it better.

"Why is there pain at all?" he asked.

"Only when I come back. It lets me come back sometimes. But if I do anything, there is the pain."

"You are not in pain now," Eric said.

She kept her eyes on him, and he could see she was thinking.

"You're right," Carol said happily. "I'm talking with you and there's no pain. I'm me again." She giggled to herself, and it made Eric laugh too.

"Carol," he said. She stopped giggling and looked back up at him. "You know there is no such thing as demons, don't you?"

"There is," Carol objected. "They come from the devil. I saw one. I told you this before."

"Where did you see one?"

"I saw one in the movies. You know that."

"You know that movies are make-believe. Like cartoons. Like when you play with your friends and make up stories."

"No," Carol said firmly. "My mother told me there are demons that come for little girls if they aren't good. She says the devil sends them."

That was new to Eric, and it frightened him. He had tried before, but the girl would not talk about her mother. He remembered the first words her mother had said to him when he had admitted, to her obvious disdain, that he was a psychiatrist. "As wax melteth before the fire, so let the wicked perish at the presence of God," she had warned. Eric sighed and looked at Carol. There was a pleading in her eyes now. At least it's something to work from, he thought. That's more than I had before.

"Your mother is wrong," Eric said bluntly. He didn't know any easy way to do it.

"No," she whispered.

"What?"

"She's not wrong," Carol said. "I know. I'm possessed."

"You're not possessed. You just think you are. It's a game, Carol. Just another game. Like playing house. It's make-believe. It's not real."

"They believe I'm possessed too," she said quickly.

"Who?" Eric asked.

"The nuns. They're going to bring in a priest. I heard them talking about it."

"It's not true," Eric said. He felt the anger grip his ribs and he hunched over to ease the squeezing. "You are not possessed. They are just doing that to be safe. It's a game. That's all." Eric wished he could believe that.

Carol shrugged but said nothing. Then there was a knocking at the door.

"Dr. Loman, you have a call," a nurse said from behind the door.

"Thank you, I'll be right there." Eric watched Carol watching him. Then he took a deep breath. "Carol, I have to be honest with you. You know that I'm always honest with you, don't you?"

Carol nodded and watched his eyes intently.

"I don't believe in this exorcism. You aren't possessed and I'm going to try to keep them from bringing in that priest. If I fail, they may fire me and I won't be able to see you then."

Carol's eyes tightened and her hands balled into fists. Eric felt as if he were hurting her now too.

"You're not going to see me anymore?" she asked. Eric could see she was near tears again. He knew it was a hard thing to say, and harder still for her to understand, but he had a policy about being honest that he could not break. He shoved his hands in his pockets to conceal their shaking.

"I'll sure try. You can bet on that."

"I'm scared," Carol whimpered. He could see her closing up, shrinking away from him. "You're the only one who makes the pain go away," she cried. She was beginning to rock as she lay in bed.

"I don't make the pain go away. You do. I just help. But you're the one who does it. It's all inside you, Carol."

Her rocking grew frenzied, then she bolted upright.

"Damned right, fucker. I'm inside her," the low voice bellowed. "I'm her life now. She is nothing. Nothing but a hollow, disgusting shell for me to fester."

"You're nothing," Eric screamed back. It had startled him, but he used his temper to hide it. "Carol is real. You are nothing."

"I'll kill her," the voice warned, crackling. Blood started to push through her teeth as she hissed, and there were red lines running down to her chin.

"You have no power," Eric said calmly. Don't let it get to you, Eric told himself. You'll give it power if you do.

"I'll kill you too," the voice warned. Then there was the loud haunting laughter again, and she spat at Eric. It hit him in the shoulder. "I'll kill her. I'll kill her!"

"Liar," Eric yelled back. The confrontation was past logic now, past being careful, and he knew it. "You have no power. You just make me sick." Eric jumped off the bed and Carol pulled up into a ball against the wall. Eric saw now that he had scared her, and it startled him. He decided to go with it again.

"You're nothing! *Nothing!* All I see is a scared little girl. No demons. No devils. Nothing but Carol."

"Arghh." The sound was more animal than human. It made Eric's skin tighten over his body. "I'll kill her," the voice cried.

"No, you won't," Eric yelled back, moving toward Carol.

"Keep away," the voice hissed.

"Why?" Eric yelled. "Are you scared of me?"

In answer, she spit at Eric.

"Is that it? The big power? Spitting?"

Eric laughed, pushing himself closer to her.

Carol turned away. She started to cough and began to choke. Blood flooded up out of her mouth and down, like a river, across her chin. She tried to scream but nothing came out. She could not take in a breath. Her face turned white, then a light yellow-blue, and her eyes bulged out wide and red.

"Nurse," Eric screamed, dashing to the door. "Bring something to open her throat. Bring twenty-five milligrams of Thorazine, too."

The little girl was frozen tight against the wall, terrified, gasping futilely for her life. Eric could barely look at her as he tried to force her mouth open. Then two nurses came in with metal clamps and a hose. One pried open Carol's mouth while the other, with Eric holding the arm, gave Carol the shot. Slowly, the child loosened up. Then there was the sound of air passing through the hose and her arm went limp in Eric's hands.

Eric shuddered. He scanned the crowd again, then looked back down at Lisa. She had big green eyes and short brown hair. His arm trembled as he put it around her, pulling her close. To Eric, she was the most beautiful woman in the world, and just looking at her now made him feel better about yesterday. He still wanted to argue, though, that a hospital was no place for superstitions, religious or otherwise, and that being a nurse Lisa should understand that. It was a place for facts and for science and for caring. But before he could, Sherry Mellany, the new hospital's director, tapped the microphone and the amplifiers screeched, causing the crowd to jerk their heads and become immediately silent. He decided it was not the time to argue anymore. He had done too much of that already.

"I'd like to welcome all of you here," she began. "Hapsburg Hospital is a progressive step for our ever-growing town . . ."

"A bunch of zombies," Eric filled in quietly through the side of his mouth. Lisa smiled and slipped her hand into his. Then she stood up on her toes to try to see the podium.

"It must be nice to always be able to see a crowd," she said. A man in front of her turned and glared. Lisa and Eric glanced at each other, both raising their eyebrows to comically imitate the man's disdain. But the playful look faded from Lisa's face as she saw a man approaching behind Eric. She gripped Eric's arm tightly with her free hand. He did not have to turn around to know who was there.

"Hello, kid," John Loman said.

Eric's eyes stayed fixed on the podium.

"Hi, Dad," he said.

John Loman pushed two people to the side to face his son.

". . . Now, too, we will all feel safer, better protected . . ." Sherry Mellany lectured over the loud-speaker.

"Bullshit," John announced.

A few heads turned, but John glanced around as if someone else had made the remark, and they looked away.

"I thought you were supposed to be on the podium too," Eric said quietly. Lisa felt his hand tense up in hers. She decided to stay out of it. She already knew how it would go.

"I am." John laughed and Eric could detect the strong smell of bourbon.

"It's not even noon," Eric said, still not looking at his father. "A little early to be drunk."

"I didn't know there was a specific time. When is that? I'll make a point of getting drunk then too. I'd hate to miss it."

Lisa kept both hands on Eric's arm and stayed between him and his father. A pleasant fall breeze curled down over the crowd. Lisa glanced up at Eric and saw the sweat rolling down from his forehead. She wished there was some way she could help, but she knew there wasn't. It was like this every time the two men saw each other.

". . . and now I'd like to introduce to you the builder of this fine hospital, John Loman. I see he's in the back with his son, who, I might add, has been offered a job here as our first resident psychiatrist."

There was scattered applause and a couple of cat calls. The town liked John Loman almost as much as he liked the town. It was a mutual hate relationship.

"I'm leaving," John mumbled.

Eric grabbed his father's arm as he tried to make his way out the back of the crowd. Lisa could see Eric was enjoying his father's sudden discomfort.

"They're all waiting. Come on, Dad. You've got to go up there and give a speech. You promised her."

John hesitated, glaring angrily, then yanked his arm out of his son's grip and shoved his broad shoulders through the crowd.

"This should be good," Eric said under his breath.

"I don't even want to hear it," Lisa answered.

But Eric laughed.

"I do. Come on. Let's move up to the front."

"I don't know—"

"Come on."

Eric tugged her by the arm. They slid in and out of the crowd until they were on the bottom steps below the podium. There were a few big clouds pushing down through the open sky above the hospital. The wind picked up again, blowing the red, white, and blue banners out straight above the speakers' heads.

"Ladies and gentlemen of Hapsburg, P.A.," Loman began. "I'd like to welcome you all here. I'd also like to say that this hospital has all the most modern facilities and equipment available."

"You tell 'em, load-head," a heckler yelled. The crowd laughed uncomfortably.

Eric looked over his shoulder at the people around him. A few feet away, a man was laughing hard, his son by his side. Eric glanced down at the child. He was about ten years old with a beautiful oval face accentuated by glossy black hair and glistening black eyes. The child peered up, confused. There was a sadness to his look, an old, tired sadness, that reminded Eric of how he had felt during most of his youth. He smiled and nodded. The little boy looked away quickly.

"Daddy," he said quietly as he pulled on his father's shirt sleeve. Eric pretended to gaze up at the podium as he leaned slightly to hear the boy.

"What is it, Peter?"

"Why didn't Grandma come with us?"

"She doesn't like this place."

"The hospital?"

The child was frowning, trying to understand.

"Yes, the hospital, this whole place. She's superstitious. Besides, she had a bad experience here once, in the old hospital that used to be here. It scares her."

"Like the way Mom scares me sometimes?" Peter's voice was soft and tentative.

The father suddenly grabbed his son's arm. Peter gasped.

"That's no way to talk. Your mother doesn't scare you or anyone. You understand?"

Eric could see the little boy was frightened. He stared up at his father and said nothing. His father squeezed harder.

"Do you understand?"

"Yes."

Then the man let go of his arm.

"There used to be another building here?" Peter asked shyly, trying to make amends.

"Just be quiet."

"As usual," John Loman was saying, "this building was erected by the best crews in this town. Loman Construction. You are all familiar with us and know, from our track record, that we use only the finest materials. I'd also like to add that we finished the hospital two months ahead of schedule."

"Hey, Loman," the man near Eric yelled. He edged his son back behind him to get a better view. "This ain't no commercial. Quit the bull."

John stared down at his new heckler, then swayed to focus. He had to grab the microphone stand to keep his balance.

"Hey," he said, pointing at the man. "You want to

come up here and give a speech? Come on, Delmont. Come on up."

Sherry Mellany edged in front of John and politely took the microphone out of his grip.

"Thank you, Mr. Loman. We are all pleased that the hospital was built ahead of schedule. Now let's hear from Mr. Compton, Vice-Chairman of the Board, and President of Hapsburg Savings and Loan."

John Loman backed away from the edge of the podium. One of his employees, Joe McFarland, a huge, hard-looking man, was waiting for him by the ladder at the side of the podium. He raised his hands to help John as he began to descend.

"Good speech," the big man snickered.

John waved his hand at him, disgusted.

"They're going to serve champagne in the second-floor lounge. We might as well start without them."

John Loman paused. "Might as well."

In the second-floor lounge there was a large table spread with food. The centerpiece was a cake made in the shape of the hospital, and surrounding it were small delicate sandwiches. Banners with "Good Luck" written on them were tacked to the walls and balloons dangled from the ceiling.

The bottles of champagne were in an antique wash basin filled with ice. McFarland grabbed one of the bottles, unwrapped the wire and popped the plastic cork. When it began to bubble over, he put the bottle to his mouth and drank until the foam stopped. Then he passed it to John.

"Here's to another building finished," John toasted, raising the bottle up above his head.

"And another check in the mail," the big man grinned.

John laughed, then drank and passed it back to Joe, his foreman of the last twenty years. He surveyed the room and rubbed his face as if he were washing it.

"Some speech, huh?" he sighed.

"The hell with that Delmont guy," Joe added, passing the bottle back.

"The hell with the whole town."

John put the bottle down on the table next to the big white cake. He glanced seriously at his friend, then walked to the large metal-framed window that rose up almost to the ceiling. It was nearly seven feet tall. He leaned forward, his hands on the windowsill. The foreman watched his shoulders tense down through the muscles in his forearms.

"They hated me ever since I could remember," John said, staring down at the crowd, then past them to the small town and the thick, green, slow-arching mountains that surrounded it. "They never gave me a chance, Joe. Never."

The foreman was curious because he had never heard John Loman talk about anything even remotely personal before. He breathed through his mouth to be extra quiet. He did not feel uncomfortable, but he did not dare interrupt. To him, John Loman was, and always would be, the boss.

"I tried at first. I built hard and well and nothing came of it. They tried to break me from the start. Twice I almost went bankrupt—until I learned to beat them at their own game. Now they do what I say and hate every minute of it." John turned from the window and stared at Joe. "And I'm glad as hell. They made the rules, but I learned quick and now I hold the cards. I deal to *them* and if they don't like the hand they got, they can fold for all I care."

Joe nodded as Loman offered him the bottle of champagne.

"To our next building," Joe announced.

He raised the bottle high to toast, then drained it in one gulp.

"I suppose we should get out of here," Eric said.
"Right."

Lisa took his hand and led him around the front of the crowd to the parking lot. She was glad to be away from all the people. A relative newcomer, by Hapsburg's standards, she had moved there after getting her nursing degree over eight years ago, but she still did not fit in. For the most part, strangers were not trusted; certainly not young women without families. Lisa's father had been dead for six years and her mother, who still lived in New Jersey, rarely came to visit in Hapsburg. Lisa thought the land was beautiful and the weather was good, and for the last seven years Eric had come back from Philadelphia almost every weekend to visit and that was wonderful too. But the people were still unfriendly and hard to get close to, and although they were never openly hostile, neither did they go out of their way to speak to her. For most people, that would have driven them away, but for Lisa, the anonymity, the personal seclusion was something she had grown accustomed to and enjoyed. It was a welcome relief from the constant gossip she had grown up with in her small hometown in New Jersey.

"Sherry certainly tried to put you on the spot, didn't she? Announcing your job offer in front of the town before you had given her your answer."

Eric Loman smiled.

"She's a smart businesswoman. She knows what she wants and how to get it."

"You are talking about a job now, aren't you?"

Eric put his arms around Lisa and she leaned up close against his chest.

"What'd you think I was talking about?"

Lisa stood up on her toes and kissed him quickly.

"Your body."

Eric laughed and they hugged.

"It would be wonderful if you took the job here at the hospital. We'd be together all the time then. Not just on weekends. We'd even be working together. That'd be fun. I miss you so much sometimes."

She intertwined her fingers in his and squeezed. Eric gazed down into her face.

"I miss you too, but . . ." Eric sighed and looked up at the sky, then down at the asphalt. "But I have a job to do in Philly. There's Carol and . . ." He couldn't finish so Lisa did it for him. She had heard it before.

"And then there's your father here. And the town. Neither of which you think too much of." She put her other hand over the one already locked in his. "But you don't have to see John if you live here. We could be alone together. It's not that—"

"I see him everywhere, Lisa. Besides it's not just him. I don't know. I have bad memories of this place. It's hard sometimes when every street reminds you of things you'd rather forget."

Lisa leaned her head against his chest. She knew he did not want to talk about it anymore and understood why.

In the front of the crowd, Peter was staring up at the big window on the second floor of the hospital, above the antique oak doors. He could see the man who had frightened him earlier when he had yelled down at his father. Peter glanced at the other windows across the hospital. The two huge windows above the oak doors were twice the size of any of the others and Peter, squinting now to look up as the sun reflected off the glass, thought that the entrance to the hospital looked like a gigantic and terrifying face. The boy shivered.

The last speech was over and the crowd was beginning to disperse across the lawn and the parking lot when Peter yanked on his father's sleeve. The man glanced down.

"There's the man you don't like, Daddy. The one who yelled at you," Peter said, pointing to John Loman through the second-floor window.

Delmont peered up above the oak doors. He was still angry after being confronted, almost challenged, by John Loman, and seeing him now behind the window, a bottle in his hand, he decided to get even.

"Hey, Loman," he yelled. "Isn't it a little early to be hittin' the sauce? I heard you like to overindulge, even when you're on the job. What's the matter, can't you cope?"

"Did you hear that?" Joe McFarland asked, opening another bottle and handing it to his boss.

"What'd he say?"

"I couldn't get all of it."

Joe undid the latch of the window and pushed. The window was heavy, but slid easily. He gripped the bottom edge and pulled it up.

"Damn," he muttered. "We sure found some cheap shit."

John glanced over and saw blood dripping out between Joe's fingers.

"That goddamn metal was never finished. It's sharp as a razor. Full of small pointed edges and heavy as hell too." Then he snickered. "When it comes to cheap material, you're the master, John. I don't know where you find half this crap." He shook his head as he grabbed a paper napkin to wipe off the blood.

Loman laughed. "My secret."

Then he walked toward the huge open window and quickly examined Joe's hands. "Are you all right?"

"Sure." He threw the blood-soaked napkin on the floor and wrapped a clean one around his fingers.

John Loman leaned his head out the window and scanned the crowd. Delmont was walking up to the stairs. His son was following, an embarrassed look on his face.

"You got something to say?" John taunted, staring down at him.

"I said you're a drunk. But everyone already knows that, don't they?" Mr. Delmont laughed and turned to the crowd for approval. There were a few snickers.

Hearing the commotion, Eric turned to watch. Lisa stood behind him. She was tired of the ceremony and of the crowd and of John Loman and his hecklers. She just wanted to go somewhere in the hills with Eric and be alone, away from other people's problems.

"They keep trying to get him," Eric said. "One constant battle. I don't think he'd like it any other way."

Leaning out, John Loman felt a sudden dizziness. He slipped down on his elbows, stretching his head further out the window.

"You're no teetotaler yourself, Delmont," he yelled. "But at least the town buys me champagne. That's more than they'll ever do for you!"

Peter was frightened. He stepped sideways to avoid Loman's gaze. Then suddenly the boy's face changed.

He stared fearlessly up at the open window as his small fists banged against his hips.

"You'd better watch your mouth, Loman," Delmont called.

"We're gonna get him," John breathed, glancing back in at Joe. Joe grinned.

"Hey, Loman," Mr. Delmont yelled again.

John stuck his head out further and stared. The Delmont boy was looking him square in the eyes. His cold, unflinching face startled John.

"I just wanted you to know that . . ."

Joe saw the window twitch just before it went. He leaped forward but was too late. The huge metal-edged window slammed down like a guillotine, slicing through John's neck as if there were no bone there to stop it.

The boy saw it too, and then the blood gushed out like a broken fire hydrant and John Loman's decapitated head splattered onto the stairs, rolling down to the boy's feet. For a moment, the boy just stood silent, smiling, staring at the white, bulging eyes, still pounding his hips with his fists.

Then Peter saw the puddle of blood around his feet and the blood splattered on his shirt and pants and he began to scream.

CHAPTER II

Eric Loman did not sleep much that night. The next morning he rose before the sun and watched it slowly creep up through the pines on the eastern range of mountains. The sky became gray, then gray-blue, then turquoise, and the heavy, low-hanging clouds from the northwest were streaked with orange and yellow. Eric was trying not to think, really, only to feel the new day.

He had thought too much all night.

Then a hand clutched his shoulders and he flinched. Lisa smiled down at him and he took her hand in his.

"You had nightmares," she said quietly. The day was too still and too new for anything but whispers.

"I don't remember."

"You cried out once and I held you, but you never woke up."

Eric squeezed her hand gently. He was feeling that strange hollowness again and it hurt inside like a long, terrible hunger. There was no one left now. Good or bad, it didn't matter. He was the only Loman left. It was a deep, cutting pain to know that and finally declare it to himself. There was no hiding, no strong shadows to pretend in, and that was why Eric had sat by the window for the last hour. He was saying goodbye.

"No one will come," he said, staring at the thick rolling clouds, almost black now on the west side, bright orange and gold on the east.

"I'm sure they will," Lisa lied. She did not think anyone would want to go to John Loman's funeral either. "At least that man Joe, his foreman, and the crews and the people he built buildings for."

Eric looked up over his shoulder and smiled. There was still that sadness lined in his face that Lisa had watched all last night. She sat on the arm of the chair, her hand on the back of his neck, caressing him gently.

"No one will come," Eric repeated. "Hell, I don't really want to go either. It doesn't seem right. But . . ." Eric sighed and leaned back in the chair. Lisa moved her hand away and watched as Eric quickly wiped his eyes. "Mom would have wanted me to go. She loved him. I don't know why, but she did. I'll go because of her. Not because of him."

Lisa slid down onto Eric's lap and he held her close as if she were the only thing left in the world that mattered. Feeling her body, soft and warm against his, took the empty chill away. The sun pushed up bright and yellow-round and clear as the clouds moved below it. Soon Eric and Lisa were asleep in the chair.

An hour later the phone woke them. It was Lisa's apartment so she answered it.

"It's for you. It's Bob." She handed Eric the phone. He stared at it before he lifted it to his ear. He did not want to hear what Bob was going to say. Too much had happened already.

"They're bringing the priest in today," Bob announced. "He's going to perform the exorcism. He's got permission from the top."

"Who, God?"

Eric stood up and walked the phone around the coffee table. He sat down and lit a cigarette.

"You said you wanted to know."

"Thanks, Bob, I'm driving there now. Good-bye."

"Carol?" Lisa asked.

"They're going to do it. The fools."

Eric hurried into the bedroom to finish dressing.

"Lisa?" he called. She walked over and leaned against the door. "Would you take care of the details for the funeral? It's pretty much all arranged, but there's still the flowers to get and . . . Hell, this thing with Carol couldn't have come at a worse time. I'm sorry."

"I know you have to go to Carol. Don't worry, I'll take care of things here."

"Thanks. I'll be back tonight—I hope. If not, early tomorrow. Before—before the funeral."

Eric put on his jacket and hurried to the door. He stopped suddenly and looked back at Lisa. His face was pale and Lisa saw how his hands fumbled nervously at his coat buttons.

"I'll be all right," he said as she ran to hug him. When she let go, Eric held on and squeezed her against him again, then backed away.

"Well," he said, trying to smile. "Here goes my job. I never liked Philly anyway."

The Jesuit priest was huge, almost six-eight, and wore an enormous gold cross on a chain around his neck. He walked silently into the hospital, his hands held before him as if in prayer.

Dr. Robert Thompson watched him as he nodded to the nuns, then was escorted to the Sister Superior's office. When he passed, Bob glanced up at him. The priest's big sunken gray eyes stared down through him. Bob was not sure if the priest had even seen him. That made him shiver. He wondered how much longer it would be before Eric arrived.

It was over an hour before the priest and the nun came out of the office together. Bob had been called on the intercom and met them outside the security ward.

"Dr. Thompson," the sister introduced, "this is Father Gregory."

There was no handshaking, only a nod.

"Please help him in every way possible," she instructed him.

Bob knew why she had chosen him for this, but it did not make him angry. He had not let himself get angry at things like that for a long time.

"Is it a little girl?" the priest asked. His voice was heavy and distant. Bob wondered if he were deliberately trying to make it sound that way.

"Her name is Carol," Bob answered.

"Then I will need a nun present," Father Gregory commanded.

Bob nodded and looked at the Sister. She smiled and walked away to choose the proper nun. Bob could see she was enjoying the priest very much.

"I have been told there is a small chapel here," Father Gregory said.

"On the first floor," Bob said. He was beginning to feel a twinge of anger now. He did not like the way the priest talked down at him without even the courtesy of looking at him.

"The girl must be prepared and brought there. Sister Superior knows what to do," he said. "I will wait in the chapel. One more thing, Doctor. No one will be allowed in once she has been brought down. And another thing, since you are one of her doctors, exorcism is not a miracle. It takes time. To rid the girl of her demon will probably not be achieved with one rite. It is a delicate and terrible ordeal. And we are not fully convinced, yet, that she is possessed."

Already setting himself up in case he fails, Bob thought. Can't lose either way now. Bob wondered if he were being unfair. He knew he didn't want to like the priest from the beginning.

Bob showed Father Gregory to the small chapel which contained only six pews and a small pulpit up front. There were two long windows and a silver cross on the wall.

Father Gregory watched two orderlies wheel Carol in, strapped on the bed. He was standing behind the pulpit with the big silver cross above him reflecting the light from the windows. Bob stared at the priest, noticing that he did not change his expression when he looked down at Carol. That surprised the doctor. It was not easy for anyone to look at Carol now. He wondered if the priest saw something the rest of them did not, and wished Eric were there already. He did not know what to do without him.

When Sister Patricia entered, Father Gregory asked Bob to leave the chapel. The doctor looked back at Carol and realized he was glad to be told to go.

The priest caressed the gold cross on his chest as he walked toward Carol. She did not move her head but watched his approach with her red, swollen eyes like a cat watching its prey approach unwarily. Sister Patricia stared at the priest because she could not look at Carol without wanting to cry. She had to remain strong now and she knew it. Her job was to restrain the child when needed because the child was female, and it was not for the priest to do.

Father Gregory began to chant a prayer, then another and another. Then he read psalms from the Bible. He called to the unholy spirit as he read, and from outside Bob could hear his resonant voice pounding against the walls of the chapel.

Then the Father asked the nun to unstrap the girl. It frightened her because she had seen what Carol could do and she tried to protest, but Father Gregory glanced at her with his deep gray eyes and she did as she was told.

Carol watched them, her head flickering now from one to the other. She did not move or speak. The Sister unstrapped her without looking at her face, and when she undid the last strap, she jumped back. Carol did not move.

Father Gregory held out his cross from the chain around his neck and began to chant. He reached out slowly with his other hand to place it on Carol's forehead. Instantly Carol sprang at him with a scream that ran down Bob Thompson's spine like ice. She gripped the priest's outstretched hand and bit him viciously between the thumb and forefinger. He did not cry out. Blood trailed down the sides of her mouth as she ripped at his flesh.

Sister Patricia screamed and grabbed the girl's mouth, trying to pry it open. Bob rushed in to the chapel, an orderly with him, and together they held Carol down, limb by limb, on the bed.

"You shouldn't have unstrapped her," Bob said. Then he saw the priest's hand, dripping blood at his side.

"I'll call a nurse in for that hand," Bob said.

"No," Father Gregory said.

"But it'll need stitches," Bob argued.

"Please leave and take this orderly with you. We do

not need your help. Do not return unless I ask you to."

"But she was—"

"Please," Father Gregory emphasized.

Bob shrugged, looked at the orderly, and gestured toward the door. They left abruptly.

"I did not want to reprimand you in front of them," the Father said, glaring at the nun. "But you should not have screamed. You proceeded quickly to do what you are here to do, but you should not have screamed."

"I'm sorry, Father," she said. It hurt her to have him say that. She had wanted to please him because she had heard of his reputation and also because she was chosen by Sister Ellise especially for this job. Then she looked down at Carol, her face splattered with blood, those eyes poking up hatefully from their sockets, and she realized something she should have seen before. This was not a job. It was something completely different. They were battling something too horrible to imagine, and they were battling that horror for a human soul. Sister Patricia believed that now and found she could look at Carol without turning away. She wondered why she had not believed it before.

"Can you control yourself now, Sister?"

"Yes, Father," she said. He nodded to her without looking up from Carol's face.

Eric parked the car and ran into the hospital. He bounded up the stairs, not wanting to wait for the elevator, and stopped at the locked door of the security ward where he pressed the buzzer. Old Tim sauntered to the door, smiled, and waved at Eric.

"I want to see her," Eric said.

"Not here," Tim replied.

"What?" Eric yelled.

"Not here," he said again. "They come and took her

away. Got a priest for her today. She's gonna get—"

"Where did they take her?" Eric asked. He was shifting his weight from one foot to another as if he were still running. He could not slow himself down.

"Don't know," old Tim said. "Gonna get exorcised. Nobody tells me nothin'."

"Damn." Eric turned and began to stomp away when his mind registered the hurt on Tim's face when he had sworn at him.

"I'm sorry, Tim," Eric said. "Good to see you again. How's Della?"

"Doin' fine. Real fine," Tim said. He grinned then and, shaking his head, turned to walk back to his chair.

An exorcism, Eric thought. You can't perform an exorcism in a hospital room. He began to walk toward the elevator. But you can do one . . . Eric pushed the down button on the wall and waited for the elevator. No, he thought, they wouldn't take her home. Her parents are too afraid of her. Besides, Sister Ellise likes her jurisdiction. It's her power.

Eric took the elevator to the first floor, then turned left toward the small chapel at the far end of the next wing of the hospital.

The Jesuit loomed over the little girl, making the sign of the cross above her.

". . . Listen and be filled with fear, O Satan, enemy of the faith, enemy of the human race . . ."

Sister Patricia watched the priest. It was as if he were growing larger with each word. His black robes covered the little girl with their shadow. His eyes beamed down at her, gray, and then yellow and glowing. The shadows of the afternoon closed in around them, and the tall silver cross stretched out above his head.

". . . Fear him who was sacrificed in Isaac, sold in Joseph, and slaughtered in the Lamb, crucified in Man, and yet is triumphant over hell.

"Depart, therefore, in the name of the Father and the Son and of the Holy Ghost. Make way for the Holy Ghost, by the sign of the cross of Jesus Christ, our Lord . . ."

Father Gregory held the heavy cross out from his neck and passed it over the contours of the little girl's frail body. Carol stared up, and the nun saw the terror that seemed to explode in her eyes.

Then Carol howled like a wounded dog. "Mother fucker," she rasped.

The priest pulled his cross close to his chest again and held it.

". . . Tremble at his arm, he who led the souls to light after the lamentations of hell had been subdued. May the body of man be a terror to thee, let the image of God be terrible to see . . ."

Carol pulled her head down across her shoulder to gnaw at her straps. Her mouth was bleeding now, and her body kicked and shook. Then she heaved and began to choke on her own bile. The nun hurried to her side, trying to turn her head enough to stop the choking.

"Get back," the priest commanded.

"She'll drown in her—"

"*Back!*"

The priest pushed Sister Patricia away and shoved the gold cross up against Carol's throat. The girl tried to scream but her throat was blocked. Then she vomited and could breathe again in short fits. Her little body heaved. She was crying and moaning, and the sister could see the awful pain ripple up through her body, torturing her blistered, bloody face into screaming contortions.

". . . For it is God who commands thee . . ."

"Bastard," Carol yelled. Suddenly there was no longer the anger or the terror or the strange wildness in her eyes.

"Father, she's . . ."

"Quiet," he barked.

Carol pulled and yanked her body under the straps until there were lines of blood soaking through her clothes and down onto the bed.

". . . The majesty of Christ commands thee. God the Father commands thee."

A terrible cold crept into the chapel, like a shadow whirling and twisting around them. Sister Patricia stepped further from the bed and held her hands tightly together in fear.

". . . God the Son commands thee. God the Holy Ghost commands thee. The sacred cross commands thee. The faith of the holy apostles Peter and Paul, and of all other saints, commands thee . . ."

The whirling made the nun dizzy, and she closed her eyes so she could remember her praying.

"Unstrap her," she heard a voice command, a voice that seemed to originate somewhere else. Her eyes popped open. The priest was pointing down at the girl and staring at Sister Patricia. She moved cautiously over to the bed and freed the little girl.

The priest, still clutching his crucifix, stood beside her, chanting in a monotone. The nun finished quickly, her hands red from the blood on the straps. Father Gregory removed a small silver vial from inside his robe and began to sprinkle holy water on Carol's face.

His chanting grew louder, the words became distinct again.

". . . that you depart from this creature of God, Carol Lake, and return to the place appointed you, there to remain forever . . ."

The nun began to feel dizzy again, and she held herself steady by staring at the priest's gray eyes, wide and angry and powerful now, like the eyes of a night animal caught in a light.

Eric spotted Bob outside the door of the chapel, pacing. He quickened his walk.

"What's happening?" Eric asked impatiently.

It startled Bob, and his head spun to look.

"He's in there ranting and raving! Carol was screaming, but it's quieter now. I don't know what's going on. I think she was choking once, but . . ." Bob looked at the door, then looked back at Eric and shrugged, embarrassed, helpless.

Suddenly a scream ripped through the walls. Eric froze, his eyes staring at the door, as if trying to penetrate it.

The nun screamed too, and there was the sound of a struggle followed by more screams.

"I can't take that," Eric said and barreled through the door.

Carol ripped the gold cross off the priest's chain and cut him across the eyes with it. The nun tried to step in but was cut with the corner of the crucifix across the cheek. The Jesuit held his hands to his face, stumbled, tripped over the bed, and fell over onto the floor.

"Carol!" Eric yelled.

The little girl's head cocked to see him.

"I can't see," the priest was screaming.

Bob ran in behind Eric and held the priest, trying to wrench his hands from his face. The priest would not let go of his face.

Carol's eyes darted to the door, then back at the others. She saw a clear path and she ran for it. Frantic, Eric tried to grab her, but the nun was in his way. Carol disappeared out the chapel door.

Eric ran outside but could not find her. He flipped on the intercom and called security. Then he looked both ways down the corridor and decided to chance the shorter end. It would have been easier for Carol to have made that corner before he got out the door.

All free staff members were put on alert, but the search still took over a half hour. Eric was in a near frenzy when he was called by an orderly to an empty operating room two floors above the chapel.

Carol was on the operating table. Two orderlies were restraining her while a doctor gave her a shot of morphine. Another doctor was wiping the blood off her body. She had sliced her face and arms and chest with the huge gold cross until the skin hung down in flaps. Eric looked at the white of her ribs pushing out through torrents of blood. He caught himself on the edge of the table and closed his eyes to keep from vomiting. His head spun, and he dug his fingers around the corner of the table to catch himself when his knees buckled. Then he opened his eyes and looked into Carol's eyes.

She was staring at him, her eyes red and wet with tears. There was no demon in her now, just a terrified little girl. Her eyes pulled at him. He held himself up weakly, feeling the whole storm of terror inside her grab him, making him know things he could never face.

"Let me . . ." she mumbled, her voice only a whisper

now. Then her body heaved in pain and she tried to scream. There was no sound to the scream, but Eric felt it tearing at his heart.

"Let me . . ." she cried again, pushing out a small gust of life from her lungs, "die. Please."

She tried to sit up and Eric took her in his arms. Gently, he caressed her cheek. She gasped and there was a terrible gurgling in her throat. Eric felt her small body tense up and he held her tight. She glanced up at him. There was almost a smile of relief on her face. Eric tried to smile reassuringly back at her but even as he did, her throat spasmed and her head fell limp against his arm.

Eric peered up at the doctor. The doctor shook his head slowly, his hand on her wrist. Eric felt his heart open up as if it were bleeding inside his chest as he fought back the tears.

The little girl was dead.

CHAPTER III

Eric did not blame the Sister or the priest. He wished he could, to take it away from himself, but it wasn't in him to do that. He only blamed his inability to cure her. She was not the first patient he had had who died from a mental disorder.

Eric drove back to Hapsburg the same day and stayed that night at his father's house. He had told Lisa he wanted to be alone. Now the loneliness was too quiet, too thick and damp around him, and he was glad to see Lisa's car pull into the driveway.

He unlocked the kitchen door and let her in. Her big green eyes sparkled in the brightness of the kitchen and Eric hugged her. She was wearing a black dress and a black lace veil. Her face seemed to glow inside the dark frame.

Eric had his dark suit on already and a black arm band.

"Nice day," he said.

"Sure," Lisa answered.

They walked slowly through the kitchen, big and clean and unused with no food smells in it, then through the dining room under the crystal chandelier, past the big maple table, and antique cabinet with the glass doors to showcase his mother's old family dishes.

In the living room, Eric stopped and stared out the

big picture window at the trimmed bushes and planted trees. The split-level house was sculptured into the land and then the land had been re-formed to the sculpturing.

A live-in showcase, Eric thought. He was gazing at the easy roll of the lawn with the square-cut bushes on the left before the row of willows blocking the neighbors from view. It was all too precise, too exact. Eric looked up from the willows to the dark sky. The black-gray clouds tumbled in over themselves and the rain began. It spotted the big window, and Eric looked away.

"It's a cold place, isn't it?" he said suddenly.

"It's a beautiful house."

Lisa stepped up behind Eric. He could feel her closeness without any touching.

"She's been dead nine years and now he's dead too." Eric watched the rain splash onto the window and run in waves down the glass. He felt an old sadness creep into his stomach. "She was special. She believed in the good in people and always went out of her way to see that. It killed her. That and my father. He killed her too. I used to wish he would die so Mom and I could be happy, but . . ." Eric took a long, slow breath. "It doesn't matter now. They're both dead. Everyone dies. It's only a matter of time, and of waiting."

Lisa squeezed Eric's shoulder lightly. She knew he had to go through this.

"She always had something nice to say to everyone. He never had a kind word for anyone in his life."

Eric turned from the rain on the window, perused the room, then looked at Lisa.

"I do not come to praise Father, but to bury him." Eric shook his head slowly. "I'm glad he's dead."

"Eric?"

Lisa did not like to hear him talk like that.

"It's terrible to say, but it's true. I'm rid of him and his hatred and his cynicism and his . . ."

Eric's face contorted. He sat down on the sofa and put his head in his hands. He was remembering what it was like living at home when he was a boy.

Eric was sitting by the small pond in the park, staring into the clear green water. There were water spiders on the pond and they darted away as he leaned closer. A bullfrog, big and brown and slippery-looking, watched him with one eye.

There were other boys playing football behind him and he heard their yelling, then the close stampeding as they ran an end sweep toward him. Eric slowly reached down behind the frog and was about to grab at it when they came crashing over him in a gang tackle. The frog leaped out into the pond and dove under water.

"Darn you guys," Eric yelled, one leg slipping past his knee into the mud.

The boys laughed and ran back to set up another play. Eric turned from the pond and started to walk around the football game. Then he saw his father.

Eric smiled and ran toward him.

"I almost caught the big frog," Eric said proudly as he neared his father.

"I thought you were going to play football with your friends," his father said sternly.

"I was, but then I remembered the frog and I . . ."

"You lied," his father interrupted. "You were supposed to play football. You need the practice if you want to go out for the team."

Staring up at his father, Eric felt terrible. He could see the growing anger in his father's eyes, and he knew it was best not to tell him now that the boys didn't want him to play on the team, that he had no friends.

"I like to play by the pond," Eric said. He wanted so much for his father to understand about the pond and the frog and the water spiders, but, looking up again, he knew he wouldn't.

"You're coming home with me right now," his father said. He grabbed Eric's wrist and tugged. It hurt, but Eric did not cry out. He knew that would only make things worse.

When he got home, half walking, half being carried under his father's arm, he knew he was going to get it. His father yanked him into the living room and threw him over his lap. Then he began to spank him hard. But he did not stop this time.

"I'll teach you never to lie to me again," his father grunted, the words punctuated by slaps.

Eric was screaming now between the tears. His mother ran into the room, a fearful look in her eyes.

"That's enough, John," she said.

"He lied. He's got to be taught a lesson."

Eric felt the sharp, cutting pain shoot through his thighs and up his belly and he screamed again, hearing his mother's voice.

"John, stop it!"

Eric's mother reached over and grabbed John's arm. He pulled away from her and she tumbled over the coffee table, cutting her forehead on the glass corner. Blood streamed down over her eye.

Eric saw the blood and began to scream even louder. He tried to reach out to her, but John grabbed his arms, pulled them back, and continued to spank him.

*   *   *

Eric shuddered at the memory. Lisa sat next to him. She had watched him drift away in his mind and saw his mouth slowly curl down in a painful frown.

"What were you thinking?"

Eric leaned back and sighed.

"I was remembering a time when I was a kid. It's not worth repeating. How much time do we have?"

"A half hour before we have to leave."

"I'm not ready yet."

Lisa reached out and took his hand in both of hers.

"I told Mom when I was thirteen and home from my first year at prep school that I hated Dad. That he hurt her too much and I wouldn't let him hurt her or me or anyone. I asked her to run away with me. That was the first time I ever saw her actually get angry with me."

Eric glanced at Lisa, then stared back across the room again. Lisa knew the talking was good for him and she did not interrupt, not even during the long silences between thoughts.

"She told me it was wrong to say I hated my own father. She got really angry when I tried to argue. Then she told me Dad had had a hard life and that he wasn't to blame for how he was sometimes. It was the people of Hapsburg that did it to him. They used to pick on him a lot worse than they picked on me. She told me how he had to fight all the time in high school because everyone teased and humiliated him."

"Why did they hate him . . . and you, so much?"

"I guess I should have told you years ago, but it's not something I like to remember." Eric paused and looked away. "My grandfather, my father's father, was a psychiatrist in an insane asylum here in town. It was built right where the hospital is now. They used its foundation to build part of the new hospital on.

Anyway, it burned down. Over a hundred people died. Only one woman and my grandfather escaped alive."

Eric ran his free hand up through his hair. "The town thought he started it. Rumors spread like crazy. It would have died out maybe, but then my grandfather started to go insane. Other rumors began then. Rumors about some of the women patients and my grandfather. Nothing specific really, but they didn't help. He started wandering the town late at night, talking to himself. Then one night he sneaked out of the house, went up to the ruins of the asylum, and hung himself on a big oak tree." Eric's voice became a whisper. "It's still there, the tree. My father heard him leave and went searching for him. He was the one that found him hanging there. He couldn't get him down alone and no one else, when daylight came, would help. They let him dangle until the sheriff cut him down, after the whole town had gathered to watch. That proved to the town that all the rumors must be true and they made it hell for his family. It was hard for me too, but times had changed a little then. Dad had it a lot harder than me. They used to say he was crazy too, that anyone related to my grandfather was insane and probably dangerous. I never wanted to live here, but Dad wouldn't leave. He stood his ground and fought them all, inch by inch, until they could only say things behind his back because they were too scared—no matter how much they hated him—to say them to his face. That was how he got back at them. He loved to rub their faces in his own success. But the hate ate away his heart."

Eric let go of Lisa's hands and leaned forward to light a cigarette.

"And now he's dead. It's all over, I guess. No more

'Loman curse' so to speak. The town's running out of scapegoats. Too bad, huh?"

"Eric?"

Lisa turned sideways on the sofa close to him. He put his cigarette in the ashtray and looked at her. She was beautiful in her shyness and her concern, and Eric lost himself in her moist, green eyes.

"I love you," she said. It was quiet and strong and touched deep inside Eric. He smiled.

"I love you too. You're all I've got left. All I've ever had, really. I know that now." He stroked her cheek gently. "Don't ever leave me, Lisa. I need you so much." Then they kissed hard and desperately, with an aching that pulled them together and would not let them go.

Eric pushed away finally and took a deep breath.

"I guess it's about time."

Lisa nodded.

"There's one thing he did do for me that I'll always be thankful for, though."

Lisa stood up and smoothed her long black gown.

"What's that?"

"I used to get bullied a lot as a kid. They called me Looney Loman because of my grandfather and maybe my father, too, because he was drunk all the time. But Dad made me fight back. I hated him for it, but he made me stand up for myself. Now, at least, I know I can always do that. Always. No one will ever push me down without a fight. I guess his only legacy to me, really, was stubbornness. That and the town's distrust, of course."

Lisa smiled sadly. "You want me to drive?"

Eric shook his head yes.

* * *

It was drizzling as they drove to the funeral at the town's only cemetery. There was no procession, only the hearse and two cars, Eric's and Joe McFarland's. As they turned onto Main Street, a few people stared, then turned away. Eric watched them but his thoughts were wandering. He was remembering the time the three sixth graders encircled him and danced around him, singing Looney Loman, Looney Loman over and over again. He had tried to move and they had held hands to keep him imprisoned. Then he kicked one and there was a hole in the circle and he ran. He ran across the playground, then out through the lot where the car dealership was being built, then down the stream that led home. When he saw his mother in the backyard, he rushed to her and then he was smothered in her embrace, and it was safe and warm and he could not stop crying long enough to tell her what had happened. When he finally told her, he saw his father looking down from behind the screen door to the kitchen.

His father took him inside and lectured him about running away. He told Eric that if he ran away, they would only do it again and again. Then he took out the brush and spanked him for not confronting the three boys. It took years, Eric remembered as they wove through the narrow roads in the cemetery, to forgive him for that. Or maybe he was just finally forgiving him now. Eric was trying hard to forgive his father for many things, as the memories flooded through his head. They were too quick now, too precise. He pushed them all away to be able to end it with his father once and for all. He did not want to live with the hatred or the accusations or that constant, gnawing apprehension anymore.

He told himself he would bury all of that today.

* * *

The minister stood at the head of the grave and four men, using red straps looped under the coffin, lowered it into the ground. Then they left. The clouds were low and dark and quick moving in the wind. The trees shook morosely, their wet green leaves trembling as the wind circled down in hard gusts, making the drizzle snap into their faces.

Eric watched how fast the sky kept changing. The thin, gray foglike clouds, under the thicker, heavier ones, reached out like vanishing fingers as they blew over him. Then he glanced around the coffin. Joe, an old woman, and a young boy were standing on the other side of the grave. Eric did not recognize the old woman, but he knew the boy. It was Peter, the one at the opening ceremony of the hospital. Eric questioned Lisa with a look, but she just shrugged. She had no idea why the boy or the old woman were there either.

The minister quoted the standard funeral rites quickly, then took a handful of dirt and tossed it onto the coffin. He nodded to Eric. Eric knelt, took a big handful of wet, black dirt, stood up, stared down for a moment at the brown coffin with the brass handles shining gold in the drizzle and told himself that it was over now, the family horror, everything; that he would start fresh and life would be good now and full, without the old scars to trouble it any longer. Then he dropped the heavy dirt onto the coffin, turned, and slowly walked away.

A cold breeze swept down between the big oaks and up the path, causing the rain to dart into Eric's face. He lifted his chin to feel the full power of it. The sharp, wind-hurled drizzle felt good to him, cleansing him.

In a moment Lisa was next to him. He reached out,

the wet earth still stuck to his hand, and she took it in hers. They walked past the cars and kept walking up the hill to the oldest section of the cemetery. Before they were too far up the hill, a huge hand grabbed Eric's shoulder. He shuddered and spun around.

"I'm sorry he died," Joe McFarland said quickly. Eric looked at him silently. "He was a good boss."

Eric opened his mouth, but there was nothing he could say, really, so he nodded and shook hands. Joe smiled uncomfortably, then left.

"What's the matter?" Lisa asked, watching Eric stare down the hill.

He turned to face her.

"All I feel is relief. There should be more to it than that."

Lisa leaned her head on Eric's shoulder and held his arm as she watched the old woman and the boy by the grave. The boy lifted a handful of dirt and tossed it down. The old woman did the same, then wiped her eyes. That startled Lisa. She watched over Eric's shoulder as they continued up the hill.

The old woman grabbed the boy's hand and hurried him down the far path that came out two blocks from Main Street.

"Don't feel guilty, Eric," Lisa said as they walked. The silence had become too uncomfortable. "You don't have to feel anything except what is there. If it's relief, fine. You're free now. It's only natural to feel relieved."

"But there should be more. Sadness, pity, a feeling of loss. *Something*."

"Why?"

"It seems appropriate. No, there's more to it." He stopped again and held Lisa by both shoulders. "My father just died and no one cared, except those who were glad, like me."

"And Joe McFarland? Was he glad?"

Eric remembered the big hand clutching him tightly and the sadness in Joe's rough face. At least there was one person who mourned the death of John Loman.

"He was truly sad. I saw it," she said.

Lisa began to walk more briskly and pulled Eric with her. The drizzle had stopped now and the clouds were breaking up on the horizon.

"I used to come here a lot," she said suddenly. The statement startled Eric.

"To the graveyard?"

"I like the graveyard. Down this hill is the oldest part. I like to read the tombstones and look at the dates. It's kind of interesting."

"In a ghoulish way," Eric laughed. It pleased Lisa to hear him joke again.

"I just find it interesting that we erect monuments to the dead. If they're made to last, then someone should take notice. Why else put them there?"

"To mark where someone is buried. So those who are alive can have a symbol to mourn."

"That's too pat."

Lisa squeezed Eric's arm and smiled when Eric laughed. She was relieved to see the distance and the numbing pain slowly fade from Eric's eyes.

"It's fun, sometimes, to imagine what the person was like, how he or she lived. Come. Look over here."

Lisa led Eric by the arm to a high-curved gravestone. It was ornately carved with leaves all around it and so worn down it was hard to read. Lisa knelt and wiped the lettering clean.

"Seventeen ten to Seventeen fifty-six. Imagine that,

Eric. Think back to those times, how they dressed, what the land was like, the people, the Indians. Now listen. It says: 'Tears Cannot Restore Her; Therefore I Weep.' I can't make out the name. Mary something."

"That could go either way," Eric laughed. "It sounds to me like he might have been glad she was gone finally."

"Maybe. Who knows? But it's fun to guess. Come on. Look at this one."

Eric crouched down and cleaned the lettering by tracing it with his fingers. It was a short, thick grave-stone and the grass had grown up over the dates. He ripped the grass out to see.

"Seventeen thirty to Seventeen seventy-five." Eric glanced up at Lisa. "He probably died in the war."

"Why is it automatically a he?"

Eric snickered, then brushed the dirt from the name. "Because they didn't name women John back then. Unless they were a true feminist."

Lisa swatted Eric on the head playfully. "Read what it says."

Eric squinted, leaning close to the stone. "If there is a future world, my lot will not bliss; But if there is no other, I've made the most of this." Eric shook his head and laughed as he stood up. "Now that's one that tells it like it is."

Lisa was already wiping off another. "Look at this," she called. Eric hurried over. "Died seventeen eighty-seven. Can't tell when he was born. This one's real poetry: 'Owen Moore, Gone away, Owin' more, Than he could pay."

"Even the dead have debts," Eric laughed.

They walked together up the next hill to the clump of tall pines. The ground beneath them was almost dry. Eric spread his jacket over the thick, soft-matted

needles so they both could sit on it. Below, the graveyard stretched out green and wet, the rows of white
stones glistening now as the sun broke out, then dark-
ening quickly when the shadow of a great cloud rolled
over the ground and covered them.

"I was fired, you know," Eric said, watching another
dark cloud-shadow ripple across the rolling land.

"You thought there was a good chance of that."

"Yup."

Eric saw Carol's face again, the pleading, the fear,
the death creeping up into her small eyes. He leaned
back and sighed. Lisa lay on her side and ran her
hand lightly over Eric's ribs.

"Did Carol . . ."

"I've had too much death," he whispered.

Then she kissed his ear and Eric sat up suddenly,
taking Lisa with him.

"I'm going to accept the job here. I'll call Sherry
later this afternoon. There's no reason not to live here
now. I don't mean that I . . . I mean . . ." Eric did not
finish it. He watched the small yellow bulldozer push
the final pile of dirt over his father's grave, then run
back and forth over it to smooth it down.

"You mean you didn't get along with your father
and now that he's gone you can live here without all
the emotional hassles. That should be good. Don't let
it be anything else, Eric."

"Bob Thompson offered me a job too. He's opening
a therapeutic clinic in Philadelphia and wants me to
work with him. It's all set up, but I told him I had to
take the job here. There's something I have to finish
here. I'm not even sure what, but it's necessary. Besides, I want to be with you all the time now. No
more weekend relationship."

He looked down into her eyes. There was no mistaking the love he saw there. He smiled and stroked her cheek.

"I've got a big house now and no one there to make it feel like home. Would you like to live with me? I love you, you know."

Lisa reached up and held his face. She kissed him deeply and for a long time.

"I'd love to live with you," she said afterward.

Eric grinned. Then they were kissing again and the touches grew bolder, desperate, more urgent.

"Love me now, Eric. Please."

Eric unzipped the back of her black dress as she unbuttoned his shirt and loosened his tie. They fumbled with each other's clothing until it was no longer in their way.

"I love you," Eric whispered as they stretched out half naked under the pines, the softness of her breasts swelled tight against his ribs.

Their lovemaking was not slow and smooth but quick and insistent. They needed the closeness and the release, and when it came neither Eric nor Lisa relaxed their embrace. In a while, they dressed and walked, arm-in-arm, around the other end of the old section of the cemetery to get to the car.

"I've never been in this part before," Lisa said. The sky was closing again and it was dark in the small valley.

"There's going to be a storm tonight," Eric said. A changing coolness to the wind bit their faces as they walked. The graves surrounding them now were all the same, in long rows, close together. They were much closer than any of the other graves in the cemetery. Lisa stopped suddenly, then began to cut through the tight rows of gray, flat headstones.

"None of them are marked," she said. "They're all the same, but none are marked. There's hundreds of them. Hundreds."

The wind blew up through her dress and Lisa shivered. Eric walked over to her, examining the small stones as he went.

"I don't like this place," Lisa announced quickly. "Let's get out of here. Okay?"

"I thought you liked cemeteries."

"Not this part. I just don't like it here. It's creepy. I'm cold, Eric. Let's hurry, please?"

Eric put his jacket over her shoulders and they walked back to his car. Making love in the pines had taken away that damp, chilling feeling of death that had stalked Lisa all day, but after being in the middle of the strange unmarked graves, it all came back to her again. She could not shake it off, no matter how hard she tried.

CHAPTER IV

The leaves were almost ready to turn colors in Hapsburg. The northwest fall wind blew down out of the mountains making the big-branched, wide-leafed old oaks next to the hospital billow like the sails of a clipper ship. Eric Loman had worked two days after having the rest of last week to prepare himself and to relax. Eric was not good at relaxing and he was glad to be back at work. He was also glad to be the only psychiatrist in the new hospital. In effect, he was the psychiatric department. The only one he had to report to was Sherry Mellany and part of his contract stated that his judgment was final, unless Sherry Mellany or the Board of Directors disagreed, which, she promised, would probably never occur. Eric was thinking about that and about Carol as he walked down the second-story corridor past the staff lounge.

A tall nurse with thick round glasses that made her eyes seem much too large was calling to the maintenance man. Eric saw a puddle of water outside of the men's room. It stayed in the slight crevice of the hall where a crack had begun.

"It's still leaking," the nurse said as Mr. Gibbs scurried next to her.

Mr. Gibbs was an old man with gray hair, bald

down the middle, and always that two-day gray stubble on his wrinkled chin and neck.

"I fixed the darn thing twice already," he complained. Sherry Mellany was right behind him. Eric stood by the men's-room door and nodded to them. Mr. Gibbs merely shook his head. It was his way to always be disgusted and grumbling about something. He wouldn't be happy any other way, Eric thought. If you can call that happy.

Sherry Mellany edged around the puddle to stand at Eric's side. She was in her late thirties and extraordinarily beautiful. She looked like an Italian movie star and had the figure to back up the comparison.

Mr. Gibbs jammed the door open with a triangular piece of wood and examined the tile floor of the men's room. There was a puddle that grew everytime the two urinals flushed. When it was high enough, it spilled out over the edge of the doorway into the hall.

"Finally happened," Mr. Gibbs stated. "Look at that." He pointed at the crack in the hall floor. "This place is built with balsa wood and cardboard, for Chrissake. They don't take their time anymore. There's no pride in what a man makes with his hands. No pride anymore."

Sherry had heard the speech often. She smiled at Eric and rolled her eyes. He smiled back.

"Think it's funny, huh?" the old man threw up his hands and shook his head. "Kids. What would they know anyway? They just don't build 'em like they used to. Now in my day, when we started construction and I—"

"Can you fix it this time?" Sherry interrupted.

Mr. Gibbs's head cocked to look at her.

"I can fix anything they make nowadays. There was a time, though, when—"

"I suggest you try doing it before we have to rent dinghies for the patients who might have to use this bathroom."

Mr. Gibbs grunted as he ambled between Eric and Sherry to look over the urinals.

"Nurse Baker," Sherry called, turning to a uniformed woman nearby.

The nurse had been staring out the window. She quickly stood at attention and waited for the coming order. She looked around for something to do.

"You have duties, I suspect? Unless, of course, you know how to fix a leaking urinal?"

"Yes, Mrs. Mellany," she stammered. "I mean no. I . . . I don't know how to fix it, but yes I have duties. I have to go . . . ah . . . check Mrs. Delap. Her temperature."

Sherry smiled and nodded. The tall nurse hurried down the hall and around the corner. Eric laughed slightly, then saw Sherry watching him. He swallowed the laughter.

"I've got paper work to do," he said quickly.

"You don't have to run away too." She patted Eric's arm.

"Thanks."

"My pleasure."

Sherry Mellany peeked in to see how Mr. Gibbs was doing. The urinals flushed again and water bubbled out onto the floor. Mr. Gibbs swore under his breath and pulled the stool closer, so he could stand on it and see into the flushing unit near the ceiling.

Eric and Sherry smiled at each other, then she took his arm and walked him down the hall.

"It's good to have new blood here. Someone young, fresh from the city, and pretty fresh out of school and his internship too."

Sherry let go of his arm when they reached the stairway door.

"There are a lot of old doctors here. Country doctors. They're used to their ways, not to change." Sherry leaned closer. "They are a lot like Mr. Gibbs."

"Change isn't always for the best," Eric added. "You need that kind of people to hold on to the good things that others want to change only for change's sake."

"Point taken." Sherry opened the door, then turned to look at Eric. "But you need both. In society or a hospital. I'm glad you're here. Besides, as an old widow, it's nice to have a handsome young doctor to look at."

"I wouldn't exactly call you . . ." Sherry was already going down the stairs and the door swung closed. ". . . old," Eric finished.

"They think it's for the best," he said. "But they don't know. I don't want to be here. I had friends in Molbrook. I don't know nobody here."

Lisa helped pack the old man's clothes in the closet, then handed him his aluminum walker. The man grinned toothlessly and leaned down onto it, relieved.

"You'll make friends here too, Mr. Klein," Lisa said. "I'll be your friend."

The old man hobbled out into the hall and Lisa walked slowly beside him. He was as old as anyone she had ever met. Ninety-six his chart said, and he looked it. His face was a mass of wrinkles like the furrowed land he had tilled for over eighty years.

"They took away my pipe," the old man grumbled. "I've smoked that pipe for eighty-one years and now some little girl in white takes it away. Says it's bad for my heart now, for God's sake. Let me choose which bad things I want. I'm too old to give up smoking for my health."

Lisa thought about that, about being ninety-six, as she walked with him out onto the sundeck on the third floor. She was wondering what it was like to be born before cars or airplanes, to have plowed your land with horses and your own muscle, to have watched the world change so much. This man had been through two world wars and seen airplanes being born, then turned into jets, then spaceships.

The old man tottered next to the stiff wooden chair and slowly let himself down. Lisa grabbed his arm to help his descent, but he yanked it away and quickly dropped into the seat.

"Never needed no help sittin'. It's just like fallin'. 'Course gettin' up—now that's another ball game."

They looked out at the small town with the big trees around the houses and arching low over the winding roads. A river spilled out of the northern mountains and curved around the side of the town, always on the edge of the valley. It was shallow now, the white, smooth rocks pushing out of the brown swirling water.

"It used to be crystal clear," he said.

"What?" Lisa asked, startled at the break in the silence.

"The river. Used to be clean, clear. Then they started mining and building that pulp mill . . ." Mr. Klein sighed and his head bobbled like one of those cheap plastic dolls with the spring necks.

Lisa sat down next to him. She liked the old man very much and was glad to have the time to sit with him. To her, it was a privilege, not work at all. She also knew he wanted to talk because he felt strange and out of place here. His family had insisted he be moved to Hapsburg now that the hospital was completed. They wanted him closer to home. Lisa wondered whose convenience that was for, his or theirs. She felt sorry for him, but knew better than to show that in any way. The old man would not put up with pity. She could tell that within the first five minutes of meeting him.

"Who's running your farm now?" Lisa asked.

"Little Tommy Stiller." The old man cackled. "Little Tommy must be sixty now." He peered over his shoulder at Lisa. She could hear the sadness in the way he spoke. That struck her deeply and she could not look away from his eyes. It was as if he could read her past and her future, watching how she was now. It was eerie, but nice.

"Is he related?"

"Nope."

He looked back at the mountains and she watched him out of the corner of her eye. His face changed as if he were with old friends again.

"The family sold it last year to pay my hospital bills." Slowly, he looked back at her. She could tell he was deciding something about her then. "They don't understand about land. My father understood. He taught me. But things are different now. The land isn't the same to young people. Maybe to some it is, but mostly they look at it as an investment. Real estate, they call it, not land anymore. Even the name changed. If anything will destroy us, it's the way we look at our land. When you lose the feeling for it, how it grows, what lives on it, you lose your own identity too." He stared back at the mountains again and was quiet for a long time.

"My father knew," he said suddenly. "He came here as a prisoner of war. The Civil War."

The old man closed his eyes to see the things only he understood, that were gone now forever. Then he opened them again.

"It was a terrible place. Right here, it was." He pointed down at the floor. "Right here on these grounds. The Union officers got rich trading food and medicine on the black market. They even sold wagonloads of supplies to the blockade runners down in Virginia.

"My father was in that prison over a year. He was from Georgia. Most of them died within six months. Starved to death or died of some disease. The guards sold most of the blankets and winter coats, the bastards. It took my father almost seventy years before he told me about it. He needed that long, that's how horrible it was. After he told me, he went crazy. It was like he was always holding it in, keeping it hidden, even from himself. Then he finally had to let it out and he couldn't control it anymore. They had to put him in the insane asylum. He was reliving that year in the camp over and over in his head. He died in the fire."

The old man paused, then caught Lisa with his eyes and held her.

"This is bad land right here, missy. The camp was bad. The asylum was bad. Land is good, but sometimes man destroys it with his own insanity, then it goes bad. This land went bad over a hundred years ago. Anything built on it won't stand long. Too many people suffered here, too much blood soaked into the soil. This land's been cursed with the evil side of man. It's no good anymore! You can feel it right up through your legs if you know how. If you've lived all your life with the land, working it, loving it, fighting it, praying to it, then you can feel those things. They're in you like the seed of a great tree in your belly, always growing, always growing."

Lisa was frightened by what he had just said. She could see the huge window slamming down on John Loman's head, and she could almost picture the old asylum and the prisoner-of-war camp. She knew it was illogical, just an old man's fantasy, but the way he said it, she almost believed him. "Why did he stay around here after the war? You'd think this would be the last place he'd want to be."

Lisa wanted to talk, rather than brood over her growing apprehension.

"He met a girl. She took care of him. Fed him, nursed him back to health. A lot of the townspeople felt guilty when the camp was opened up. The Union guards couldn't lie about the living skeletons that came wandering out of the gates. She saw him and took him home and nursed him. I think they felt guilty." The old man smiled. "He married her. My mother. She owned land, good land. Her father died in the beginning of the war. She was a woman like the land itself, loving and strong and always . . ." The old man smiled. "Always full of surprises."

Lisa laughed and patted his hand. He opened his fist and they held hands gently. She could feel his heartbeat through his fingers. She had never felt that in a hand before.

"You see this?" He let go of her hand and stuck out his fingers. They were bent and gnarled, but still strong. "Look at those fingers. See the black? That's eighty-some years of dirt. Can't wash it out. It's part of me now. None of my children, or their children, have that." The man looked up at the sky and breathed in deeply. "Except Danny. He's twenty-something, maybe thirty-something now. He works the land. He sweats with it. Maybe someday he'll have the land in his hands, like my father . . . and me."

The old man could see that Lisa was really listening to him. She wasn't just humoring an old man the way his family pretended to listen. He decided to tell her the rest of it.

"I am almost dead," he began. "I'm past fearing for my life. But I still fear this place. This land I sit on now. It is evil, vengeful land. Hell, it got John Loman. That is as it should be. John Loman was part of this land, as his father was before him and his father's father. He could not escape what happened."

Lisa was not insulted or angered at this slur against the Lomans. That startled her, but there was nothing malicious about the old man. What he said, he meant, because it was his truth and he believed it in his heart.

"It is a bad family, the Lomans, the way this land is bad. Too much blood ran through their hands."

"I know about John's father," Lisa said. "The rumors. But why his father's father too? What did he do?"

"Colonel Loman," Mr. Klein sighed. "He ran the POW camp. He was the one in charge of the black market, of everything. No one ate or slept or was executed without his signature. He was a terrible, mean man. He had only one emotion, sadistic hatred. No one knows what happened to him after they opened up the camp. Some say vigilantes from town killed him."

"I can see why you feel John's father and grandfather were harmful but John never tried to . . ."

"He inherited it from his father. He couldn't live with it, so he drank and he hated. That killed people, even if he didn't do it with his own hands."

"I don't think that's fair."

"Perhaps not," the old man pondered, rubbing his wrinkled cheek. "But Teddy was bad. As bad as his father the Colonel. Truly an evil man. It's hard to get that out of the blood."

"Who's Teddy?"

Lisa felt herself sweating when the cool wind blew over the porch, making her shiver. She rubbed her arms to warm herself.

"Teddy was Dr. James Loman. Dr. James Theodore Loman. He liked his patients to use his nickname to make them feel more at home, less scared of authority. I visited my father a lot at the asylum. He hated it, but it was the state that committed him and I couldn't get him out. Mother was dead two years. He talked about the prison camp most of the time, but sometimes he would hear the clanging of keys and then his eyes would bulge out white and terrified, and he would whisper about Teddy. He was scared to death of him. My father did not scare easy. Maybe it was 'cause Teddy looked so much like Colonel Loman. I don't know. But things went on there. Horrible things. There was a room. When my father heard that room mentioned, he would break out into a cold sweat and he couldn't talk. He would just freeze up."

The old man stopped, stared out at the mountains, then wiped the sides of his eyes. When he glanced at Lisa, he saw how badly she was taking it.

"You know I haven't talked this long with a pretty girl that held my hand for forty years. Except my wife, of course. You got a husband?"

"No, but . . ." Lisa smiled.

"A boyfriend?"

She nodded yes, still smiling.

"Tell him to come and see me and I'll tell him just how lucky he is. Or does he know that already?"

"Sometimes."

"That ain't enough. Ain't enough."

Lisa put her other hand on his and felt his heart beating and the dirt on his fingers and she wanted to cry.

Dr. Eric Loman finished his first general staff meeting by giving a small speech to the other doctors. It was laced well with youthful humility and a respect for the old ways, but it also had a hint of new strength, of different ideas. Sherry Mellany made sure he included those too. She did not hire him to be like the others. She hired him to change things, things she wanted changed, because he had the energy and a willingness to go against the system. She had read his files over a month ago in Philadelphia and knew he was the one to help her with the new therapies she intended to begin.

The meeting broke up quickly, everyone hurrying back to their rounds or their appointments.

"Dr. Loman," Sherry said.

Eric stopped at the door and turned.

"If you have a moment?"

"Of course." Then he glanced at the other doctors scurrying down the hall. "Maybe I shouldn't have, though?" He smiled and looked back at her.

"They always run out after a meeting whether they have something to do or not. They've got to keep up the image."

Eric did not know if he should laugh or not, so he held it in.

"Let's go to my office."

Sherry walked past him and down the hall. Eric caught up quickly. He was not used to her pace or her quick decisions yet.

But as they passed the front door, a man cut across their path carrying a boy in his arms. A woman hurried next to him.

Eric recognized the man as the same one who had heckled his father at the hospital's opening ceremony. The boy was familiar to him too. He was the man's son, Peter, who had been at the ceremony and also with the old woman at the funeral.

"Does it hurt bad?" Sherry asked him as his father eased him down in a chair. Peter nodded. He was biting his lower lip.

"Do you have a name?"

"Peter," he said shyly, not looking up. Eric watched his lip quiver when he stopped biting it. He knew how much Peter wanted to cry and felt sorry for him trying so hard not to.

"Well, Peter, perhaps we should take you for a little ride. How would you like that?"

Peter shrugged. He still would not make eye contact with anyone, not even his parents. A nurse pushed a wheelchair up next to him and Eric lifted him onto it with the help of the child's father. Eric watched him wince when his father touched him. There was a terrible fear in Peter's face that cried out to Eric in a quiet, agonized way.

The nurse was about to wheel Peter into X-ray, but Eric grabbed her arm and shook his head.

"I'll take him."

The nurse glanced at Sherry Mellany and she nodded her permission. The nurse walked away. Sherry took the parents to the emergency desk to fill out the required forms.

"I think it's just a sprained ankle," Eric heard the father repeat as he turned Peter into X-ray. He stopped for a second and watched from the doorway. The look he had seen on Peter's face had not come from a sprained ankle. He watched the parents closely. They seemed more frightened than concerned, and Eric wondered why.

He heard the intercom call the X-ray technician. He had never gotten used to the mechanical chill of its voice.

"Fell, huh?" Eric asked as he picked Peter up and set him down on the table.

Peter nodded. Eric looked at his ankle and Peter sat up to watch. Eric noticed he was holding his left arm unusually straight as he moved.

"Arm hurt too?"

Peter froze, then shook his head no. Eric could see the question bothered him.

"Lie down flat."

Peter did, but his eyes attached themselves to Eric and rolled with his every move. Eric prodded the child gently with one finger. When he touched the ribs by the arm Peter favored, he flinched, but tried desperately not to show the pain.

"That hurt?"

He shook his head no.

"Don't talk much, do you?"

Peter looked away at the other wall with the glass cupboard against it.

"Let's see that left arm once."

As Eric walked around the table, he watched Peter cringe. He took the wrist and pulled slowly. Peter almost cried out, but caught himself.

"That hurts, doesn't it?"

"No," he said quickly. "I fell and broke my ankle."

He turned his head away from Eric and bit his lip.

Then the technician entered. Eric took him aside and asked him to X-ray the left arm and ribs too. He walked back to the emergency desk. The parents were still talking to Sherry.

"He's so awkward," the mother was saying.

"He's always falling and hurting himself," the father added. "No coordination at all. Maybe it's just a passing phase."

No one had been asking them about it, but they seemed to have a need to talk. They were obviously nervous. Their son is hurt, Eric reminded himself. But the way the mother hung her head, her eyes darting continuously from one person to another as if to check for a reaction as she or her husband spoke, bothered Eric. She looked—guilty.

Eric motioned to Sherry. She excused herself and they edged down the hall together. Glancing back, Eric saw both parents watching them suspiciously.

"I'm not so sure he fell at all," Eric said quietly.

"That's a dangerous accusation," Sherry said. "If you are implying what I think."

"His ribs and arm were bruised too, but he was too scared to admit it."

"Maybe he's just afraid of the hospital, of you. Or maybe he hurt his arm and ribs when he fell too."

"Maybe."

"Do you want to file a report on suspicion of child abuse? You need concrete proof, Doctor. It's not something to play with."

Eric nodded. He already knew the procedure and just how difficult it was to prove.

"I don't have proof, but look at the way they're acting. It's all wrong."

The technician came out of the X-ray room near them.

"Just a sprain," he said, stopping next to Sherry.

"What about the ribs and arm?"

"One rib had had a slight crack, but it's old, already healed. I looked at his arm too. There were bruises on his shoulder. He fought me to keep from looking."

Eric shook his head, disgusted.

"Thank you, Tom," Sherry said.

The technician left.

"That's no proof, Eric. I think you should leave it alone for now. I'm speaking as the director." Eric said nothing but watched Sherry walk back to the parents.

Alone in the X-ray room, the boy sat quietly staring toward the door.

"They won't hurt you again," he said.

"But I'm scared."

"Don't worry, I'm here. I'll protect you."

The boy got up slowly and slid down off the table onto his good foot.

"I don't like it here."

He glanced around the gray, sterile room with the huge metal X-ray unit and no windows.

"There's great protection here."

"They want to hurt me. Hurt Mom and Dad. I can tell."

"It's safe here."

"It smells funny."

"Cleaning stuff. I can be strong here. I can protect you."

"I don't like it."

"You will. Don't worry. You will."

A nurse walked in and the boy bit his lip again.

"Come on now. Time for another ride."

The boy sat in the wheelchair and the nurse pushed him down the hall to his parents. Eric and Sherry stood a few feet away, talking. They stopped when they saw him coming.

Suddenly there was a loud crackling and a quick snap. Smoke puffed out the doorway of the X-ray room. The lights in the hall blinked, then there was more crackling and the smoke became thicker and blacker.

"Something must have shorted out," Eric said, running to the X-ray room. Sherry was right behind him.

Where the X-ray unit was plugged into the wall, the freshly painted plaster seemed to be splintering, and smoke seeped out from around it.

"I think the fire's inside the wall," Eric yelled. "Get a fire extinguisher."

A nurse following Sherry heard him and ran for the extinguisher in the hall.

"We might need an ax too," Eric said.

The nurse handed him the extinguisher.

"I don't know where an ax would be," Sherry said, ducking under the smoke.

Eric smashed the wall with the butt of the extinguisher. Flames burst out of the hole. He banged the crack until a good section of the wall was opened Flames licked out, curling toward Eric before he turned over the extinguisher and shot the white foam into the wall. The smoke was thicker for a moment, then it was gone. Eric kept spraying the extinguisher until the space was filled with foam. When he finally stumbled out of the room, coughing, his pants soaked from the extinguisher's foam, he fell to his knees. His breath came in short gasps. Slowly, he breathed more deeply. He peered down the hall as he pushed himself up onto his feet. The boy was sitting in the wheel-chair, staring as if nothing had happened. Then he smiled at Eric, and his mother wheeled him out the emergency doors.

CHAPTER V

"So how's our volunteer fire department today?" Debbie Long asked.

Eric sat down at the table in the hospital lounge where she and Lisa were having coffee. There was no one else around.

"Lungs are a little sore," he said.

Lisa slid back on her chair to reach the big metal coffee maker. She poured a cup for Eric.

"That should give Mr. Gibbs something to complain about for a few weeks," Lisa said, handing Eric the coffee.

"Everyone in the hospital is talking about it," Debbie said. "You reacted quickly. The staff is proud of you." She got up out of her chair.

"Well, they don't know what I'm like as a psychiatrist, but at least I passed the fireman's test."

The nurse laughed and closed the door behind her.

Lisa reached across the table and took Eric's hand.

"You're a fine psychiatrist and you know it."

Lisa knew something had been bothering him last night, but he didn't want to talk about it then. He said he was exhausted from the smoke inhalation, so she had left it alone. That was what she had been discussing with Debbie, but her friend merely concluded that Lisa was being oversensitive now that she was living with Eric. She told Lisa she should try to go slowly and be comfortable, and not to expect that any time anything seemed wrong between them, they would automatically discuss it openly right away. People, meaning Eric, needed time and the right atmosphere to talk seriously about their problems.

"You know that boy, Peter, who was admitted yesterday, but only had a sprained ankle? The one who was in the X-ray room just before the fire?"

"Debbie told me about it."

"I think he may be an abused child. I have no proof, so I can't file a suspicion charge, but . . ." Eric leaned back to the table and took a sip of coffee. "What if I don't have proof and I don't file, and he *is* abused? Hurt badly sometime?"

"You can't file on suspicion, Eric. It wouldn't hold up. The parents would sue you for everything you had."

"What am I supposed to do? Wait until he's been hurt badly enough so I have the proof?"

"That's the way it is. We're not lawyers or policemen. We are medical people. We don't have the options."

"But how about a little preventive medicine?"

"Doesn't work that way."

Eric sighed loudly and put his head in his hands.

"Is that what was bothering you last night?"

"Yeah."

Lisa pulled his face up and kissed him quickly. Eric smiled and she winked at him playfully. Then she frowned. Eric was startled by the quick change.

"Something is bothering you too."

Lisa shook her head yes and stared down into her coffee cup.

"Well let's have it. Your turn now."

Lisa laughed uncomfortably. "I was talking to that old man, Mr. Klein. He's over ninety-six."

"I spoke to him in his room. I went down and got him his pipe."

Lisa smiled and looked at Eric. What he had just said reassured her about moving in with him. He might be too logical sometimes—that was part of his profession—but deep down he had a child's heart and that was the best heart to have.

"So what about him? Besides that he's full of spunk and stories."

"He told me what the graves were from."

"The unmarked ones?"

"They were Confederate prisoners. Prisoners from a POW camp built right here on this hill."

"That's a story and a half."

The door to the lounge opened and two doctors walked in.

"There's the fireman," one joked.

Eric glanced up and smiled.

The taller man who had spoken patted Eric on the shoulder as he passed. They sat at the table by the window.

"These big windows in the lounge still give me the creeps," the other doctor said.

"Jack," the taller man reprimanded, kicking him under the table. He pointed with his chin at Eric.

"Oops," Jack whispered.

Eric had heard it and so had Lisa.

"I've got to go," he said, standing up.

Lisa gave Jack a dirty look before she rose and he shrugged guiltily.

In the hall, Lisa thought about telling Eric what the old man had said about the asylum and about Eric's grandfather and his great grandfather, but decided it wasn't a good time. Then Sherry Mellany came out of the elevator with a young boy. She was holding his hand, but when he saw Eric and Lisa, he tugged it out of her grip.

"I'd like to talk to you, Sherry," Eric said.

"And I'd like to talk to you."

"I've got to go. See you later," Lisa said. She hurried to catch the elevator before the doors closed.

"This is my son, Mike. Mike, this is Dr. Loman."

"How do you do?" Her son stuck out his small hand like a miniature English gentleman.

Eric shook it and grinned.

"Fine, thank you, and yourself?"

"Fine," he answered, standing at attention.

"He's got to have his tonsils removed. They were infected twice already this year," Sherry said. She took Mike's hand again and he begrudgingly let her lead him with it. Eric followed.

"This is your room."

She opened the door to Room 204.

"You have your own private room just like at home."

"Where's the TV?"

Mike perused the room suspiciously, glad to have both hands free again.

"One will be brought up," said a heavyset nurse, walking in behind them. Both Eric and Sherry jumped, not having heard her enter.

"This is Nurse Campbell; she'll help get you settled. You're going to be fine, Michael. Now give Mother a kiss." Sherry leaned down toward him.

"Oh, Mom," he whined.

Sherry leaned closer and he pecked her cheek. Eric had a hard time keeping himself from smiling.

Then she left and Eric followed once again. He was growing tired of always being a step behind her.

"You certainly move quickly."

Sherry Mellany ignored him. She stopped after a nurse approaching them went into a room two doors down.

"He's scared of the hospital," she said. "I've tried to reassure him, but it's hard. He's been scared of a lot of things since his father died two years ago. I was wondering if you'd talk to him. Present a masculine role model."

"A father figure?" Eric injected. He was finding Sherry's proper terms slightly humorous under the circumstances. She was talking about her son now, not just another patient.

Sherry smiled. "I guess I've been a career person too long."

"You should try to relax. You dart around this hospital in high gear constantly. It's not good to be that preoccupied with business all the time."

"Maybe you're right, Doctor. But would you talk to him, please?"

"Of course."

"Thank you. Now I've got a meeting to attend. You must excuse me."

Sherry turned and started almost jogging down the hall.

"High gear. Shift. Shift," Eric called after her.

She did not look back, but Eric could see her purposely slow her pace. He smiled to himself as he went back to Mike's room. He decided Sherry Mellany was a hell of an administrator. Then he tried to imagine what she would be like in bed. Despite her looks he couldn't picture it, and that made his grin grow into a smile.

* * *

Sherry's son was tall for a ten-year-old, and skinny.

"Hello again," Mike said, as Eric walked in his room.

"Hi."

Eric sat on the opposite bed. The boy smiled shyly because of the way Eric was grinning.

"Nice place you have here," Eric joked.

"Gets cold in the winter," Mike said. "Too drafty." Then he laughed and sat up. Eric was glad to see the boy joking. It was a healthy release.

"Don't you like it here?"

Mike shrugged and stared everywhere but at Eric.

"Play any sports?"

Eric wondered what Mike thought of him because the boy seemed nervous.

"Soccer."

Mike got up and walked over to the window. He shoved his hands into his pockets, then pulled them out again and turned around.

"You like soccer?" Eric asked him.

"Sure. Better than football."

"You know, in England, they call soccer football."

Mike stopped fiddling with his hands and looked at Eric.

"What do they call football then?"

Eric laughed. "I don't think they call it anything, really. They don't play it."

"Good," Mike said.

Eric glanced over at the door, then back at Mike.

"You having your operation today?"

"Yup." Mike looked down at the floor. Eric could see he was frightened then.

"I'm sure it will be easy. Over in no time. Then you get all the ice cream you can eat."

Mike shook his head. "I don't like ice cream."

Eric smiled and decided to change the subject.

"Do you know Peter Delmont?" he asked.

"Sure," Mike said. He sauntered over to the far edge of the bed Eric was sitting on and leaned on its metal footboard. "He's in my class."

"Do you like him?"

"He's all right. He's on the team too."

That surprised Eric.

"On the soccer team?"

"Yeah."

"He sprained his ankle yesterday."

Mike's eyes widened and there was finally a hint of interest on his face.

"Sprained bad?"

"Not too bad. He'll be out for a few weeks, though."

"Darn," Mike said, as he slapped the footboard.

"Going to miss him, huh?"

"He's our best forward. The second fastest runner on the team. I'm the first."

Eric thought about that as Mike sat down next to him.

"Are you two friends?"

Mike shrugged.

"Nah. He doesn't really have friends. He stays by himself a lot. Kinda weird, huh?"

"No, not really."

"He's okay, though."

"He is?"

"Sure. We've hacked around together on the playground."

Mike looked down at the floor and ran his hand along the edge of the mattress.

"I try to be his friend," he said, not looking up.

Eric felt the sadness then.

"It's nice of you to try to be his friend. He needs that. We all do."

Mike smiled and looked up at Eric. Then the smile died and he quickly moved off the bed.

"What time is it?"

Eric looked at his watch. "Ten fifteen."

"They're going to take 'em out at eleven."

"They've been infected a few times already, huh?"

Mike nodded.

"Put you out for a while each time?"

"I missed three games 'cause of my tonsils."

Mike got up off the bed and leaned against the portable metal tray stand.

"Hurt much?"

"Yup."

Mike shoved his hands back in his pockets and began to kick one foot back and forth.

"Once you have this operation, they won't be there to get infected again. It's a little scary, I know that. But it's worth it in the long run. It'll be all over by noon and you won't ever have to worry about them keeping you from playing soccer again. Doesn't seem like such a bad deal, does it?"

"It's still kinda scary."

Eric stood up and patted Mike's head.

"You'll just fall asleep and when you wake up, it'll be over. No problem."

"It's gonna be sore. Mom told me."

"Not as sore as when it was infected."

"Really?"

Mike's eyes widened and he glanced up at Eric to reassure himself that this grown-up was on his side. He could see he was and that made him grin.

"No problem, huh?"

Mike shook his head.

"No problem."

"I'll talk to you as soon as you're back here. Man to man. Agreed?"

Eric stuck out his hand and Mike shook it.

"Agreed."

After an early lunch in town with the X-ray technician, Eric hurried back to Mike's room. He was back in bed now, still out from the anesthetic.

Eric asked the nurse how it had gone and she told him it went smoothly. Eric thanked her and she left. It would be awhile before Mike woke up but Eric decided to wait in the room so there would be someone familiar with him when Mike first opened his eyes.

Eric was standing by the window when he saw a car screech around Claton Street and into the hospital driveway. A man and woman jumped out. The man was carrying a dark-haired boy in his arms.

It was Peter Delmont.

Without a second thought, Eric rushed downstairs. When he got to the emergency room, Sherry Mellany was already there. Eric saw Peter's parents talking to her. He saw the look on their faces, and he knew. He felt his stomach tighten.

Peter was lying on a bed in a small room with a bright light over him. Dr. Jacobs was examining him. Peter's face was badly bruised. The doctor cut off his shirt to reveal large brown and yellow bruises on his ribs and shoulders. Eric stood outside the door as the doctor prodded Peter gently on the ribs. Peter was only half-conscious, but his body jerked at the slightest touch. He did not cry out. Eric wondered how anyone could intentionally harm such a beautiful and courageous child.

"You say he fell down the stairs?" Sherry asked, standing over the nurse who was filling in the admittance sheet.

"Yes," Mr. Delmont said.

Eric came up behind Sherry and stared. Mrs. Delmont glanced at him. She was crying, her eyes red. She looked away quickly. Mr. Delmont stared back at Eric, and there was no mistaking the anger in his glare.

Eric swallowed to calm his stomach. He knew what he had to do. He walked out of the emergency room and down the hall until he could control himself enough to do it. Then Eric walked to the end of the corridor and back again quickly.

The Delmonts had finished filling out the admission forms. The father was now standing outside the room where his son was.

"We'll have to take X rays," Dr. Jacobs said, coming out of the room. He did not look at the father. Dr. Jacobs had examined every inch of Peter's body and had seen all the old scars, as well as the new bruises. He wanted full X rays for evidence.

"I'd like to speak with you, Mrs. Mellany," Dr. Jacobs said. "Alone."

Sherry looked at Mrs. Delmont. She was staring at the floor now.

"In my office," Sherry said.

"Excuse me." Eric ran up to them. "I'd like to have a conference with the parents. Is there a spare office? Mine's not done yet."

"You can use Dr. Paul's," Sherry said. She questioned Eric with her eyes, but Eric's face was a mask now and she couldn't tell what he was going to do.

"Follow me please," Eric said. He walked briskly ahead of them. The mother glanced up once, and the father shook his head at her. Eric caught his threat as he turned into Dr. Paul's office.

"Sit down, please." Eric offered. They sat on the sofa to the left of the desk. Eric pulled his chair toward them. He wanted to be facing them so they could not look away.

"Who are you?" Mr. Delmont asked. There was a suppressed anger to his voice that frightened Eric.

"I'm Dr. Loman," Eric said. He was going to say "the psychiatrist" but decided against it.

"You're the son of . . ." Delmont stopped himself when his wife grabbed his arm.

"Of John Loman," Eric said. He kept his tone cold and professional. It was his way to keep a balance. "Why?"

"Nothing," he answered. "Nothing. I'm sorry about the accident."

Eric waved that conversation away with his hand.

"You say your son fell down some stairs?" Eric asked.

"We already went through this," the father said.

"Yes," Mrs. Delmont said sheepishly. "The basement stairs. It was awful. I heard him screaming and . . ." She began to cry again and couldn't go on.

"And yesterday, what was it that happened?" Eric asked.

"He fell playing," Mr. Delmont answered. His anger was growing, and Eric watched him knowingly. The anger he saw in Mr. Delmont's eyes was the worst kind, the kind that erupts from an overwhelming fear.

"He's very awkward," the mother injected quickly.

"I've heard that," Eric said. He stared at Peter's father, pushing him, taunting him. He let the silence work for him and waited.

"We don't have to sit here," the man said, "and watch you stare."

"Was I staring?" Eric asked. "Sorry. Let's get back to Peter."

"He's going to be all right," Mrs. Delmont said. There was a terrible pleading in her voice.

"Don't know yet," Eric said coldly. "He's hurt pretty badly. They've taken him to X-ray right now. We have a reserve unit." Eric smiled as he said that. Then he sat back again. He was thinking about how stupid it was to beat Peter and bring him back to the same hospital the very next day. Then he began to realize what that meant.

"I know Peter never fell down any stairs," Eric said suddenly. He watched both parents recoil. Then the father sat up stiffly, his arms tight and bulging through his shirt.

"What are you trying to say?" he asked.

"I'm trying to say that I know he didn't fall down any stairs. Dr. Jacobs can testify to that."

"Testify?" Mrs. Delmont gasped. She grabbed her husband's arm with one hand.

"Are you calling us liars?" Mr. Delmont asked. His eyes narrowed, and he squeezed the arms of the sofa.

Eric stared and waited and said nothing. He had seen what the silence had done before and he let it work for him again. Besides, he knew now that, unconsciously, this was what they really wanted. It was why they came back.

"Are you?" Mr. Delmont asked again, leaning forward on the sofa.

"Did you see him, Mrs. Delmont?" Eric looked directly at her, ignoring her husband.

"Lying there all bruised and bloody." Eric shook

his head. "God, the pain must have been excruciating."

"What are you trying to—" the father began.

"Brave little boy, though. Kept his jaw clenched. Never uttered a sound." Eric switched his gaze to the father. "You teach him that?"

"What?"

"To take pain without making any noise? You hit him when he cries?"

"I never hit that kid."

"Kids need discipline," Eric added. "You got to take them in hand once in a while."

"Never!" Delmont said loudly. "I never—"

"Why are you so defensive, Mr. Delmont?"

"I'm not defensive." He looked at his wife, then sat back against the cushions. "You're just trying to make me sound that way."

"Why did you do it?" Eric asked. "Did Peter misbehave?"

"Do what?" Mr. Delmont pushed off the back of the sofa with his elbows.

"You know."

"We don't have to sit here and listen to this," he said. He stood up and pulled his wife with him, but neither actually tried to walk out.

"Yes, you do," Eric barked sternly. His accusation caught Mrs. Delmont by the shoulders and scattered like needles down her back.

"You brought Peter in yesterday for his ankle. Today for some new bruises. He didn't get those falling down any stairs and you don't want me to believe he did. You wouldn't have brought him back the very next day unless you were trying to get caught. Trying to make it so obvious, there would be no other way. You know that, don't you?"

"That's absurd," Mr. Delmont said, but he sat down again and so did his wife. That convinced Eric he was right.

"A little boy is lying over at X-ray, beaten," Eric stated. "Beaten. And you tell me it's absurd."

"Let's go." Delmont stood again, but his wife sat stunned, unable to look up from the floor.

"He did it, didn't he, Mrs. Delmont?" Eric asked, pointing at her husband. "He can't hurt you here. Don't be afraid. But if you don't say it now, next time he may kill Peter. You know that's why you brought Peter back today. You know it."

"No," she whimpered. "No. No. No." She started to cry even harder.

"Leave her alone," the father said. "She never touched him." He stood a few feet away and Eric realized he wouldn't come any closer than that. It startled Eric. He had thought he would react. He'd thought Delmont would become violent if pushed too far. But now he saw that the father was helpless, and then he realized why. Delmont had said "she" just then. He was standing limp, drenched in his own fear, the anger diluted. He was not dangerous at all. Eric suddenly knew he'd been wrong. He looked at Mrs. Delmont like he had never looked at a woman before. She saw the look and recoiled, her head quickly retreating into her shoulder as if she had been slapped.

"You want me to know, don't you?" Eric asked her. The mother shook her head, still crying.

"You hurt him badly," Eric said softly. He saw his words cut into her like razors. "You love him, don't you?"

The woman glanced up at Eric, but her head stayed down on her shoulder. It was awful to see, but Eric had to go on. There was a life at stake.

"You do love him, don't you?" he asked again.

She nodded.

"But sometimes he's just too hard to handle. You get angry. All that responsibility. All that pain he made you go through. All those years, the best years of your life, spent on him. And he doesn't even care sometimes, does he?"

"Yes," she moaned. "No. I don't know."

"Why did you beat him?" Eric asked quietly.

The father took a step forward to protect his wife. Eric glanced at him and he stopped. Just like he did when she beat Peter, Eric thought.

"Why?" Eric pushed toward her out of his chair.

"I don't know!" she cried. She hid her face in her hands. "I don't know. It just happens. I can't help it. I never want to hurt him. I love him!"

Mr. Delmont looked at Eric. Eric nodded to him and started to leave.

"She really does love him," Delmont said.

Eric stopped at the door but kept his back to them.

"That's what so sad about it," he said as he closed the door.

The full X rays showed that Peter had been beaten often over the last few years. It made Eric sick to hear Dr. Jacobs describe all the old fractures. Standing outside Peter's room now, Eric had to wait until he could compose himself. The child-abuse charges were being filed by Dr. Jacobs. There was more than enough proof, especially with Mrs. Delmont's confession. But Eric wasn't worried about that. He was worried about Peter and how deeply the beatings had affected him. He was almost afraid to go in and find out.

It's time, doctor, he told himself. Then he opened the door.

"I hear you ate something," Eric said as he sat on the chair next to the bed.

Peter turned on his side, resting his weight on one elbow.

"It's not good. But it's food," Peter said. "Hurts to chew, though."

Eric got out of his chair and walked to the window. He was surprised that Peter was talking at all. He attributed that surprise to the skill of the nurses who had brought him up there and sat with him to make him feel comfortable.

Peter rolled over and looked out past Eric.

"You play soccer?" Peter asked.

"Used to," Eric said. "In prep school."

"I'm a forward," Peter said. "Left wing."

"I heard you're good."

"Who said?"

"Mike Mellany."

"I'm pretty good. Not as good as I could be, though."

Eric came back and sat down. He didn't know where to start. Peter watched him closely, and Eric knew he was waiting to hear something. Eric saw the painful questions in his eyes as Peter watched his every move.

"How did you get hurt, Peter?"

Eric sat back in his chair and tried not to make the question sound harsh. He had seen how quickly Peter could turn inside himself for protection.

"Fell down the stairs," Peter said hesitantly.

Eric sat up, looked straight into Peter's eyes, and sighed. Peter tried to return the stare, but couldn't. He looked down at his hand playing with the bed control.

"Who told you to say that?"

Peter stared at his hand and kept fidgeting.

"Peter? Who told you to say that? I know it isn't true. Your mother told me it isn't true."

Peter's eyes gazed slowly up through his lashes at Eric.

"Why hasn't she come to see me?" he asked. "Dad almost cried when I asked him. He came up with the nurses."

Eric watched the fear grow until a tear pushed slowly out of Peter's eyes. Eric knew how much it hurt, but there was nothing he could do. He was there to help Peter even if it hurt.

"Your father told you to say that, didn't he? So your mother wouldn't get into trouble."

Peter took a deep breath and turned his head to the window. Eric reached out and touched his arm. He tried to jerk it away, but it hurt too much and he almost cried out.

"Peter," Eric said softly. "I know what happened. Your mother told me."

Peter's head snapped back, and his eyes, wide and full of fear, stabbed at Eric.

"She didn't," he defended loudly. "I fell. Down the stairs. I fell."

"She hit you."

Eric didn't know how he would take the bluntness. He said it because he saw no other way now.

Peter cocked his head and stared, unbelieving, at Eric.

Then he began to cry, trying to stop himself at the same time.

"She loves me," he said, gasping. "She would . . . never hurt me."

"You don't have to lie now, Peter. Your mother told me what happened."

"No," Peter barked. "No."

Eric watched him and said nothing. It was up to Peter now. Eric had to know how bad that turmoil was inside. It was all Eric could do to keep from picking up the frightened, confused boy and holding him and telling him it was all right.

"Sometimes . . . I'm . . . a . . . bad boy." Peter spoke in sputters, and his head twitched with each verbal spasm. "Need . . . a . . . spanking . . . But she . . . loves me." He stuck out his chin as if to prove what he had said.

"It's not shameful." Eric watched Peter sit up slowly. "People who love other people don't always know how to treat them. Sometimes you hurt the people you love, worse than anyone else, just because you do love them, because they are so special."

Peter listened. Eric could see the slow, growing fascination in his eyes. The worst part, Eric remembered from his youth, was the loneliness, the thinking that you were the only one, that no one would understand.

"She loves me," Peter mumbled.

"She told me she did."

Peter wiped his eyes and tried to smile. "But she loves me more than anyone."

"But she gets mad sometimes. And she scares you then?"

Peter nodded.

"And she hurts you?"

Peter stared past Eric. He was pushing hard to admit something, something Eric knew suddenly he hadn't even admitted to himself. Peter stared until his eyes glassed over, but he did not answer.

"And sometimes she hits you. Doesn't she, Peter?"

The boy's eyes blinked slowly and turned to Eric, but did not look at him. There was something strange in the way the boy sat up stiff and erect and still.

There was no nervousness now and, as Eric watched, it seemed as if the boy's face changed, as if he somehow was older then, and angry, not young and frightened. Eric closed his eyes, then slowly opened them, but still the boy looked foreign to him.

"Did your mother ever hit you?" he asked, seeing Peter's eyes were with him now.

"No."

His answer was not quick or defensive, and that bothered Eric.

"She never spanked you?"

"No." Peter turned his head sideways in the pillow, curling one arm under it. "Just David. Not me."

Eric sat back and, breathing deeply, rubbed his hands over his face. He knew Peter had no brothers.

"Who is David?"

"My friend," Peter said quietly.

"Where does David live?"

Eric already knew the answer. He felt himself cringing, hoping he was wrong. Watching the boy closely, Eric felt he was no longer with Peter, but with someone else, someone he wasn't so sure he liked.

"With me."

Eric walked over to the boy. He tensed his muscles so the boy wouldn't see he was shaking as he pulled the covers up over his chest.

"You're going to be all right. No one can hurt you now. You're safe here and I'm your friend. Now get some sleep. I'll come visit again later."

Eric clenched and unclenched his fists as he watched the boy close his eyes. The situation was much worse than he had ever expected and he did not know what to do.

Eric walked out into the hall and leaned against the wall at the water fountain. A nurse walked by and asked if he were all right. He didn't say anything, just walked two doors down to the supply room and went inside. He needed desperately to be alone then. Peter had struck a chord deep within him and he had to think it out. It was hard because his insides kept tugging at him when he tried to analyze what hurt so much. It was difficult to keep a thought very long.

Lisa saw Eric go into the supply closet when she stepped out of the elevator. She hurried toward him. As she passed Peter's room, she didn't see the boy limp out of bed, hobble to the door, and watch her enter the supply room.

It was dark in the room, but she could see Eric leaning back against the large gray metal shelves. She felt for the switch and turned on the ceiling lights. "How is he?" she asked.

Eric shook his head, raised his hands as if to say something, then dropped them limply to his sides.

"Not too good, I guess," she said.

She walked up to him and put her hand on his shoulder. Eric kept his head turned away from her. When she pulled his face toward her, he yanked it away, then wiped his eyes.

"That bad?"

"Goddamn people," Eric muttered.

Lisa forced herself in front of Eric and hugged him. He held her loosely, but was not very receptive.

"You know he may have developed a multiple personality because of the horror, the beatings! It must have been awful. Just can't see how anyone . . ."

Eric moved away from her. He grabbed one of the uprights on the metal shelves and glanced at Lisa. "How could she do that to her son? I know what the textbooks say, but it's sickening. That poor kid doesn't even know what's real now and what's not. I'm not sure he even knows who he is. God, that's sick."

"You've seen worse," Lisa said. She was worried about Eric getting too involved again. He had done that with Carol and her death had cut into him sharply. She did not want to see him slowly eat away at himself because of his patients.

"But there's something about Peter. He reminds me of myself when I was his age. I can't exactly say what it is, but . . ." Eric shrugged. "I don't know."

"You shouldn't let your patients get you so emotionally worked up. You're a doctor. You need that professional distance for your own good."

"The boy needs someone desperately, and I'm the only psychiatrist here. I can't help it if I'm concerned."

"Concerned is fine. Overwrought is something else again."

"What the hell do you expect?" Eric yelled. As he did, he turned slightly and there was a quick snap and suddenly the eight-foot shelves were careening down on Lisa.

"Eric!" she screamed, covering her head with her arms.

Eric dove under the falling shelves and tackled Lisa, rolling her underneath him. The corner of the shelves crashed down on his back. He lifted himself up and Lisa pulled herself out from underneath him. Then he yanked himself out after her.

An aide threw the door open then and with Eric's help, lifted the shelves, their contents broken or spilled out over the floor, back against the wall.

"What happened?" he asked.

"I don't know," Eric said. He was helping Lisa stand up. "Are you okay?"

Lisa wiped off her stained uniform.

"I guess so. Nothing seems broken."

"What happened?" the aide asked Lisa this time. She shook her head.

"Eric was leaning on the . . ." She stopped and peered over at Eric. "I don't know really. The shelves just came off the wall. We were in front of them, and they just fell. Eric covered me with his body."

Eric put his arm around her. She turned and buried her face against his chest.

"Jesus, that scared me."

"Are you all right, Doc?" the aide asked, seeing the tear in the shoulder of his coat.

Eric felt a sharp pain ripple down his back. He moved his arm around. It was bruised, but not seriously.

"I'm fine. Thanks for your help."

"Well, I'd better get someone to clean this up."

The aide looked at both of them strangely, then walked out. Eric and Lisa followed him, but went the opposite way down the hall. As they walked, Lisa peered back over her shoulder at the aide. When she did, she saw that the door to Peter Delmont's room was open, and the boy was standing in the hall, staring.

When Eric turned to look, the boy was gone.

CHAPTER VI

That afternoon, Sherry Mellany and Mr. Gibbs checked the closet for damage. They made a list of what was broken and needed to be replaced. Mr. Gibbs, mumbling to himself and scratching his gray two-day growth, walked around the shelves. He pulled at those on the opposite wall of the accident. The whole structure pulled out of the wall and tipped slightly.

"Top heavy," he said.

Sherry glanced up from her note pad.

"Look at this crap."

Mr. Gibbs waved Sherry over to the shelves.

"See that? The shelves are screwed into the plaster." He poked his finger in one of the holes. "These screws won't hold nothin'. All these shelves could go with the slightest pull. Especially since whoever stacked 'em put the heaviest loads on top. That's basic stupidity. I learned not to do that when I was ten, piling canned vegetables for my mother in the cellar."

"I guess you'd better find a better way to secure the shelves then."

"And repack 'em."

"I'll send an aide up to help."

"Dr. Loman wasn't hurt, huh?"

"Just a sore shoulder."

Mr. Gibbs nodded. He had known Eric since he was a child, the way he knew almost everyone in Hapsburg, and he had always liked him. He knew how the other children had picked on him and how the town disliked the Loman family, and he had always felt a certain twinge of guilt for that. It was his town too and the stupid prejudices it held embarrassed him. He was glad to see how Eric Loman had gained strength from it all and was proud of him, the way an uncle would be proud, but he would never tell him that. He did not feel it was his place. Besides, he hadn't given anyone a compliment in twenty years.

The next day Peter's bruised face was puffier and the yellow on his cheek and around one eye had turned to blue-black. Eric had come in early that morning to work with him, but the boy had fallen asleep after breakfast and Eric sat in the chair by his bed to wait until he woke up again.

"Doctor Loman? Doctor Loman?"

Eric opened his eyes to see Peter leaning toward him, shaking his shoulder shyly. Eric smiled.

"I fell asleep."

"You woke me up. You were snoring."

Eric laughed and shook his head. "Sorry about that."

Peter began to smile, but his cheek hurt too much and he stopped.

Eric sat up in the chair and yawned. "How was breakfast?"

"Okay."

"Just okay?"

"Nothing special."

"Does it hurt to eat?"

"A little."

"You're a brave kid. Did you know that?"

Peter gave him a half-smile. Eric could see it mostly in the eyes.

"You feel good enough to talk for a while?"

Peter nodded. "Sure."

Then his face became rigid and he looked away from Eric over at the window.

"Am I going home now?"

"Do you want to?"

Eric watched the boy search him with his eyes. Then he shrugged.

"Would it be all right with you if you stayed here awhile?"

"Yeah. If its okay with David." Peter lay back on the bed and peered up at the ceiling.

Eric Loman was in no hurry. He would not push as hard as he did with Carol. But it was not Carol he was pondering now as he sat and watched the boy drift away in his mind. He was remembering a time in the summer of his ninth year.

Eric was playing with his trucks in the sandbox behind his house when he heard the sound of children laughing in the woods beyond their lawn.

"I'm bored playing construction," he sighed.

The boys in the woods were playing army. Eric ran up to them and asked if he could play too.

"You don't even have a gun," one of them said.

Eric found a straight stick and presented it to them. "This is a machine gun."

The boys laughed. They all had toy guns. Then the biggest of them, Fred, pushed up close to Eric.

"That's a stick," he said.

"I can pretend. Your guns aren't real either."

"You can't play with us." Fred pushed Eric back.

"My mom told me to stay away from you. She said you—"

"I didn't want to play anyway," Eric said quickly. "Teddy wants to go home and play."

"Teddy who?" Fred laughed.

"Teddy's my friend," Eric said. "I'm the only one who can see him."

Fred laughed even harder and turned to the other boys. He was their leader and they laughed with him.

"Ya see," Fred said, pointing his thumb at Eric. "He's crazy, just like my mom said." The laughter grew louder. "You're crazy as a loon," he taunted, shoving Eric hard in the chest. Eric fell back onto the ground. They stood over him, laughing.

Eric grabbed his stick and swung it at their legs. They jumped back and laughed even harder. Eric stood up, threw the stick at Fred, then dashed, crying, back to the house. He stopped before he entered the back door and waited until he was finished crying. Then he wiped his eyes.

"Don't you start crying now, Teddy," he said. "Father's in the house."

Eric felt the pain again and, looking at Peter, tried to find a way to show him he understood. Peter had rolled over on his side and Eric knew he was waiting for him to say something.

"I used to have an invisible friend," Eric said. "His name was Teddy."

Peter had watched Eric remembering and had seen the hurt on his face. It was a look Peter knew well. He pushed himself up in bed and scratched his nose. He wanted to hear more.

"I never had many friends," Eric continued, "so I

made up Teddy. He was make-believe. But he was very important to me."

"David is not make-believe," Peter said suddenly. "He protects me."

"But he is not real. He is your friend. He's nice. But you did make him up."

Peter shook his head.

"No. He's not pretend. Mom gets mad at him. He gets the beating. He would never let me get hurt."

Eric was hoping it wouldn't get to that and he was glad to see Sherry Mellany walk by the room. They both heard her talking with Mr. Gibbs.

"I've fixed it three times," Mr. Gibbs was complaining.

Peter smiled, hearing the craggy old voice. Mr. Gibbs had visited Peter last night after dinner. He had joked with him and the night had not been so lonely after that. He liked the old man because he did not talk down to him the way most grown-ups did. That's why he liked Eric too. And because he made him feel safe.

"I suppose I should see what's going on, huh?"

"I think it's the bathroom again," Peter said. He propped himself up and, leaning over the bed, peeked out into the hall. Then he lay back. "Mr. Gibbs told me last night that he was sick of that darn bathroom. It keeps leaking."

Eric smiled and stood up.

"You sure are big," Peter said, staring up.

"You will be too. I can see it in your bones."

"You really think so?"

Peter stretched out his arm and examined his wrist.

"I'd like to talk to you some more later today. If that's all right with you?"

Peter put his arm down. He was pleased to hear Eric ask his permission. It made him feel important. His parents had never asked permission for anything from him.

"Sure, I'd be glad to talk to you."

"Good. Then I'll be back. You get some rest now."

"I'd rather watch TV."

Eric showed Peter how to work the television controls by the bed, then left him watching cartoons.

"I did fix it," Mr. Gibbs said loudly.

Sherry Mellany frowned.

"Then what is this puddle in the hall? And what is this, the Grand Canyon?"

She slid the toe of her shoe along the crack in the floor of the hallway. It had grown since the first flooding. The tile was chipped and the crack was almost an inch wide. Sherry Mellany was tired of hearing that the hospital was not built like they used to build them. She was tired of slipping on water in the second-story hall. It was also very dangerous. Her sarcasm, however, did not bother Mr. Gibbs. He was glad to see that the lady who ran the place had a little spunk. It made him feel better about working for a woman.

"I put new washers in, I checked the rubber piece on the metal arm of the flushing mechanism. It all works fine."

"If you want to swim."

Eric walked out of Peter's room and closed the door gently. "You think you could argue somewhere else? This little guy needs his rest."

"I think there is nothing to argue about." Sherry crossed her arms sternly. "I think something needs fixing and I'm tired of hearing excuses."

Then she stomped away.

Mr. Gibbs glanced up at Eric. He was smirking, waiting to see Eric's reaction. Eric coughed to cover up his grin.

"She's got spirit," Mr. Gibbs said as he pried the bathroom door open. "If I were younger . . ." Then he cackled. "And had all my teeth." He shook his head and laughed to himself.

"Why do you think it keeps leaking?"

Eric walked into the bathroom behind the bent old man.

"I don't know. Why'd them shelves get screwed into plaster and not the wooden part? Why'd the X-ray unit short out and the whole wall catch on fire? Why's the floor cracked so bad? Why'd the window . . ."

Mr. Gibbs stopped and looked at Eric apologetically. Eric waved the look away.

"Well, if it keeps leaking, we should bring some sand up and charge beach rates," Eric injected quickly.

Mr. Gibbs shook his head and laughed. Then his face grew pensive and he began to talk as he pulled the stool over to get at the plumbing system above the urinal.

"I fix things good. I've fixed things for fifty years. I've fixed things here, but nothin' stays fixed." He ran his crooked hand over his chin. "It's like this building don't want to be fixed. It wants to fall apart. I know that sounds strange, but this here hospital is strange. Can't quite pin it down, but somethin' ain't right here. Just ain't right."

Mr. Gibbs took the wrench out of his back pocket and set it on the sink. He climbed up on the stool, then turned and stared down at Eric.

"I know you're a shrink and this may sound crazy

to you, but . . ." He stepped down off the stool and rubbed his bald head. "When I'm here at night, down in the basement, alone, tinkering, I hear things."

"What kind of things?"

"Don't know. Sounds like voices, distant, faint cries maybe. Then . . ." Mr. Gibbs exhaled loudly. Eric could tell he wasn't sure he should go on. But he did. "Sometimes I hear deep, slow breathing. I know all this sounds like I'm goin' loony. But that's what I hear. Sometimes I think maybe I *am* a little wack-o."

"It's probably the ventilation system. You could hear voices from upstairs through it."

Mr. Gibbs grinned.

"Yup. That sounds good. Don't believe it, but it's a better answer than any of the ones I've come up with."

Eric sat on the sofa by the window in the third-story staff lounge. Lisa sat next to him. The only other person there, Debbie, winked at Lisa and left. Lisa smiled to herself and moved sideways on the sofa next to Eric. The smile did not hide the worry in her eyes, but Eric did not notice.

"Eric?"

Lisa lightly caressed his arm. Eric pretended to peruse the empty room suspiciously.

"You mean me, lady?" He leaned over and kissed her.

"Peter Delmont. Isn't he the boy we saw at the funeral?"

"I think so."

"Do you know why he was there?"

"I haven't asked. He's in bad shape. I don't know whether he's made up a 'pretend friend' like I did when I was his age or . . ." Eric hesitated. "Or if he has two completely separate personalities. It's rare.

We don't really know that much about it. It can be treated, but . . ." Eric sat up straight, his hands on his knees. "Carol might have had the beginnings of a split personality. It was the only explanation I could come up with."

"He frightens me." Lisa sat close to the window. "He was watching when we came out of the closet after the accident, but he jumped back before you looked. There was something cold in his eyes."

"He's one terrified kid. If I had heard all that noise, I would have gone out and investigated too."

"It's not that he was looking, it was the *way* he was looking." Lisa shook her head, confused. "It's hard to explain. But he frightens me. I know it sounds silly, but . . ."

Lisa shrugged and stood up. A group of doctors opened the door and entered, talking and laughing. They sat at the table by the coffeemaker. Then two nurses came in too.

"I have to go."

Lisa straightened her uniform and Eric watched the thin white material stretch over her bottom as she bent to pick up a chart.

"I think you're worrying too much," Eric whispered, standing up next to her. "He's only a kid."

Lisa was remembering the old woman holding the boy's hand in the rain and staring hatefully at John Loman's grave. She could not get the image out of her head.

"Maybe you're right," she said. She squeezed his hand quickly and left.

Eric watched her long legs pull at her uniform. He was thinking how lucky he was to have her love him and worry about him.

"Dr. Loman?" A big, heavyset doctor called to him from across the room.

Eric walked over.

"Dr. Smith," he said, very officially.

The other doctor laughed.

"All right, all right," the big doctor apologized, holding up his hands as if surrendering. "Eric, then. I have a patient in one-fifteen. A Mrs. Wilcox, in for a gallstone. She's overly nervous. Never been in a hospital before. I was wondering if you . . ."

"I'll go see her right now."

"Thanks."

The younger of the two nurses leaned over to her friend and whispered.

"I think he's adorable."

"He's Lisa's," the other whispered back.

The doctors heard them and Dr. Smith shook his head. Eric smiled and nodded to the nurses, then left. He could hear them giggling with embarrassment as the door closed.

Mrs. Wilcox had already been given 2cc's of innovar and .04 milligrams of atrophine before her gallstone operation.

"How are you this fine day?" Eric asked, walking next to her bed.

She was a plump woman with a round, cherublike face.

"A little tipsy," she said. "They already gave me a shot."

"Good stuff, huh?" Eric smiled.

She laughed.

"I hear you're not so sure you want to go through with this," Eric said.

"I never had an operation before," she said. "I've never even stayed in a hospital overnight."

"At least they serve good food," Eric said.

"I wouldn't know. They won't let me eat because of the operation. Gallstones." She glanced up at Eric and liked what she saw. He gave her strength just by standing there looking calm and handsome.

"They should have more doctors that look like you," she giggled. "I would have come sooner."

Eric laughed with her. Two compliments in one day, he thought.

"They asked me if I wanted to stay awake and watch the operation. God, how morbid."

"I wouldn't want to," Eric said.

"Will you be operating on me too?"

"No, I don't operate."

"I bet you're a good operator," she said, and giggled again.

Eric understood that her joking was a way to avoid the fear.

"It's a simple procedure, you know," he said.

"That's what they keep telling me. But I've never had one before . . . an operation. Sometimes I feel like . . ." The smile drifted from her face and she pushed her head back onto the pillow.

"Like what?" Eric asked. He sat on the edge of her bed.

"Like I'm going to die if I let them put me to sleep. My sister died from an operation."

"A gallstone operation?"

"No. It was her liver. It wasn't functioning. Or something like that. I saw her the day before, and then . . ." She looked up from deep in her pillow at Eric. "Two days later she was dead. Complications, they said."

"Well, gallstones aren't complicated."

She shrugged and tried to smile. "Everyone tells me not to be scared, but I can't help it."

"Then be scared."

She questioned Eric with a glance.

"There's nothing wrong with being scared about something you don't know about."

"I don't want to be scared," she said.

"Then don't be," Eric said bluntly. "It's up to you. Do you have a good doctor?"

"Dr. Kirby. He's supposed to be very good."

"He's the best," Eric said. "So trust him. If you walked outside and got into a car with your husband, would you be scared?"

"Only if he'd been drinking again," she teased. Eric smiled.

"There's less of a risk to this operation than to driving home."

"They say that about airplanes too, but you wouldn't catch me on one."

"Well, you could always live with the pain you've been having."

"No, thanks," she said.

"So what's our choice here?"

"Have the operation."

"For a scared person, you seem awfully brave to me." Eric held her hand for a moment and then got up.

"The doctor made it sound like you were terrified or something," Eric teased.

"I was. But I'm not now."

"Still a little nervous?"

"Yup."

Eric winked at her, and she smiled.

"I'll come back and visit after the operation," Eric said. "All right?"

She nodded, and Eric left the room, wondering when the older doctors would accept him enough to ask his assistance in something more than just making their patients feel more comfortable in the hospital. But, he thought, at least this is a beginning.

Sarah Bingham put one more bobby pin in her gray hair, then held her purse with both hands. She looked over at the big oaks next to the hospital. She knew which one it was that he had hung himself from. She knew which branch. She stared at it to gather strength. It helped her ignore how the hospital seemed to watch her, waiting, almost beckoning, and she strode forward up the stairs. When she got to the doors she felt like turning and running.

All the others, she thought, all dead.

But somehow they didn't feel dead to her then. Suddenly she knew that if she went in those oak doors, she would never get out again alive.

But my grandson is in there. I must go see him. She felt all the years of guilt surge up into her throat. She knew the girl she had given birth to was never really stable, but she had always loved her and helped her and then, when the girl grew up and was married, everything seemed better. Until Peter was born. Then she started drifting off in the middle of conversations again and becoming overemotional about everything.

The old woman reached for the door of the hospital and tugged it open. It is my fault. I must see the boy and reassure him that I love him. I must, she thought.

Then she walked in, her head high and proud, her gait strong, strong enough to push her past her fears.

* * *

Lisa was carrying a tray with medicine and hypodermic needles when she saw an old woman standing outside Peter's room.

"Can I help you," she asked as she approached.

Sarah Bingham turned to face Lisa. Her face was white and frightened and she was holding her hands together in the loop of her purse. When Lisa saw her, she almost dropped the tray. It was the old woman she had seen at the funeral.

"Hello." Lisa forced a smile. "Can I help you?"

The old woman shook her head, then went into Peter's room, never uttering a word. She closed the door.

Lisa stood, confused, gazing at the door. Her heart was jumping against her chest. She squeezed the tray to keep from shaking.

An aide, pushing a metal cart full of heavy steel oxygen tanks, dug his feet into the tile to stop the cart before it hit Lisa. He slipped on the still moist floor by the long crack in front of the men's room, but regained his balance. The metal tanks clanged together and Lisa spun around, startled. She was pale and her mouth was hanging open.

"Are you okay, Lisa?" the aide asked.

Lisa took a deep breath, then exhaled.

"I'm fine. Just fine."

"Good. Now do you know where I'm supposed to store these oxygen tanks? They're too heavy to keep pushing around and, to be honest, I don't know where they go."

"Ask Mrs. Mellany. I don't know either."

The aide grinned. He had always liked Lisa and was secretly jealous of Eric, but had never told anyone.

Lisa held the tray and smiled. He grinned sheepishly.

"Well, I suppose I should find Mrs. Mellany. You don't think anyone will mind if I leave this cart here? It's too heavy to lug around while I look for her."

"Sure. It'll be all right there. Besides, it will warn people about that crack in the floor."

Peter sat up, overjoyed to see his grandmother. She was always the one who comforted him when he was hurt or scared of his mother. She understood things before he said them and she never judged him. Everything he did or felt or cried about was important to her.

"Hi, Grandma." He grinned and the pain in his left eye and cheek shot through his skull. He turned his head and tried to hide the bruise with his hand.

Sarah sat on the bed next to him, took his hand from his face and held it. Peter had been holding back much of the pain and the fear since he had come to the hospital and now, with his grandmother there, it all welled up inside. It was more than he could control.

She stroked the hair off his forehead and smiled that smile he knew so well, the one that meant everything in the world was safe, at least for the moment. He threw his arms around her frail body and cried. She held him close while he wept for nearly half an hour.

"Everything will be all right," she cooed as the sobs began to subside. "I'm here now. I'm here."

Peter's chest heaved and he started to choke, he had been crying so hard. Slowly, she laid him back on the bed, holding him close to her each time he gasped for air.

"Now is that any way for my brave man to act? You're suppose to be taking care of me now, remember? You promised. I'm the one that's too old to get around."

"Mom didn't mean that," he defended.

"I know. But she's right. I am. And I do need you." Peter smiled slightly as he wiped his eyes.

"So," the old woman said, wiping her eyes too. "Are they treating you like the hero that you are?"

Peter beamed and shook his head yes.

"They like me here. They're real nice to me. There's a doctor who always comes to talk. He's my friend."

"You like him?"

"He's real neat. He doesn't talk to me like I'm just a kid."

"Well, you're not. You're pretty near grown-up now."

The old woman looked around the sterile white room. She was beginning to feel it again. There was a strange, terrible thickness to the air. It was becoming hard to breathe. She tried to tell herself she was being foolish, superstitious, that there was nothing to fear, but the feeling did not go away. When she looked back at the boy, Sarah gasped. She knew it was her grandson and yet she hardly recognized him. The more she looked, the more she thought he was someone else. She held her purse tight to keep from trembling.

"You don't like it here, do you?" the boy asked, watching her turn pale. His voice startled her too. It didn't sound like her grandson. It sounded more like a voice from her past, a voice she tried hard to forget.

"Why do you say that?"

She rubbed her moist palms together and set her purse on the table by his bed.

"I know," the boy answered. He was looking at her strangely now, as if he were challenging her. There was no innocence left in his face. "You've been here before."

Sarah felt her heart cringe and she edged back away from the boy. The horror she had felt outside, looking up at the hospital, now loomed around her in that room. She felt cold fingers ripple down her spine.

"Why do you say that, Peter?"

"I'm not Peter."

The boy grinned and the bruised side of his face puffed up, thick under his eye. But he didn't seem to notice the pain.

"What do you mean?"

The boy sat up, the grin still plastered like a mask on his face, haunting her, his eyes staring angrily, ripping at her heart, killing what was left of her stubborn bravery. She had never seen the boy look so cold and hateful. Her chest began to pound painfully.

Still, the boy did not answer her.

"We're glad you finally came back," he said, watching how that terrified her.

"We? What do you mean we?"

The burst of laughter was deep, terrible, teasing, and suddenly Sarah knew where she had heard it before.

"No!" she cried. "Get away!"

She stood up weakly, feeling dizzy as she backed away from the bed. She was sucking in hard trying to catch her breath.

"You know you had to come back," the voice told her. "You and the doctor."

"No," she screamed. She shook her head and forced herself to walk back up to the boy. She grabbed him by the shoulders and shook him. "Peter? What are you doing? Is this a game? Peter? Peter?"

The boy sprang up in his bed and laughed even louder. Sarah gasped and fell back against the other bed. The laughter echoed in the room and her head began to spin. She pushed off the other bed and, reaching out in front of her as if she were blind, stumbled forward toward the door.

The boy rose out of the bed and followed her. She could hear him breathing horribly behind her. She glanced over her shoulder and screamed for her life. Grabbing the door knob frantically, she twisted it and the door flew open.

Sarah stumbled backward down the hall toward the cart with the oxygen tanks. The boy stopped and stared, close-mouthed, at the crack in the floor.

Suddenly, there was a snapping sound. One of the wheels of the cart slipped into the crack. It widened, breaking under the weight. Then the cart snapped again.

Sarah spun toward the noise. She slipped in the puddle and fell backward onto the floor. The cart creaked, its metal leg dropping further into the crack before it collapsed. The cart flipped and the oxygen tanks spilled down in procession on top of her. They shattered her arm and shoulder and bounced over onto her ribs. She tried to cry out, but there was no sound. Sarah went limp as the heavy steel tanks buried her upper torso.

Lisa rushed out of the room down the hall in time to see the tanks crash down on the woman. She ran to her and began to lift off the tanks.

"Help me," she yelled.

Looking up, she saw a boy watching her as if she

were crazy. She wondered what he was doing there. Then his whole face seemed to soften and change. Lisa stopped picking up the tanks and stared.

Only then did she realize it was Peter.

CHAPTER VII

"It's beautiful," Lisa sighed.

They were sitting at a table in an elegant restaurant in the big north mountain above Hapsburg. There was an open air porch with a dozen tables that leaned out above the sheer cliff. A stream wound down below and when the piano player took a break, you could hear the water rippling over the rocks down into the valley.

The dinner had been wonderful: fresh asparagus, veal Oscar, a good Sauterne. It had relaxed both of them. The clear fall night shone dark and bright with stars, and Eric pointed out a big white-winged owl that circled below them, then dove and disappeared into the trees.

"Want dessert?" he asked.

Lisa reached across the table and took his hand.

"I'm full."

"Drambuie and coffee, then."

Lisa smiled and nodded.

The waiter brought the drinks. Glancing around, Eric noticed they were the only ones left on the porch.

"Did I tell you how beautiful you look?"

Lisa squeezed his hand.

"Tell me again."

She was wearing a light blue gown that clung to

her lithe curves when she moved. Eric loved the way her breasts pushed the material up and held it like the tucked wings of a dove.

"You look like a queen," he said.

"That sounds kind of old."

"All right, a princess."

Then he kissed her hand. Lisa laughed. She sipped the Drambuie. It was sweet and sticky and felt good as it heated her throat.

"Eric? How long will Peter Delmont be in the hospital?"

"I thought we weren't going to talk shop anymore."

Lisa shrugged and stared up at him through her long black lashes. Watching her face in the gentle glow of the candles, the moon perched in the sky behind her black, glistening hair, Eric thought he'd never felt such contentment, such perfection. But the mention of Peter somehow dampened his spirits.

"I don't know exactly." Eric wiped his mustache with the linen napkin. "It's not a matter of physical disability or recovery. It's a matter of the mind."

"He still bothers me."

Eric sat up and shook his head, about to argue. Lisa put her hand up to stop him.

"I know it sounds ridiculous to you, Mr. Facts Only, but there's just something wrong. It's not only the boy, it's the hospital itself. Eric, your grandfather died on those grounds, your father died there. Neither in exactly normal ways. I know that sounds brutal, but . . ." Lisa leaned closer across the table. "Eric, Peter and his grandmother, Sarah, were at your father's funeral. She wasn't there because she liked him either. It was easy to see that."

Eric waved that away. "A lot of people hated my father. Maybe she had a special grudge."

"And Peter. He's so cold sometimes. He just stared today, watching as if he had expected what happened to happen."

"You're losing me now."

"The accident in the closet. He was watching. His grandmother's accident. He was right behind her. He didn't even try to help. He just watched."

"He was probably in shock."

Lisa sighed and leaned back in her chair.

"He was there when your father died and when the X-ray room caught on fire."

"The whole town was there. Lisa, this is getting out of hand. We've discussed it before. Peter, I believe, has two, separate, distinct personalities. He developed the David personality as a defense mechanism against the horror of his mother beating him. Peter needs to love his mother and he cannot accept the fact that she could hurt him. I'm not sure, but I don't think he believes he's ever been beaten by her. Only David has. I'm speculating, but . . ." Eric sipped his coffee quickly. "The boy seems strange because he's scared. Scared of the hospital, of his parents, and worst of all, scared of himself. In most multiple personalities, the original personality has no knowledge of the other or others, although they have complete knowledge of him. But, with Peter, he knows David. That's extremely unusual, but I'm hoping it's a good sign. Maybe he doesn't have two completely separate personalities. Maybe he just forced a make-believe playmate to its farthest extreme, considering the environment he had to deal with."

Lisa finished the Drambuie and, pushing out from the table, crossed her legs. Eric lost his train of thought seeing the long, dark-stockinged leg slip out from the slit in her gown.

"Maybe I'm being too sensitive. I don't know," she said.

Eric slid his chair toward her and caressed her thigh. Lisa rested her arm on his shoulder. Then they kissed. It was quick at first, but neither drew away and then they were kissing deeply and that wonderful aching grew intense.

"Let's go home," she said, pulling away to look shyly at the grinning waiter.

"Why? Don't you want another drink?"

Eric clenched his teeth to keep the teasing from showing.

"I want you," Lisa whispered, letting her fingers drift up Eric's leg under the table. "Now."

Eric smiled and overtipped everyone on his way out the door.

Mike Mellany woke up with the sun. It was rising over the mountains as he listened to the morning sound of birds. His throat was sore and swollen, but Dr. Loman was right, he thought. It still didn't hurt as bad as the infections.

Mike pressed the bed controls so he could be sitting up to watch cartoons. The controls didn't work. He pressed them again. Suddenly the radio blared on through the speaker in the wall behind him. The noise frightened him. Then it shut off and the television turned on. It did not come into focus and the static grew louder and louder.

Mike worked frantically with the controls, but was only able to change channels from one blank station to the next.

Then the nurse came running in.

"Did you buzz me?"

Mike spun his head toward her. "No."

His face was pale and his eyes were wide and jittery.

"What's wrong with the TV?" the nurse asked. She walked over and tried to get it in focus. She couldn't. "You'd better turn it off. We'll get you one that works." The nurse smiled her well-practiced smile, the one she could summon under the most dire of circumstances. "Now don't press this." She held up the nurse's call box. "Unless you want me. You understand?"

Mike nodded. He knew better than to try and convince her he had not pressed it the first time. The nurse hurried out of the room and Mike sighed with relief.

Five minutes later she came running back in. She did not looked pleased.

"I didn't touch it," Mike pleaded.

"It just doesn't go off by itself, young man."

"But I didn't. I didn't turn on the radio either." The radio had come on again just before she entered. It was playing a taped revival sermon. The nurse shut it off with the manual controls in the wall next to the speaker.

"Now quit these shenanigans. This isn't the time or place for boys' games."

Mike nodded and looked apologetic. It was a look as well practiced as her nurse's smile. Both were learned survival techniques.

After she left, Mike pressed the bed controls again. The bed began to respond. The top half lifted and the bottom half bent at his knees. He let go of the buttons, but the bed kept compressing, like an accordian. Mike felt himself becoming entrapped. He curled up and jumped sideways off the bed. He was trembling now, and his throat was aching badly.

Suddenly the television screamed on again and the

radio began to preach the worth of hard work and self-sacrifice. It was a deep, southern male voice and he yelled as he sermonized, the cackling of the television backing up his fervent conclusions.

Mike's head snapped back and forth between the TV and radio wall speaker. He was too terrified to move. He felt like he had just been invaded and his legs began to quiver down through his knees.

Then the door flew open and smacked against the wall. Mike gasped and jumped back. The nurse barged in, her face no longer under its usual control. Mike could see she was definitely upset, but when she saw the boy's horrified look, her face changed. She knew the boy was not being a prankster.

"Wiring must be wrong," she yelled above the howling electric cacophony.

Her voice soothed Mike. He tried to smile. He had felt like he was being attacked, but there was nowhere to flee, and he was glad not to be alone now in that terrible threatening noise.

"I don't like that room," he said, walking out quickly, gratefully holding the nurse's hand. She had unplugged the television, but she could not turn off the blasting sermon.

"We'll move you into another," she said. She let him sit with her at the nurse's station and watch as the day shift arrived. Then his mother scurried down the hall and he waved to her. By that time he was not scared anymore. He had been having a good time with the nurse at her desk.

"Would you like to have a roommate?" Sherry asked as she led her son down the hall. The nurse had called her at home and told her what happened.

"Sure," the boy said. He did not want to be alone in a room anymore.

"Is Peter Delmont all right with you?"

Mike shrugged. "He's all right."

"Good. Then that's settled. We'll move you in with him. I'm sure he'd be glad to have you. Dr. Loman said it would be good for both of you, and I agree."

Sherry halted her march and looked seriously down at the boy. He knew the look and kept still, waiting for his mother to speak.

"Now, Mike, I want you to be nice to Peter. He's had a rough time. He's still very sick. He's scared and he's not always thinking the way he should. He's very sick inside like you were when your father died, but for a different reason. So be nice, and be careful too. You're a big boy now. I expect you to act properly."

Mike grinned and shook his head. Then they started down the hall again and Mike grabbed his mother's skirt to get her attention. She stopped.

"My throat hurts. Maybe I'd like ice cream now."

Sherry patted his head and smiled. "Well, maybe I'll just go to the kitchen right now and get you some."

Eric stopped by Peter's room after having coffee with Lisa in the lounge. He felt good now after last night. And again this morning, he thought, smiling to himself. As he approached the room, he heard Mike and Peter giggling. That pleased and reassured him that moving Mike in was a good idea. It had suddenly occurred to him that he had not heard Peter laugh before, not a real boy's laugh.

"What's the joke?" he asked walking in between their beds.

They laughed again together, and Eric knew he would not get an answer. Then, scrutinizing Peter, he suddenly wondered if something was wrong. There was something in the way the boy looked at him that made Eric feel like he was the vulnerable one, not Peter.

"What's up, Doc?" Peter giggled, pretending to chew on a carrot. Mike tried to hold back, but he burst out laughing. Eric smiled.

"Feeling better now, I see."

The boy grinned. "Sure. As good as always." There was a strange positiveness to the way he spoke now too. Eric did not show the sudden twisting in his gut as he recognized that.

"Mike told me before that you two were friends," Eric said. He tried not to be obvious as he watched Peter's actions.

"We're good friends now," Mike said with a grin. "I didn't know he was so funny."

Eric couldn't imagine the shy, frightened little boy he had been working with as funny.

"So Peter's a comedian now?" Eric smiled and glanced from one child to the other. The joy he had experienced hearing the boys' giggling was gone now.

"No not Peter," Mike laughed, then took a breath. "David." Then he burst out laughing again.

Eric turned to Peter but the boy wasn't laughing. He was staring at Eric, and there was no fear in his eyes like there was before.

"David, huh?" Eric kept his eyes fixed on Peter's.

A slow grin spread across the boy's face but there was no humor to it. Eric coughed. His throat had gone dry and he couldn't swallow. The grin widened.

Mike laughed again, and suddenly Peter began to laugh too. It was a terrible, haunting laugh, and it grew as the boy watched Eric's face. Obviously this was no time for Eric to work with Peter. He decided it was best to come back later.

"Take it easy, Mike," Eric said, heading for the door. "You, too, Peter."

"David," Peter corrected.

Eric did not turn around to see the cold smiling hatred in the narrow black eyes.

When Eric was gone, Peter got up out of bed and walked to the window.

"I wish we could be playing soccer instead of sitting in this dumb place," Mike announced.

The boy turned and glared at him. Mike recoiled as he laid in bed. He pulled the covers up farther on his chest.

"I like it here," Peter said. He ambled over to Mike's bed. Mike grinned. Then, seeing no humor in his friend's eyes, he frowned and looked away.

Peter laughed; it was a forced sneering laugh. It made Mike's skin crawl. "Let's play."

Mike slowly looked back at his friend. The sneering was gone now. "Play what?"

"Let's explore. I can show you all kinds of neat places here."

"I . . . I got to stay in bed. Mom told me. She said I'd have ice cream sent up soon. Let's wait. I'll share it with you."

"What are you, chicken?"

Mike sat up and looked hard at Peter. He was surprised at the boy's authority and strength. He had always been quiet at school and easily intimidated. He was always running away from the older boys on the playground. Mike did not understand the abrupt change.

"I can't go," Mike said. "I have to stay here. I just had my tonsils out in an operation."

The other boy stared at him, then shrugged indifferently. "I'm going exploring. I'm no scaredy-cat."

"Neither am I," Mike said loudly as Peter slipped out of the room.

Lisa had tried to talk herself out of it, but she was still nervous when she entered Sarah Bingham's room. She did not like to admit it. Eric and she had talked more about her fears of the hospital and Peter and the old woman, and she knew he had logic and reason on his side. In her head, she could even admit he was right. There had been a strange set of circumstances and that was all it had been. There was no strange force at work. Intellectually she knew all that, but in her heart she was not convinced.

Sarah's face was white and heavy with wrinkles. The old woman turned her head slowly as Lisa entered the room.

Lisa smiled politely, then took the chart from the bottom of the bed and read it. Sarah had broken her upper arm and eight ribs. The shoulder had a hairline fracture and the side of her head had a few bad contusions. They were still testing for internal injuries.

"How do you feel?"

Sarah stared up at Lisa but said nothing. Lisa reached for her good wrist to check her heartbeat, but the old woman jerked it away.

"Don't let him get me again," she cried suddenly.

"Who?"

Lisa saw the blank, glossy, distant look in Sarah's eyes. She wondered if the old woman even knew where she was now or what had happened to her yesterday. She appeared close to being in a state of shock.

"He'll lock me up. I tried to run away. He found

out. He's going to lock me up again." Her head cocked off the pillow. "I can hear him."

"No one is going to lock you anywhere, Mrs. Bingham. Calm down. This is a hospital. You're safe here."

Lisa reached to pat her reassuringly on the shoulder.

"Don't," Sarah cried. Her voice was weak, but the terror was real enough and Lisa recoiled immediately.

"I'm here to help you."

"No. Don't let him. No."

Sarah rolled her head on the pillow, and the tears streamed down her cheeks.

"What's wrong?"

Lisa leaned forward, being careful not to get too close again.

"They think I'm crazy. I'm not. He wants me here. Like the others. He keeps us for that." Sarah stretched her head back. "Oh, God. Please." Then her face fell limply to one side and she peered up at Lisa out of the corner of her eyes. "Sometimes it's a curse to be young and pretty. It's the war. It took away everything. It took away my Bobby. He'll never come back. All the men stare at me in town. I know what they're thinking." She shook her head and the tears dropped onto both sides of the pillow. "He forced me. I hated it. But I couldn't stop him. I couldn't." Sarah sat up and the pain shot through her body. Lisa quickly helped her lie back down.

"Don't try to move. You've been hurt. Try to keep still."

The old woman reached up with her good hand and wiped her eyes. "They don't know. Nobody knows what he does."

* * *

Peter crouched behind the half-open door to Room 228 as an aide sauntered by. Then he sneaked along close to the wall and dashed up the stairs to the third floor. Opening the stair door, he peeked down the hall. No one was there, except the nurse at the station with her back to him.

He watched an old man hobble with the aid of his walker out to the sundeck. Slinking along the wall, eyes glued to the nurse's back, Peter followed him. He was intrigued by the old man. He had never seen anyone or anything move with such steady persistence. Except, he remembered, the big snapping turtle he had seen crossing the road that summer.

"Hello," Peter said, standing next to the old man. The sun was higher now over the mountains and the shadows of the town were short and dark. There was a cool west wind that blew through the trees.

The old man gazed up at the boy and nodded, grinning through his hard-wrinkled face.

"Can I try it?"

Peter ran his hand along the cold metal of the walker. The old man was sitting in a chair. He pushed the walker closer to Peter with his foot.

"It's all yours," he answered. "I don't much like it myself. It makes me feel like a robot."

Peter smiled and held it the way he had seen the old man hold it. He began to mimic his stride, pretending to be a mechanical man. His head moved in short, quick-angled jerks like a nervous bird feeding on the ground.

"That does not compute," Peter stuttered. "Calling R2D2." Then he laughed and the bruised side of his face twitched, but the pain was not so bad. The old man watched the twitching and the laughter. It was both sad and pleasant to him at the same time.

"How'd you hurt yourself up? Crash on your bike?"

Peter stopped suddenly and put the walker back next to the old man.

"I fell down the stairs."

"The first step is always the hardest." The old man leaned to one side, grabbed the arm of another chair, and slid it next to him. "Sit down. Take a load off your mind."

Peter put his feet on the chair and sat on its arm.

"Never used one of them before, huh?" the old man asked.

"Used what?"

Peter glanced at the old man to see if he were making fun of him. The old man looked very serious.

"A chair. It was built to put your can where your feet are."

The old man laughed kindly and Peter, sliding down into the seat, laughed too.

"You live here?"

Peter peered back at the hospital, then looked at the old man.

"Not here." Peter pointed out at the town. "There."

The old man grinned and his eyes danced playfully. Peter giggled.

"It's a different world. Young people take everything too literal." The old man pulled himself up and, holding his walker, edged over to the porch wall. "Which house?"

Peter scurried next to him and stared down at Hapsburg.

"That one there," he pointed, "with the green roof. Behind the new grocery store next to the apartments. And you?"

The old man pointed north at the mountains.

"There," he said.

Peter stood up on his toes and squinted. He could only see trees and the big rock cliff that had multicolored graffiti on it.

"I can't see it."

The old man stared at the mountains and Peter watched his face slowly sag. He did not interrupt because he could see the importance of the silence in the man's eyes.

"I can," the man said quietly. The boy cocked his head to one side the way a puppy does when it's confused. The old man laughed and tapped his bald head. "In here. I can see it in here. At my age, just the seeing is important. Don't matter too much whether it's in the head or through the eyes anymore. Both gettin' to be pretty much the same now."

Peter looked at him sadly. The old man ruffled his hair.

"Ain't nothin' to frown about. It's quite a nice thing, really. Don't take so much effort when you use the remembering."

He hobbled back to his chair and waved Peter over. They sat side by side again.

"Ya see, when you're young, you ain't got much to remember, really, so God gives you a hell of an imagination to play with. Then ya get older and you ain't got time for playin' anymore, you're so busy livin'. Tryin' to make something concrete for yourself, something you can say you've done, and done well, as well as any man. Then ya get older still and you start gettin' as much joy out of what others do, as with what you do. Then if ya live long enough, you got a whole world to remember. That's enough too, at least almost, if you're content with what you've done. Then the imagination ain't so necessary anymore."

Peter did not understand what the old man meant, but he liked the way he spoke and he shook his head knowingly.

A nurse came out with a small paper cup and a glass of water.

"Time for your pills, Mr. Klein."

The old man sneaked a quick glance at Peter and winked. The nurse put the glass on the table next to his chair and handed him the small cup. Then she stood behind him and waited. Peter was slightly disappointed that the nurse had not asked him how he had gotten out on the porch.

"I'm old enough to take my own medicine without you starin'," he barked. The nurse shook her head and left. The old man looked over his shoulder, then handed the cup to Peter.

"Go dump these over the wall."

Peter smiled and did what he was told.

"They're for my heart, they say. My heart's been goin' for ninety some years on its own. It don't need no help now."

"But you might get sick."

"Don't you fret. You want the pills, you take 'em."

"I didn't mean . . ."

The old man shrugged. "You got a lot of livin' to do. I did mine. More than most. I don't want no fancy medicine to keep me alive past my time. My time is between me and God. We got a contract."

Peter smiled. He walked around the perimeter of the porch, watching two squirrels on the lawn chase each other, then dash, circling, up a tree.

"You gonna get out a here soon?" the old man asked.

Peter shrugged, his back to the old man. He was

staring at Main Street and his stomach ached in a numb, sad way. He had just seen his father's car go by, but it did not turn in. His mother was not in it.

"What's the matter?"

The boy turned and glared at him. "What's the matter with you?"

"They say I'm too old."

The old man saw a distance and an anger in the boy's eyes. The joking was gone. "You are."

"Now don't you get disrespectful, boy."

The boy walked up to the old man. "Why? You're not my father."

The old man had been through too much in his life to be frightened now, but he still felt a quick tingling run down into his fingers. He was startled and hurt by the coldness, the lack of emotion in the boy.

"But I can still put you over my knees if I had to."

Peter laughed nastily and took a step back. "You couldn't catch me. Not with that dumb cage you need to walk in."

Angered, the man lunged out at Peter but the boy was just out of reach.

"My grandmother's pretty old too," Peter said. "Maybe you'd know her. Her name is Sarah Bingham."

The old man felt the shock ripple through his brittle torso. He remembered Sarah well from the rumors after the asylum fire. She was the only one, besides Dr. Loman, who had escaped the holocaust. The old man had always felt deeply sorry for her because he knew what the rest of the town suspected. Then, looking over, seeing how much the shock pleased the boy, he became truly scared. He had contented himself with death long ago, but this was more horrible than that. It was sadistic.

He began to sweat coldly and his heartbeat quickened.

"You like it here, don't you?" he asked, hoping he was wrong.

"Yes," the boy answered proudly, a strange, sickening smile on his bruised face. "It's my home now."

The old man felt a sharp, jabbing pain. It cut through his chest and he doubled over, gasping for breath. He tried to stand, but couldn't. He looked over at the boy, his mouth twitching, trying desperately to speak, but there was no breath to make the words. His face turned white and his eyes grew yellow and wide and terrified. One gnarled, spiderlike hand reached out, trembling, toward the boy. He watched it. When it got close enough, he stepped back.

The old man fell forward out of the chair, coughing, gasping, shaking on the cement floor.

Then Peter saw death in his eyes and heard the terror in his wordless gasps, and suddenly he was frightened for the old man. He ran into the hall and yelled frantically for the nurse.

Sherry Mellany called Dr. Philips, the heart specialist, to come to the hospital immediately. Mr. Klein had a coronary thrombosis and occlusion of a main blood vessel by clotting. His condition was critical. Philips argued with her, after he arrived at the hospital, that the old man should not have the coronary bypass operation, but Sherry had a strict policy that, to her, was a moral imperative. She believed everything should be done to save a patient no matter how old or sick he was. Besides, the old man was still strong. Death was a hospital's enemy, even if some might consider it a relief, and it was to be fought to the end, no matter what. Dr. Philips could not argue that with her and when she quoted his Hippocratic oath, he left to scrub up.

Dr. Jacobs was already scrubbing, waiting to assist him.

Mike was asleep. Peter sat on his bed, staring blankly at the floor. He was trying to piece together what had happened. He remembered talking with the old man, and even sneaking up to the third floor, but he couldn't remember how the old man was suddenly on the floor, gasping, his eyes bulging out. Peter could see that death-mask face in his mind and he shivered. He was becoming frightened now of the things he could not remember.

Then Mike rolled over and Peter decided to walk out into the hall. He wanted to be alone. Two nurses rushed around the corner and down the hall toward him. He quickly bolted into the men's room. There was a small puddle by the urinals and he slid on it, but caught himself on the sink before he fell. The nurses passed by. Lifting himself up by the sink, Peter stared into the mirror. He did not like looking at himself and that scared him. But it was not the bruises that bothered him. He made himself stare into the mirror to face it. He felt like he were splitting in half.

"I don't like you," he whispered, staring. The face looked back at him, bruised and swollen and smiling. He did not feel like he owned that face anymore. Then the eyes in the mirror grew cold, capturing Peter. He could not turn away.

"He teased you. He tried to grab you. He was going to spank you."

"I like him."

"He's a mean old man."

"Go away. You're hurting me. Go away."

"I'll protect you. Take care of you."

"No!"

Peter shook his head violently but his eyes never left the mirror. Slowly, his arm muscles spasming, he lowered himself back down on his feet. He couldn't see the mirror anymore.

"Must get clean," he mumbled quietly. "He touched me."

The boy turned on the hot water and began to wash his hands. As the water grew hotter, almost scalding, he smiled and kept talking to himself, never removing his hands from the water.

"He's over ninety, for God's sake," Dr. Philips said. He was spreading the soap up his forearms.

"If Sherry Mellany thinks there's a chance, then there is one. He's a tough old coot. We could buy him another six months, maybe longer if he's lucky. I think its worth it. Besides, we're not judges, just doctors."

Dr. Jacobs ran his arms under the sink, then began scrubbing all over again.

"The heart massage strengthened him. Heartbeat's up, blood pressure's better, he's a tough cookie. If we can clear out the blocked artery without complications, he'll be ready for his walker in no time."

Both doctors leaned down together to wash off. Suddenly the water was boiling hot.

"Jesus!" Dr. Philips screamed.

Looking down, they saw their hands and wrists had second-degree burns; the blisters would not be long in appearing. Steam rose up thick and hot into their faces. They stepped farther back from the sink.

"Nurse. Nurse!" Dr. Philips yelled.

A nurse ran in.

"Call the ambulance. They'll have to take the patient to Anville Hospital. Call Dr. Linhouser there. Quick. We've been burned at that damn sink and can't operate."

"I'm telling you, it's more than coincidence. Peter was with him when he had the attack," Lisa argued. She was taking Eric to see Sarah, but stopped on the stairs to finish her thought.

"Now how could the boy give him a heart attack? How can that be his fault. Even you have to admit when Nancy came out to give him his pills, she said they were having a nice time talking together."

Leaning against the rail, Lisa looked two stories down between the stairs. She was angry inside. She liked the old man and did not want him to die.

"And what about Dr. Philips getting burned? How was the water boiling hot all of a sudden?"

"A malfunction. Mr. Gibbs said the cold waterline clogged. You can't blame that on Peter too."

"It's just . . ."

Lisa shook her head. She was frustrated but she fought back the anger. Eric took her in his arms.

"It's just what?" he asked.

Lisa took a slow easy breath and tried to recover her composure.

"I don't know. Everything keeps going wrong here. One thing, two things, all right, but . . ." She pushed away to look up into Eric's face. "Too many things have happened here."

"It's a new building. Things go wrong."

"It's more than that."

"Then what? What is it?"

"It's like he said. It's evil. The land is evil. The

foundation of the hospital. It's all been soaked with too much blood. And Peter's part of it somehow."

Eric wrinkled his eyes disapprovingly as he stared down at Lisa.

"Come on now. That's ridiculous. Land isn't evil. This hospital is just a building, like any other building. I'll admit some odd accidents have occurred. But that's all they were . . . accidents. You can't blame any of that on a ten-year-old boy."

Eric lifted her chin and smiled. Lisa turned her head away.

"Now let's go see Sarah and find out what's wrong. We've got work to do. We're medical people, not witch doctors. There are patients who need our help. Right?" He pulled her face back gently until she was almost looking at him. "Right?"

Lisa nodded, but avoided making eye contact. It was just not that simple and she knew it.

Sarah had been given a sedative. She was half asleep when Lisa and Eric entered her room.

"Sarah, this is Dr. Loman. He's going to talk to you, if that's all right?"

Eric moved a chair next to the bed and sat down. Sarah slowly moved her head to look at him.

"Doctors," she mumbled, shaking her head.

Lisa forced herself to smile as she helped Sarah prop herself up on the pillow. Then she raised the bed with the controls.

"Who's there?"

Sarah's eyes moved sleepily from Eric to Lisa and back.

"I told you. A doctor."

Sarah pushed up weakly and tried to focus. Her eyes were glassy. Slowly her face began to tremble.

"Doctor?"

"Dr. Loman," Lisa answered.

"No!" Sarah moaned. "No. No. No. No." She banged her fist on the bed with each exclamation.

Eric reached out to touch her reassuringly. He was surprised and confused by her reaction.

"Maybe we should be alone," he said, glancing over at Lisa.

"Don't leave me," Sarah screamed. "Not with him." She tried to push herself out of bed.

"He's here to help you," Lisa said as she gently eased Sarah back against the pillow.

"Help me?"

"He's your friend."

Sarah turned her head and peered again at Eric. She was calm for the moment and Lisa backed away. Eric smiled and pulled the blanket up to her shoulders.

Suddenly Sarah clawed out at him. She was slow-moving and Eric jerked back out of reach.

"Keep him away from me," Sarah growled.

"I'm not going to hurt you." Eric stood close and kept smiling.

Sarah's face began to twitch, her eyes pleading with Lisa.

"Please. Not again. I . . ." Her head rolled back and forth on the pillow and she began to cry. "I'm . . . I'm pregnant. Don't. Please. Not again."

"Don't what?" Eric asked. He leaned closer to hear her answer, but she cringed under the blanket. Eric glanced at Lisa and Lisa shrugged. Sarah stared, horrified, and said nothing.

"You'll be all right," Eric said soothingly.

"No." Sarah cried. "Teddy. Please. No."

When Lisa heard that name she felt her knees give

way. She grabbed the table by the closet. Her hands were shaking. She squeezed the corner of the table until they stopped.

"No, Teddy, please! Not again. I'm pregnant. *Please*."

Eric backed away from the bed. He was startled and embarrassed that he frightened her so much. Sarah's eyes were half-closed and Eric could tell she was hallucinating. He stepped closer to her.

"Eric, we should go," Lisa whispered.

Eric glanced over his shoulder. Lisa pushed up off the table. Her face was pale.

"What's wrong?"

"She . . . she called you . . ."

Suddenly, Lisa jerked her head toward the door. Peter was standing there, watching.

"Get out," she hissed, her teeth clenched tightly together.

"Lisa, what's wrong?"

Eric tried to grab her, but she hit his hands away.

Sarah screamed. All heads darted toward the old woman.

"Not you too," she cried, looking at the boy. Then she pointed at Eric.

"You can't destroy your own flesh and blood. Even *you* can't do that. You can't!"

Then she screamed again, from deep in her soul. She tried to raise herself up. She was seeing those things again in her head, things too horrible to live with anymore.

"It's burning," she cried, falling back on the bed. "Burn the others, everyone. But not him. I saved his mother but I can't save him. Not him!"

She coughed and a terrible sound rose up from her throat. Blood oozed out the side of her mouth and her head dropped limply off the pillow, her eyes wide with terror.

Lisa gasped and put her hands to her mouth. She was still having trouble standing, but seeing the old woman's body begin to convulse, she swallowed and hurried to her. She lifted Sarah's head back up on the pillow and held her as her chest spasmed. Then Sarah exhaled loudly and did not move.

Lisa glanced back helplessly at Eric, then at the boy. He was staring at the bed. Eric saw Lisa's eyes fix on the door and he turned.

The boy slowly gazed up from the bed to Eric. Then his eyes turned up into his head and he fainted, crumbling heavily down onto the floor.

Eric had worked late with Peter after his grandmother's death. The boy did not remember going up to her room. All he could recall was her death. That was terrible for him. His grandmother had been his emotional buffer, the only one he could truly count on when it got too rough at home. Eric talked with him about her for hours, then gave Peter a sedative and sat with him until he was sound asleep.

The sun was setting now and the clouds, low over the western mountains, were streaked with orange and gold. There was no wind and the air was deathly still.

Eric parked his car and went into the house. Lisa was waiting for him in the living room.

"How is he?"

Eric went to the bar and poured himself a scotch and water. Then he sat on the sofa beside her.

"I'm not sure." He took a long pull on his drink. "His grandmother was extremely important to him. She was a strong surrogate mother. He looked to her for praise and for protection when his mother beat him. He was never David when he was with her, he made a point of telling me that. Except, he thought, but he's not sure, in the hospital. That part is blurry. He can't seem to sort it out."

Eric took a long sip from his drink.

"Why was he there, Eric?"

He could hear the threatening tone in her question and was not ready for another confrontation.

"Just wandered up, I guess."

Lisa swirled the ice in her glass.

"Can I get you another?" she offered.

"Sure."

Eric gulped the rest of his drink and Lisa rose to make two more. She stumbled, catching her balance on the chair next to the coffee table.

"How many have you had?" Eric tried to keep his tone polite. He did not want another argument.

"Not enough."

Lisa turned, leaning like a sailboat tacking in high wind, then balanced herself back upright, put the drinks on the coffee table and slumped down on the sofa. She was still in her nurse's uniform. Eric waited until she looked at him, then put his arm along the top of the sofa, his hand resting on her neck.

"What's wrong? Is it still Peter?"

Lisa gazed down at the drink she was twirling in her hands. She did not look up when she spoke.

"She thought you were Teddy."

"Who's Teddy? I had an invisible friend when I was a kid named Teddy, but I . . ."

Lisa peered up at Eric in a way that caught his full attention.

"That's what the inmates at the old asylum called your grandfather."

Eric felt it slowly sink down his throat. He took a

quick gulp of scotch, but it did not wash away the heaviness now in his stomach.

"Eric, she thought you were Teddy. She was pleading with you not to kill your own flesh and blood. She meant Peter. I've heard the stories, Eric. Sarah must have been raped by your grandfather and had a child: Mrs. Delmont. Don't you understand? Peter is *related* to you. He's a Loman through your grandfather. You're not the only one left."

Eric had kept himself from analyzing what had happened in Sarah's room because he was concerned about Peter. He realized, suddenly, that he had stayed with Peter, not just out of professional or human concern, but because he did not want to face what Lisa was saying. Eric downed his drink, then went for another.

"There's more, Eric. Did you know your great-grandfather was the colonel in charge of the Union prisoner-of-war camp we talked about?"

"What?" Eric put his glass on the coffee table and sat down.

"Colonel Loman. He ran that horrible camp Mr. Klein told me about.

"I never heard about that."

"I wasn't sure when or if I should tell you, or if you knew already, but that's what he said."

"My father never spoke about him."

"Maybe he didn't know. It was a long time between the Civil War and when John's father started working at the asylum."

"My grandfather was sixty, Dad said, when he remarried and opened the asylum," Eric said, twirling his fingers in his drink. "Dad said grandfather was a powerful older man when he knew him, which was not that long. His wife was young, though."

"I am sorry, Eric."

"That's all right. It has nothing to do with me or you . . ." Eric glanced slowly up at Lisa. ". . . or Peter. I've contended with having a morbid family tree all my life. One more bad branch really doesn't bother me anymore."

"Peter's a Loman too, Eric."

"So? Mrs. Delmont is also, if Sarah was telling the truth."

"I know," Lisa sighed, watching her hands intertwine with each other.

"There's more, isn't there?"

Eric reached out to touch her arm. She quickly took his hand in hers and finally looked at him.

"Eric, you know Peter was declared a ward of the state until after the trial. The outcome was pretty certain, though. Mrs. Delmont would get three-to-five-years probation with enforced psychiatric care."

"I heard, but . . ."

Lisa held up her hand.

"The deputy called Mrs. Mellany a little while ago and she called here. I took the message."

"And?"

Eric sat up straight on the sofa.

"Mrs. Delmont died this afternoon of an overdose. She committed suicide a few hours before she was to be sentenced."

Eric took his hand away from Lisa's, quickly picked up his drink and gulped it down.

"Are you all right, Eric?"

"I'm not going to tell Peter. Not yet. It would be the last straw. He couldn't take it. And I'll keep Mr. Delmont from being allowed to see him, just to make sure. I didn't want him to see either of his parents for the next few weeks anyway, not until he's been

able to confront what's already happened to him."
Eric finished his drink. "God, that's sad. Poor Peter.
Nothing goes right for that kid. His grandmother,
now his mother. Jesus."

"Eric?"

Lisa put her hand on his knee and stared at him
until she had his full attention.

"Eric, your grandfather hung himself because he
went crazy, crazy with guilt. He started that fire to
protect himself because of the horrible things he was
doing in the asylum. Then your father builds a hospital on the same foundation to save money. A foundation that once was a Union prisoner-of-war camp run
like Auschwitz by your great-grandfather, for God's
sake. Then he gets killed. After that, one accident
after another. It's like the Lomans are doomed. Mrs.
Delmont killed herself. Now it's just you and Peter."

Lisa took a long breath, then put her drink down.
Tears rolled down her cheeks.

"Eric, it's going to get you too. I know it. Peter is
part of it. Somehow he is the catalyst. He makes
things happen. Every accident that occurred, he was
there."

"Not when Dr. Philips got scalded."

Lisa turned her head and let out a deep breath.

"Eric, take me seriously please. Peter is part of the
Lomans too. That hospital, that foundation. It wants
you dead. Eric, I know it sounds crazy, but . . ."

She was crying too hard then to finish it. Eric slid
across the sofa and held her. She shook as she cried,
but the tears subsided quickly. Eric did not say anything until she calmed down. Then he put her head
on his lap and stroked her hair. She turned and dried
her face with a napkin from the coffee table, staring
up at the ceiling.

"Lisa, you're drunk and overemotional. It is startling and, I'll admit, frightening—or maybe sickening would be a better word—if what Sarah said was true. But who knows? She was psychotic. And she was full of drugs. She was living in the past. In her mind. Who knows what part was real and what was her imagination? Her subconscious had taken over. The deaths of my grandfather and father were horrible, but not 'predestined.' Not planned by vengeful land or an old asylum foundation. That's childish. That's for fiction writers. It's not reality. We've gone too far to fall back on black magic, curses, witchcraft, or anything like that. There has been a strange set of circumstances, no doubt about it. But I'll bet it can all be explained logically if we look for the answers. And whether or not my grandfather raped Sarah, and whether or not Mrs. Delmont and Peter are related to me makes no difference as far as the hospital, my work, your work, our lives together, is concerned, Lisa. I lost Carol to an absurd superstition. I won't lose Peter the same way."

Eric lifted Lisa's head up and kissed her quietly. She slid her arms around his neck and held him tight.

"Lisa, I love you. I need you. You are the most important thing in my life. I wouldn't risk you or me or anyone else if I thought our lives were in danger. Peter is a hurt, scared, sick boy. He needs my help. That's all. It's my job, what I've devoted my life to. If I accept superstitions as real, I might as well quit, and I can't do that. And neither can you. Especially now that his mother did what she did." Eric shook his head. "I can't feel much sadness for her or her husband, but that's one more horror Peter will have to contend with at some point. He needs me more than ever now." Eric kissed Lisa again softly. "And I need you."

Lisa looked up and kissed Eric hard. Their bodies entwined in the darkness, and Eric held her close until her breathing was slow and even. When he was sure she was asleep, he carried her upstairs and laid her gently on the bed.

"I love you," he whispered, looking down at her as if he had never really seen her before. He sat for a long time on the corner of the bed watching her sleep. A terrible feeling of loneliness crept over him. It was as if he was looking at her for the last time.

CHAPTER VIII

In the morning, the second-floor staff lounge was full. Lisa and Eric entered to a constant buzzing of voices. It stopped when they walked in, but resumed right after they had sat down with their coffees.

One of the night nurses moved from her table by the window and sat with them.

"Mr. Klein died," she said sadly, knowing how Lisa had liked him. "Even though he was in his nineties, they thought he would make it."

The news was not a shock to Lisa. Somehow she knew he would not live and had expected to hear that when the nurse sat down. Neither the booze nor Eric had been able to wash away her fears last night, but she didn't want him to know that. She knew it was a disagreement that would not be resolved until something horrible enough happened. She didn't dare imagine what it would be.

Dr. Jacobs leaned back in his chair, gesturing toward Eric. The morning coffee breaks had turned into a daily information bank for hospital news.

"You remember Mrs. Wilcox?" he asked.

"Sure," Eric said.

"I don't understand it, but she developed a severe infection after the operation. It's getting worse. This whole goddamn hospital is going haywire."

Lisa glanced at Eric, showing him with a look that what had just been said further proved her assumption. After Dr. Jacobs moved back to his table, Lisa edged closer to Eric.

"You see?" she whispered.

"No," Eric said. He did not want to hear it all again. "I have to go and check on Peter."

When he pushed his chair out from the table, Lisa grabbed his arm.

"Eric. Will you meet me for lunch? Take the afternoon off?"

"I have work to—"

Lisa squeezed his arm.

"Please, Eric. For me. I need it, even if you don't. Please?"

Eric smiled and patted her hand.

"All right. I'll meet you at noon by my car."

Then Sherry Mellany walked in. Eric got up out of his chair and walked to the door. Sherry stopped him from leaving.

"Ladies and gentlemen. Or should I say doctors and nurses," Sherry announced. All heads turned. The room was instantly quiet. "I'm wondering if I really should say doctors and nurses. I've been listening to the rumors and they're getting absurd. Medical professionals talking about a hospital as if it were alive. Really! I thought I hired scientific personnel, not frightened children. Do I need to go on?"

Sherry slowly scanned the room, making eye contact with each individual in it. They all looked away.

"Then let's act like doctors and nurses. We have jobs to do here and if we start gossiping about ridiculous things like that, what patient would feel secure in coming here? You've already upset the few patients we do have now. Is that what you're here for? Is it?"

She stared over the crowd again. Most of them shook their heads. Then she glanced down at her watch.

"Then let's go to work. We're wasting time."

Peter and Mike were talking when Eric entered. They both stopped when they saw him.

"When do I get to leave?" Mike asked. He trusted Eric and no one else would give him that answer. Even his mother gave him vague answers and made no promises. "It's hurting worse than before."

Eric sat on the corner of Mike's bed.

"There's a slight complication. Nothing serious. Your mother wants to keep you here for observation until . . ." Eric rubbed his chin and stared up at the ceiling, overdramatizing, as if he were pondering a great dilemma. "Until . . ." Mike watched apprehensively, then Eric grinned. "Tomorrow. How's that?"

"Oh, boy! I'm getting out of here."

Mike clapped his hands and smiled at Peter. Eric glanced at Peter when he saw Mike's smile sour.

"I'll come and visit every day, Peter," Mike said quickly. "We're buddies."

Peter faked a smile, then looked away from both of them. Mike glanced at Eric helplessly. Eric patted his ankle and winked, then stood up.

"How'd you like to go for a walk, Peter? Get out of this joint for a while?"

Peter slowly turned back to face him.

"We'll head up the hill behind the hospital. Check the woods out."

Peter tried to seem aloof, uncaring, but watching Eric make silly faces as he waited for an answer forced him into a big grin.

"Can I really?"

"Put on your pants and shirt and let's go."

Mike and Peter burst out laughing. Eric glanced from one to the other, confused. Then Peter pushed the covers off to show he was already dressed, shoes and all. Eric laughed and headed for the door.

"See ya later, Mike," Peter called as he ran out into the hall after Eric.

Eric and Peter hiked up the hill past the maples and the patch of white birch. It was rocky and they hopped from one stone to the next. Then they were in the soft shadows of the big pines and the wind was blowing hard and cool in their faces as it came down off the top of the hill.

There was a small cliff to their left and Peter climbed it easily, then waved at Eric to follow him. As Eric climbed, Peter spilled loose dirt down on him playfully, pretending his foot had slipped.

"A wise guy, huh?" Eric grunted, finally reaching the summit. They were above the top of the pines then and they could see the whole valley. Peter smiled and stared up at Eric. They both sat on the edge of the cliff, dangling their feet in the air. Looking at Peter now, the bruises almost gone from his face, Eric was reminded of Carol when she had first come to St. Mary's. There was an innocent beauty to their youth, and it saddened Eric to know it was only a mirage. Peter had lost most of his childish innocence, his trust in the world, years ago. It was a terrible realization, and Eric felt his throat tighten. He hated to think of all the things the boy needed emotionally and psychologically. A goddamn waste, Eric thought. He felt great pity for the boy, but, he thought, this is not the time for pity.

Eric had decided he would push the boy about his

mother today. Twice Peter had almost admitted what she had done, but always "David" had stopped him. It was a powerful defensive mechanism, and Eric realized how hard it would be for Peter to face the beatings. But he also knew it was the only way to link the two personalities. Eric had been researching multiple personality cases with a vengeance, but Peter did not seem to fit the term. Usually the original personality knew nothing of the other, or others, but Peter had confessed his knowledge of David from the beginning. Neither personality seemed in control to Eric, and the quick switches from one to the other did not always make sense. Eric didn't believe Peter was really a multiple personality. It was like nothing he had ever seen or read about before. And the relationship kept changing. Peter could not remember what David did since he had entered the hospital, but before that he knew every detail of David's escapades.

At first Peter had talked about David as his escape, the one who took the beatings. But now David was an aggressor, not just a defense mechanism. The change seemed too fast and too easy. It was as if David had changed into someone else since Peter had been admitted to the hospital.

Eric was willing to admit that Peter meant a lot to him. He tried to understand why this particular patient was so special. Maybe it was because Carol had died or because he had become a symbol to Eric, a symbol of Eric's ability as a psychiatrist. It was a way to prove to himself that he wasn't a failure. Eric felt as if everyone he had treated in the hospital had not recovered, and Peter was . . . his last chance.

Peter smiled as Eric glanced at him. The doctor always felt his own childhood again through the boy and now Eric had to help him in order to resolve his own past as well as Peter's. And, Eric realized, Peter may be family. That pushed Eric's need to help the boy into a passion he could not control.

"Does David like your mother?" Eric asked. Peter was used to the sudden questioning and he sat up straight.

"He hates her," Peter said.

Eric wondered again if David was more of a defense mechanism, a fantasy Peter had made up, than a true split in his personality. It seemed unlikely that Peter could talk about him like this unless that were true. Eric still felt David was like his Teddy—at least he hoped so.

The questioning was difficult for Eric now. He had to keep reminding himself to speak about Mrs. Delmont in the present tense. He had already warned the nurses who took care of Peter to do the same.

"And you hate her too?" He watched for Peter's reaction.

Peter shook his head. "I love my mother."

"But?"

Peter shrugged. Eric saw he was remembering something as he turned and stared out at the valley. Eric let him go with it and did not interrupt until he saw Peter grimace. He knew he had remembered something.

"And she loves you?"

"Uh-huh." Peter kept his eyes straight ahead.

"And she loves David?"

Peter rolled his head back to look at Eric.

"She hates him. That's why she beats . . ." Peter could not finish it. He closed his eyes tight and held his arms out straight between his legs.

"Peter," Eric said, more loudly now. Peter opened

his eyes. "When David got a beating, did you ever hurt too?"

"I felt sorry for him. She doesn't love him the way she loves me." He scratched his nose nervously.

"And all this time in the hospital you never felt any pain?"

"Yes," he said. "It hurt awful."

"Then you had bruises too?" Eric said.

"You saw 'em." Peter stared at Eric. Eric smiled reassuringly. He knew the pain he was asking him to go through.

"Where'd you get the bruises?"

Eric leaned over and kept his eyes glued to Peter's. Peter blinked and jerked his face away.

"Where'd you get them, Peter?"

"Don't know. Fell down the stairs, I guess."

The lie did not sound convincing anymore and Eric was glad. It was the first time Peter said he wasn't sure.

"But they hurt?"

"I told you that."

Peter looked at Eric, frustrated. The defenses were building quickly now. Eric wished he could stop them.

"She beat you."

"No!" Peter yelled.

"And it hurt awful."

"No!"

"And she loves you."

"No!" Peter shook his head. "I mean, yes."

"And she hates you."

"No."

"And she hit you. And she hit David and it hurt. And you—"

"Just David."

Eric could see the panic in Peter's face. He hated to, but he decided to use that. He stood up, towering over Peter.

"And you make David take your beatings for you. You, Peter."

"No," Peter moaned. "He was bad. Not me. She loves me."

"She beat you!"

"She didn't mean to," Peter cried. When he heard what he had said, his eyes widened. He began to shake his head, no, again and again. Eric saw the battle inside him. He wanted to hold Peter, to tell him it was all right, but that would not help either of them. Instead he sat still and watched. It was horrible.

"Didn't she mean to beat you, Peter?" Eric finally asked. Peter stopped shaking his head and turned his huge, terrified eyes at Eric.

"She . . ." Peter pulled his legs up and wrapped his arms around them. He began to rock.

"Peter," Eric prodded, "you have to admit it. It will be better inside once you get it out. It's not David now. It's you. Only you."

Peter stopped rocking and let his knees down. His eyes were not petrified anymore. He stared at Eric coldly, and there was hate in his gaze.

"You can't do that to him."

Eric knew it was David who was speaking, but he tried not to show it.

"Do what to who?"

"Hurt him like that. Peter. I won't let you. You're as awful as his mother."

"I'm trying to help you, Peter."

"I'm not Peter."

"Look like him to me."

The tension drew the boy's face taut. Eric could

see his anger building. Then the small face relaxed into a smirk.

"Just wait," the boy said, chuckling. A cloud moved over them. It was suddenly dark and cold on the cliff.

"For what?" Eric wiped the sweat off his palms onto his pants.

The boy grinned.

"Even the innocent must die."

Lisa had left work an hour before lunch and had prepared a picnic meal with two bottles of cold Chablis. She knew exactly where she wanted to go and directed Eric there as he drove over the eastern mountains above the valley. The farmland spread out beneath them in geometric patterns of yellows and greens.

They parked the car at the top of the pass and walked along the tree-shaded path to the wide stream that circled under a huge boulder, then slowly arched down toward the valley. The water was high and fast-rushing under the boulder, then widened and curved in gentle swirls between the few big jutting rocks where it was deepest. There was a small, still pool blocked by a fallen oak and two large flat stones. That was where Lisa spread out the blanket and uncorked one of the cold bottles of Chablis.

"This is where we . . ." Eric began.

Lisa put her finger to his lips and smiled.

". . . the first time," she said. "You brought me here and we got drunk and were swimming and . . ."

Lisa peered up at him flirtatiously, her big green eyes glowing under their long lashes. Eric leaned over and kissed her gratefully. He realized just how glad he was to be away from the hospital. The sight of the sun filtering through the thick trees on the other side of the stream, and the sound of the water as it harmonized with the wind made Eric forget all about Peter and his fears and that dull aching sadness that had been with him for days.

"Eric?"

He had been staring for a long time and Lisa had been watching him. There were still things she needed to say. Eric looked over at her as he relaxed on the blanket, his head on his hands.

Lisa stretched out next to him and tickled his ear with a long blade of grass. "Two more coincidences," Eric said. He did not want to discuss what he knew she was going to bring up. He hoped his bluntness would end it.

It didn't.

"Eric, I think it's gone too far for that. You can't keep calling it coincidence."

"That's what Sherry Mellany would call it. What else can you call it? I don't believe in ghouls."

"No one is getting well in the hospital. That's not just coincidence. We are trained personnel and we can't heal anyone. People are dying when they shouldn't. Please, Eric, try to keep an open mind. Maybe there are things in this world that we don't understand yet, that aren't scientific or logical. People, civilizations down through the centuries have believed in . . . in . . ."

Eric sat up and pulled the blade of grass out of her fingers. He was remembering how Peter had threatened him on the cliff. It suddenly made him angry.

"In *what*, for Chrissake? In evil children? In vengeful buildings? In doomed generations, for the evil of their fathers? What?"

"I don't know exactly. But there's something wrong. God, Eric, you can't deny that."

The wind blew through the trees, cool and refreshing. Eric stood up and drank from the bottle of wine. Then he paced around the blanket uncomfortably.

"Fear is what's wrong," he said. "That's what we should be afraid of. It can turn into an epidemic. That was why they had witch hunts. Drowned people, burned them. Fear, Lisa. Nothing else. Just fear."

"But the boy. He's—"

"He's just a boy. Like I was a boy. The more people feared the Lomans, the more they hated. Don't make Peter go through that too. He's had enough bad luck already."

Eric dropped to his knees beside Lisa. She rolled over to look at him and he stroked her hair.

"When I was a child, the other kids liked to pick on me. They did that because of their parents. They wouldn't get into trouble. No, it was safe to pick on the Loman kid. All because of how they viewed my father and especially my grandfather. They hated us because we frightened them. My father realized that quickly and used it to frighten them. He knew fear that well. I didn't understand that when I was young. I kept trying to make friends and I never could. If I was pushed by a bully, I ran away. My father was a bastard, but eventually he taught me something. Never to run away. I have a patient, a frightened, sick boy, and he needs my help. I don't give a damn what the hospital staff thinks. I'm going to help that boy recover. I couldn't live with myself if I didn't. He's touched me, Lisa. I'm fighting for my childhood, instead of running away, through him. I need to help him as much as he needs my help. Can't you understand what that means to me?"

"I know he means a lot to you," she said. "But it's frightening."

"I can't deny it's a little scary. Not so much the boy, but the way the hospital is falling apart. I blame that on my father. I wouldn't put it past him to have used cheap materials to increase his profits." Eric fell silent, wondering. "And if my grandfather did do that to Sarah Bickham . . ." He took another slow breath. "There's just something about Peter. I can't let him down. I'll admit his David personality is becoming extremely psychotic—he could be dangerous—but I've got to save him. I *have* to. I feel like what has happened to Peter is partly my fault. My family's fault. I have to right an old wrong."

Lisa saw how much that meant to him as he said it. She reached up and caressed his cheek, smiling. She decided not to talk about it anymore. No matter what she felt, what deep, hidden, instinctive fears still gnawed at her, she would trust him and let him do what he had to do. But she would still be watching, waiting for evidence he could not deny; waiting to protect him if something terrible happened. And somehow, she knew it would.

They ate the chicken and the salad and opened the second bottle of Chablis. Eric took off his shoes and socks, rolled up his trouser legs, and went to wade in the stream. It was cold and the clear green water swirled hard against him, pulling him like a small undertow.

"Can't swim," he called, stepping back up onto the bank. "It's real cold."

"Like the first time?" she asked, slipping her uniform off her shoulders.

"Mom told me I'm leaving in the morning, just like Dr. Loman said."

Mike looked past Peter at the window. The moon

shimmered through the clouds, making a small green haze high up in the corner of the window.

The nurse had been in and turned off the lights, and since then the two boys had been talking steadily. Peter could tell Mike was still nervous because of the pain in his throat.

"I didn't want my tonsils removed," Mike said. They were both sitting up in their beds with the covers off. "Mom said I had to, though. I couldn't get out of it."

"I know what you mean," Peter agreed. He was remembering his mother's anger and how his father would leave when it got bad. He would stay away for a long time, and when he returned he would be drunk. Peter tried, but could not remember what happened when he and his mother were alone.

"I don't know what's so good about them anyway," Mike said.

"Who?"

"Parents."

Mike lay on his side, his elbow deep in the pillows, his head on his hand.

"Did you ever see Peter Pan?" Peter asked.

"Sure. When I was little. Saw it on TV."

Peter turned and sat with his feet hanging over the side of the bed. He was glad to have a real friend, and he was bubbling over with all the things he still had to say. He had never had a friend to say them to before.

"I always figured it was out there somewhere." Peter held his hands together on his lap. "Never-Never Land. It's got to be."

"Where there's only kids and no grown-ups?" Mike asked. Peter nodded. "Grown-ups never understand. Especially parents. They never have any time for us."

Mike scratched his nose. "The maid plays with me more than both of them put together. I mean, when Dad was alive. He was very important. He was always very busy."

"You got a maid?" Peter looked at Mike in awe.

"Sure. A gardener too."

"Gees." Peter shook his head. Then he went back to what he had been saying. "Don't need maids in Never-Never Land. Don't have to clean up after yourself, ever. Don't have to do anything but fight Indians and pirates and fly around a lot." Peter and Mike laughed.

"I can fly," Peter said.

"Come on. Nobody can fly. It's make-believe."

"I can." Peter sat up straight. "In my dreams."

"That's different."

"Someday I'm going to fly away in a dream and never come back," Peter announced after a short silence.

"How?" Mike asked doubtfully. "Dreams are like TV. It's all make-believe."

Peter lay back down on the bed and stared at Mike.

"You don't believe there is a place like Never-Never Land, do you?"

Mike shook his head

"Do you believe in ghosts?"

"Nah." Mike answered.

"They're here, you know."

"Who?" Mike glanced at the shadows in the room.

"People from another world." Peter could see the interest on Mike's face as the moonlight illuminated his small features.

"Aliens?" Mike couldn't sit still on the bed. "From a UFO?"

"No." Peter said. "From another world. Right here. Ghosts, I guess."

"I don't believe in ghosts. Mom said that ghosts are for stupid people that need to believe in things like that 'cause they don't have anything else."

"They're here in the hospital. I've seen them."

"Mom said that—"

"Who cares?" Peter interrupted. "Moms don't know." Peter thought back to his mother and felt the sharp tugging sadness in his chest. She had never come to visit him in the hospital. If she really loved me, she would have come, Peter decided. If she loved me, she wouldn't . . . He tried to finish his thought but he didn't know how. He tried to concentrate. Then he saw that hand, white and huge and mean, swinging down at him. He pulled his knees up to his chest. He began to rock, and Mike watched him. He had seen the quick panic on Peter's face and had turned to see if someone had entered their room. When he looked back, Peter was holding his knees tight against himself and rocking. Mike watched the way Peter stared at the door. He had grown accustomed to the eerie change in Peter's face and he saw it again now.

"What are you looking at?" Mike asked. The boy stopped rocking and let his knees down. Mike glanced over at the door again, then back at Peter. "It gives me the creeps."

The black eyes slowly turned on Mike.

"Are you playing again, Peter?"

He didn't answer.

"Do you want to hunt for those people?" Peter asked. The boy's voice was heavy and unemotional.

"What people?"

"The ghosts."

"I don't believe—"

"Scared?"

Mike jumped off his bed.

"I'm not scared." He stuck out his chest.

"Are too."

"Am not."

The boy slid down off his bed, walked to the door, and peeked out. Then he looked back at Mike.

"You're too young anyway."

"I'm as old as you," Mike defended.

"No, you're not."

He sneaked out around the door and down the hall. No one was at the nurses' desk. He walked by quickly on his tiptoes. Then he heard Mike following him. He smiled and slowed down.

He would show Mike now.

He tiptoed to the stairs and opened the door cautiously. It did not creak. As he closed it, he saw Mike sneaking down the hall, keeping close to the wall. He started up the stairs slowly. He did not want to lose him now.

Mike watched the nurses' desk as he followed along the corridor. He was a little scared, but it was a game to him, like hide-and-seek, and he liked it. He pretended he was a secret agent following a spy. He slipped through the door silently and heard footsteps above him. He held his breath and listened. The door to the third floor shut.

Mike peeked up the stairs. They were empty now. He ran up them and stopped to look out the glass window in the door. The hall was empty. Mike took a deep breath and opened the door.

Suddenly a hand flashed out in front of his face and he gasped. Then the boy leaned around the edge of the wall by the door and laughed. Mike was shaking, but he pretended it hadn't scared him and laughed too.

"Shhhh."

Mike nodded and fell silent.

"There was an old woman up here," whispered the boy. "She could see them too. She's one of them now. She's waiting like the others."

"The ghosts?"

The boy nodded, then waved at Mike to follow. They stopped outside the room Sarah Bingham had died in.

"They frightened her, but they don't frighten me. They're my friends. I know them."

Mike was getting scared again. He didn't like the way Peter looked at him now or the strange dullness to his voice. It was not like the Peter he knew before, or like David either. There was something different now in Peter's eyes.

The boy leaned over Mike. "They don't like Peter. But they like me," he whispered.

"When you pretend you're David?" Mike asked.

"I am not. I never pretend."

The cold voice and accusing eyes frightened Mike. He wanted to go back to his room, but he was too scared to do it now. He didn't know why, but he knew better than to make Peter angry. They weren't playing a game now.

"The ghosts are in there," Peter said, pointing at Sarah's door.

"I still don't believe it," Mike countered shakily.

"I'll prove it."

The boy slowly twisted the knob on the door and opened it. It squeaked once and he stopped. Then he pushed it far enough to slip inside. He grabbed Mike's arm and leaned his face close to his ear.

"Watch," he whispered. Mike stayed where he was and watched his friend walk up to the foot of the bed. It was dark in the room and the light from the hall cut across the bottom of the bed. The boy stood in the line of light and stared at the empty bed. Mike's eyes adjusted to the dark and suddenly he thought he saw a face—old and wrinkled, the eyes closed, the mouth gaping open. He almost thought he could hear breathing. He looked out the window, then back at the bed, and saw it was only the shadows from the moon and the dim light from the partly opened door.

Mike held his breath and listened for footsteps, afraid they would get caught. It was still quiet outside the door. But inside the room, the boy was beginning to breathe loudly, almost moaning when he exhaled. He sounded like a big grunting animal to Mike, who grew even more frightened. His eyes were glued on the bed. Mike thought he saw something jerk under the covers. He stepped backward toward the door.

Suddenly the boy's eyes flashed open and turned on Mike. All Mike could see in the dark were those white, glowing eyes. "Let's get away," he pleaded. Peter did not move. He just stared at the bed as if in a trance. Then suddenly, he screamed.

Mike gasped and his heart leaped up into his throat. He threw the door open and ran out into the hall. A nurse yelled down after him and, hearing that, Peter dashed out in pursuit.

"Wait," he called.

Mike glanced back over his shoulder but didn't stop until he was on the other side of the door to the stairs. He leaned against the wall and tried to catch his breath. His heart jabbed against his ribs and his side ached. He had never been so scared in his life.

Then the stairway door swung open and Mike felt a gust of cold wind pushing him tight against the wall. Peter stood in the doorway laughing horribly and pointing. Mike felt the wall, cold at first, now burning against his back. He gasped, but his lungs were on fire and he couldn't breathe. Then the light on the ceiling exploded and he screamed. Suddenly the wall cracked behind him. He leaped away, but he tripped and smashed head first into the railing. The railing snapped, and he grabbed out for help as he fell. The last thing he saw was Peter standing there, laughing, with the light from the hall behind him. He felt the quick-rushing terror as he dropped down between the square open space between the three stories of stairs. It seemed as if he fell for a long time before he landed sideways onto the first floor. Then there was nothing. His skull cracked on impact and blood oozed out in a large puddle under his frightened, mangled face.

The boy stared down between the stairs at the small crooked body.

No one will leave here, he thought. Ever.

CHAPTER IX

Eric parked his car in the hospital lot. They had called at midnight to tell him about Mike's death. Sherry was already there. The nurse who had called informed him that Sherry was hysterical and they couldn't calm her down. She asked him to hurry because the police had just arrived too.

It had taken Eric less than ten minutes to get to the hospital. Now, outside the huge oak door, he gathered his thoughts and prepared himself for the confrontation. His first fear had been for Peter, but he was trying to push that aside so he could help Sherry.

The hallway was crowded with the night staff and the police, and Eric had to shove himself through them to Sherry's office. A nurse was sitting on the arm of the sofa where Sherry was lying.

"I'm glad you're here," the nurse said as she stood up. "We gave her a sedative, but . . ." She glanced back at Sherry, then looked at Eric and shook her head sadly.

"It's all right. You can go now. I'll stay with her."

Sherry had cried so hard that she was still fighting for her breath as Eric slid a chair up next to her and sat down.

"I'm sorry."

Sherry moved her arm away from her face and looked at him.

"Oh, God, Eric. He's dead. He's all I had left and he's dead. How can that be? Why? Why?"

Her throat tightened and she choked as she began to weep again. Eric knelt next to her and took her in his arms. She cried even louder, her chest heaving in painful spasms against his. Eric wished he had an answer to her question, but there was none. There was nothing that he could say that would take the terrible hurt away. He held her tightly and whispered over and over that it would be all right, rocking her slightly as she cried.

"I want to walk. I don't want to be here. I . . ."

Sherry pushed away from Eric and stood. She felt the dizziness sweep down through her legs and she swayed back, catching herself on the top of the sofa. Eric pulled her back up.

"You should just lie here now. Let the sedative work. Relax. It'll make you feel better."

Sherry glared at him and ripped her arm out of his hands.

"Feel better?" she yelled. "It's that Peter. *He* did it. He was with . . ." She began to choke again. She put her hands over her face.

Eric tried to hold her, but she backed away.

"The police are talking to him now. That little . . ."

Sherry stormed out the door and Eric rushed after her. He was suddenly very frightened for Peter. He knew the child could not handle that type of confrontation, not with the police.

There was a nurse with Peter, holding his hand as an officer spoke, continuously writing on his pad. Sherry stormed past the policeman, stopping in front of Peter.

"You killed my son," she screamed. She tried to grab him, but the policeman restrained her. "He killed my Mike!" She fought against the officer's grip. "Let me go. He killed my Mike!"

Eric pushed between Peter, Sherry, and the officer. The little boy jumped over and clutched Eric, clinging to him in terror.

With Peter behind him, shaking, Eric inched by Sherry and the officer.

"He killed him," Sherry screamed again, pointing at Peter. Eric could feel Peter's body shudder.

Eric looked at the nurse and directed her with his eyes toward Sherry. The nurse hurried over and helped the police officer lead her back to her office.

When Sherry was out of sight, Eric pulled his patient around to face him. Peter glanced up, his big, wet eyes pleading for help and reassurance.

"Don't be scared. She's hysterical. She doesn't mean what she said."

Peter wiped his eyes, still clutching Eric by his jacket and leaning as close to him as he could.

"He was my friend. My friend," Peter blurted between breaths.

"I know."

Eric swept the boy up in his arms and carried him through the crowd to the stairs, then up to his room.

"She wants to hurt me," Peter said as Eric put him to bed.

"No one's going to hurt you. I'm here. You're safe."

"I didn't do anything. I didn't. I . . . I don't even remember what happened. All . . . all of a sudden the nurse grabbed me and started yelling and . . ." Peter was crying and Eric sat on the bed to be near him. When the tears subsided, he put the boy down and covered him with the blanket.

"What do you remember?"

Peter took a deep breath, his eyes staring out at the wall.

"Just standing there. On the stairs. And Mike was lying down there all bloody and . . ." Peter pulled his arms over his face and began to shake. His whole body trembled. Eric gently pulled his arms down and held his hand.

Then a nurse came in.

"I thought you might want to give him this."

She handed Eric a sedative, which Eric gave to Peter with a glass of water. He choked, but finally swallowed it.

"What's happening to me?"

Peter looked up at Eric. His small face was pale. His eyes were huge and red.

"You'll be all right. It's not your fault. It was an accident. Just try not to think about it now."

Peter's body twitched as his eyelids slowly closed. Eric put the hand he was holding lightly back under the covers. He sat in the dark until he was sure Peter had fallen asleep.

"The police want to talk to you," the nurse said, opening the door.

"I'll be down. How's Sherry?"

"She's resting now. Dr. Jones, her family doctor, is going to drive her home and stay with her."

Eric nodded and the nurse left. Then he closed the door and slumped back down on the chair next to Peter. His head felt heavy and his chest ached. Slowly his head dropped down into his hands.

Then he cried.

He hadn't felt so helpless since his childhood, but he fought the feeling with everything he had. He rubbed his face hard and stood again.

He would not give up now, not for anything.

The police chief was a rough-looking, heavyset man in his fifties. His uniform pulled tight at the buttons stretched over his huge belly.

"I'm Dr. Loman," Eric said. "You wanted to see me."

"The name's Haggar. Come with me."

The chief waddled down the hall to the stairs and Eric followed. He thought the chief probably resented him because his father had bought him off years ago and had used him often since then to get what he wanted.

They walked through the door and Eric stopped suddenly. There was an outline of a body chalked on the floor and the dried brown blood was still caked around the head. Eric swallowed to keep from being sick.

The chief glanced back at him and Eric couldn't believe he was smirking. He felt like punching that smug look off his face. He clenched his fists and followed the chief, until they stopped on the third floor.

"Railing broke right off," Haggar said. He knelt by the short, hollow metal stumps where the railing had snapped. "Cheap crap." He shook the remaining section of the railing with his big, pudgy hand. It rattled, but held.

Eric walked down a few steps and kicked the railing hard. It quivered but gave no indication it would break.

"Don't make sense," the chief said, pushing himself back up on his feet.

"What do you mean?"

"It's lousy railing, but it still should hold," the

chief shrugged, "at least two or three hundred pounds of force against it."

"So?"

"So Mike Mellany weighed about eighty pounds. He couldn't have broken it himself."

Eric felt the back of his neck tighten. He tightened his fists again after shoving them into his pockets.

"What are you trying to say?"

"I'm saying that someone had to have pushed him real hard or already have weakened the railing."

"Maybe these few pieces were weak to begin with."

"It's a possibility, but doubtful."

"It's more of a possibility than saying Peter pushed him. Peter is smaller than Mike."

The chief raised his eyebrows and stroked his chin.

"Got a point there. But he was seen going to the stairs with Mike. No one else was there. The nurse will testify to that."

Eric walked up the rest of the stairs past the chief to the door, then leaned back against it. He was doing all he could to control his temper.

"I'd like to speak to the Delmont kid."

"He's sedated."

"You're his doctor, they tell me."

"That's right."

"A psychiatrist?"

Eric stared, disgusted, and said nothing.

"The boy's crazy, huh? Must run in the family. I mean his mother killing herself like that. I hear Mr. Delmont hasn't been sober since."

Eric turned his head away. He was afraid he would lose control and punch the heartless, brainless son of a bitch.

"The child has been abused," Eric said, trying to be patient. "He needs emotional and psychological treatment. I'm trying to help him cope with a lifetime of fear and confusion."

"I heard he was a little crazier than that. I also heard he always seems to be around when something goes wrong in the hospital, or when someone has an accident."

"That's a bunch of paranoid bullshit," Eric said loudly.

Chief Haggar grinned.

"So what do you want from me? You seem to have it all figured out," Eric barked.

"I wanted to talk to you, John Loman's kid." He shook his head. "I know he falsified contracts to build this hospital. I know these railings are illegal."

"So arrest him."

"I just wanted you to know he didn't get away with anything."

"So now I know. But it seems to me he got away with everything all his life." Then Eric grinned, taunting him. "With your help."

The chief stormed up the last two steps and grabbed Eric by the shirt. Eric shoved him back.

"Don't ever touch me again."

He was hoping now that the chief would. But Haggar backed away and there was no longer that smug look on his face. Eric could see he was still afraid of John Loman even though he was dead. Obviously the chief thought Eric knew more than he actually did about his father's affairs. Eric smiled, glad to use that power now.

Police Chief Haggar pointed at him angrily, trying to win back his authority.

"I can prove the boy's death is linked to—"

"You can't prove anything unless you want to go down with it."

The chief put his hand down and looked away. Then he glanced back up at Eric's cold, set face. Eric knew his bluff had won.

"I still want to talk to the boy," the chief said, more politely now.

"When he's ready. Not before."

Haggar grunted, turned, and started down the stairs. Halfway, he stopped and looked up.

"Don't push me," he warned, feeling safer with the distance between them. "I'll be back in the morning to see the boy."

"Like hell you will," Eric snarled. "You'll see him when I give you permission and not before. You got that?"

Eric listened to the echo of the chief's heavy steps disappear and felt his insides tighten into a knot. He knew the chief would try to get at him through Peter and it made him sick to know there would always be people like that, especially people in positions of authority. At that moment, Eric was actually glad his father had been such a bastard.

Eric left strict orders that no one was to see Peter unless he was there, then went home and slept a few fretful hours. First thing in the morning, he went to talk to his patient.

He had told Lisa about the accident and she had tried to use it as the concrete evidence she needed to prove her point, but Eric argued that even the police chief thought it was probably the faulty railing that killed Mike. He did not, however, tell her the chief suspected Peter too. He was tired of arguing.

But more than that, he did not want to tell her that he knew his arguments were losing at least some of their validity. He did not want to admit that even to himself.

When he walked in the open door, Peter turned to see who it was and Eric examined the anxious hurt in Peter's eyes. He knew it had been horrible for him. He walked between the two beds and sat on the empty one.

"I'm sorry about your friend," Eric said. Peter was staring across at him. Eric could see the terror and the pleading in the way he stared. He wished he knew what to say to soothe that, but it wasn't that simple.

"Are you all right?" he asked softly. Peter's eyes widened, wet and trembling. Then the tears started. Eric sat next to him and Peter leaned forward to reach around his neck. He shook and cried, then wiped his face gently with the back of his hand.

"It's going to be all right," Eric said. "It hurts to lose a friend. But he'll be with you in your memory. So it's not really like losing him." He knew there was more to Peter's crying than losing Mike, but he didn't know what to say about that now.

"They killed him," Peter said.

The words gripped Eric's throat, remembering his use of "we" the last time David had threatened him. He tried to tell himself it was just a child's imagination.

"Who?" he asked.

"Mike."

"Who killed him?"

For a second, Eric hoped Peter was going to say the Loman Construction Company. Then he realized he was just grasping at straws.

"David's with them now," Peter said. He stared through Eric until another tear rolled out of his eye, making him blink. Then he was looking at Eric again.

"Your friend? Like my old friend Teddy? Is he gone now?" Eric felt a terrible chill. He tensed the muscles in his shoulder and chest to keep it from taking control. Peter did not answer. He looked back at the wall. "David is your friend, isn't he?"

Peter nodded. "He's my friend."

Then he sat up and held his hands on his chest. The fear was gone from his eyes. Eric did not understand. The change was too abrupt.

"He's big now," Peter said proudly.

"David?"

"Yup. He's big and strong and no one can hurt him anymore. Or me." Peter glanced at Eric. Eric felt threatened by the quick staring. "No one."

"Why would anyone want to—"

"They did," Peter interrupted. "But they can't now. Can't. David's too strong."

Eric felt a strange breakthrough then. It was the first time Peter really admitted that someone had hurt him. He tried to go with that and see how far Peter would take it.

"Who hurt you, Peter?"

But pain clouded Peter's eyes again.

"My . . ." He tried to say it but couldn't.

"Who, Peter?"

"My . . . He choked on the next word. Eric watched him battling, trying to say it.

Then Peter sat up tall in the bed and turned to rearrange his pillows. Eric waited and watched as the boy took his time fixing his bed. Finally he turned back to Eric.

"Do you believe everything he tells you?" the boy asked. He looked Eric in the eye.

"He, who?" Eric had thought he was getting through, but now he felt totally helpless.

"Me," the boy corrected. "Everything I tell you."

Eric saw the quick apprehension on his face, a face no longer beautiful or innocent. He had tried to correct something that had not been a mistake.

"You're David, aren't you?" Eric looked at him without accusing or the judging.

"Maybe."

"So you're big and strong and can protect Peter?" Eric asked.

"When I want to be," the boy answered. "I know things. Things other people don't."

"Like what?"

"I know things about you."

"What things?" Eric felt the room grow cold and he shivered.

"Just things."

"You're not going to tell me."

He grinned as Eric looked at him disapprovingly, but it had no effect. His smile widened. Eric felt it challenging him. He knew better than to give in to that. It was just like being with Carol.

"If you don't want to talk," Eric pushed off the bed and walked to the door. "When you feel like it, press the button. The nurse will find me."

The boy laughed. It was a taunting, hollow laugh and it turned Eric's stomach. He waited at the door to be asked back, but the boy just kept laughing. Eric stepped outside and leaned against the wall. Eric felt a dizziness hit him and wondered if he had gotten up too fast. He waited until it went away, then decided to go back in to the room.

"Hello, again," Eric said, smiling, as he nonchalantly walked back in.

Peter rubbed his eyes and yawned. "I'm bored." He looked up earnestly at Eric.

"What is it?" Eric asked.

"When do I get to go home?"

David was gone as quickly as he had come.

"As soon as you're better," Eric improvised.

"I don't hurt anymore." Peter pulled his gown aside. "See, I'm not red either."

Eric smiled and sat on the corner of Peter's bed.

"Won't be long now," he said. "We just have to face some things. You and me. That's all."

"Like what?"

"Like Mike's accident, for one."

"Oh." Peter sat up and took a slow breath. Eric turned to face him, pulling one leg, bent at the knee, up onto the bed and resting his arm over it. He was not in any hurry to start. Peter waited. He was used to these sessions now. He liked Eric a lot because he said things straight out. But he always felt guilty at the end too, when he saw how frustrated Eric would get. He wished he could do better at whatever it was Eric wanted. He decided to try even harder this time. He hoped that would please Eric.

"You remember last night?"

"Some." Peter pulled himself up even higher against the back of the bed. "More than I could last night."

"You want me to crank this jalopy for you?" Eric asked, slapping the metal railing of the bed.

"No. It's fine." Peter smiled. "I wish I had one of these at home. Good for watching TV."

Eric realized why he said that. The sadness grew heavy and thick in his stomach. He wondered when he would be able to tell Peter about his mother. He wished he never had to. But it was his job. It was more than that too. That's what Peter could see in his eyes that made him trust Eric so much.

"Do you remember playing with Mike?"

Peter nodded.

"And you played outside your room? Wandered all over the hospital?"

"We were exploring. I was the leader."

Eric smiled. "Where did you go?"

"We went all over."

"Did you go to the stairs?"

Peter thought back. "I don't think so."

"Try to remember. You were on the third floor, exploring and . . ."

Peter closed his eyes and looked back at that night. Fragments of it drifted by in his mind. Then he saw a room. A big man entered. He walked over quietly and stood at the foot of the bed. Peter squeezed his closed eyes tighter, but it was blank then. He looked back at Eric.

"There was a room. But I wasn't the one that went in," he said.

"Mike went in?"

"No." Peter wished he could remember more. He closed his eyes again and squeezed his small hands into fists to help him concentrate, but there was nothing now.

"Someone else," Peter said. "Not Mike. I don't know who."

"David?" Eric leaned over. "Was it David?"

"Why would David go exploring? He knows all about this hospital."

Eric stood up. He saw no choice now. Peter fluctuated, but he wasn't getting better at all. Eric felt like they were both backed into a corner.

"Would you like to go exploring with me?"

Peter grinned. "Sure."

"We'll try to retrace your last adventure. How's that?"

Peter put his robe on, then got out of bed.

"Let's go," he said. When he got to the door he stopped, turned, and glanced up at Eric. Eric could tell he had just remembered something. And whatever it was, it frightened him.

"What's wrong?" he asked, putting his hand on Peter's shoulder. They began to walk.

"I don't know," Peter said. Eric could feel the boy shiver up through his hand. "I saw something. A fire, maybe. Something. It's gone now."

They walked slowly down the hall and Eric kept his hand on Peter's shoulder. He felt the tension mounting, but Peter strode forward, quickening his pace. Eric looked down at him proudly and Peter smiled. Eric did not want to show him that what he had been saying shocked him. He did not know why Peter spoke of a fire or why David was frightening to Peter now.

"We went up these stairs," Peter said. He remembered in flashes. He could see the stairs and the windows in his head before they began to climb. Then Peter stopped in the middle of the stairs to the third story. He shivered again.

"Do you feel it?" he asked. A cold chill ran down over Peter. It was darker on the stairs with the sun on the other side of the building. It was the same feeling Peter had had last night. He tried to keep it away.

"It's a little cold," Eric said. "Like a basement. That's all."

Peter nodded and began to climb again. Eric followed behind him. The chill did not last, and they

walked through the door to the third floor. Then
Peter closed his eyes for a moment. Eric stopped and
waited until he was ready.

"That room." Peter pointed at Sarah's old door.
"He went in there."

"Who?" Eric asked again.

Peter tried to remember, but he couldn't. He wasn't
even sure whether or not he was just imagining it all
now, and that frightened him. He glanced up at Eric
for reassurance and Eric winked at him.

They walked into Sarah's old room together and
Eric put his hand back on Peter's shoulder.

"Do you remember it now?"

Peter shrugged. He was staring at the empty bed.
He could not look at it. He wanted to run. Eric began to back away, wanting to give Peter as much room
as he needed. He was wondering if the memory of his
grandmother was bringing something out in him.
Something, he could see, was terrifying him.

"I know this place," Peter said. He looked up at
Eric helplessly. "But I wasn't here. I wasn't." He was
almost crying and Eric wished he could let him leave.
He put his hand on Peter's back and turned him
around to face the room.

"Look at it again," Eric urged.

Peter turned his head away.

"I don't want to."

"Come on. You're being brave just doing this. Look
around. See if you remember anything more."

Peter took a deep breath, held it, then stepped
farther into the room.

"I can't." There were tears in Peter's eyes when he
looked back at Eric.

"You have to."

Peter threw his arms around Eric's waist and held

him tight. He was crying hard now and Eric hugged him. Then he backed away. He hated himself, but he knew he had to do it.

"Try to remember."

"She's dead," Peter cried. "I saw her."

He tried to edge out the door. Eric turned him around and shoved him forward. Peter stood for a second, shaking his head, then pulled back his shoulders and marched up to the bed. He stood at attention and glanced around the room. When he looked back at Eric, he was smiling.

"She's with them now," the boy said confidently. Then he laughed.

"Why is it funny?" Eric knew he was talking to David. He could actually see the difference in his face now.

The boy stood where he was and laughed even harder. Eric grabbed him hard.

"There's nothing funny about it. She was your grandmother. The only one you always knew you could count on."

The boy covered his mouth to muffle his laughter. Although Eric knew it wasn't Peter anymore, he was angry, and that only made it worse. He gripped the boy's shoulders and shook him.

"It's not funny." He had shaken him harder than he had meant to, and suddenly Peter screamed. Eric saw the eyes change again and he realized he had gotten carried away. He pulled Peter close to hug him and felt the trembling and the tears again.

"He's not my friend," Peter wept. The trembling grew worse. Eric knelt and held him tighter, until Peter threw his arms around his neck and cried fitfully on Eric's shoulder.

"He's someone else now." Eric stroked Peter's head. "They took him. Now he's someone . . . else."

Peter was slowly becoming hysterical. Eric squeezed him against his chest, but he couldn't stop the child's fierce quivering.

"Who was taken? Mike?"

Eric held Peter's head in his hands and looked into his eyes. Peter stared back.

"David!" Peter cried. "But it *isn't* David."

Peter tried to hold back the tears, but they streamed from his eyes uncontrollably. 'Something horrible," he moaned. "Something horrible's happening to me!"

The look of naked terror on Peter's face was all too convincing, and Eric felt a jolt of fear. The cold logic of his profession was beginning to desert him. He moved to embrace the tiny shoulders but the instant he raised his arm, Peter doubled over, clutching himself as if in agony.

"Inside. I felt it." Peter glanced back up at Eric, his eyes like hard black glass. "I can't stop it. I can't!" Peter grabbed Eric's arms and squeezed. "Don't let them do it. *Please!*"

"Do what Peter? What?"

Peter shook his head spastically. There was a battle raging inside him. Eric could not help anymore. It was all up to him. Then Peter became very still and peered out the window. Eric watched and waited. The boy seemed mesmerized by something. He turned and his big, dark eyes fixed onto Eric's, the silent horror tearing Eric's heart.

"Mike's dead too," Peter said it as if he had realized it then for the first time.

"An accident. You were playing."

"No."

Peter was still fighting something in his head and Eric wished he could make it easier for him, but he knew he couldn't.

"It wasn't an accident?" Eric held the boy's chin up. "Peter? Was it an accident?"

Suddenly Peter began to tremble, then he screamed. "He's dead! He's dead! He's dead!"

Eric pulled the child against his chest and held him as the terrible spasms shot down through his small frame. Then Peter's knees buckled. Eric caught him in his arms and picked him up, realizing they had pushed too far, too fast. Even Peter's body was battling against him now, to keep from remembering.

CHAPTER X

"The police chief came this afternoon to see Peter," Eric said, mixing himself and Lisa a drink. A storm was brewing. The wind blew hard against the trees, and the bushes by the window scratched at the glass. The rain started to pelt the roof, and soon it was coming down so heavily that Eric could no longer see the road from the living room window.

"What did he say?"

"Not much. I wouldn't let him see him. Peter has gone through too much already. I thought he might be getting closer to a breakthrough, but . . ."

Eric handed her the drink and sat next to her on the sofa.

"But what?"

"I don't know. Now I think he's getting worse instead of better. It's not just his mother anymore. He's trying to face his grandmother's death, his only friend's death. The hospital seems to be doing him more harm than good. Even *I'm* doing him more harm than good. It's all mixed up. The poor kid doesn't know which trauma to deal with first."

Eric stared down at his drink.

"You should move him to the state mental hospital."

He was thinking and her words did not register.

"What?"

"He's dangerous, Eric. He should be in a place where someone will watch him all the time. He could hurt himself—or someone else."

"What do you mean?"

Eric scowled and put his drink on the coffee table.

"I mean just that. You're right. The hospital isn't doing him any good. It's not you, it's the . . ." Lisa almost smiled, "coincidences that are making him worse. He's getting dangerous. I don't think Mike's death was an accident and neither do you."

Eric leaned back and questioned her with a look. Lisa was surprised he didn't have an instant comeback to disprove her statement.

"The boy needs my help. I can't just send him to a place like that."

"Why not?"

"It would be too much for him to take. He's at a breaking point already. He's watched his whole world fall apart around him this last week. I'm not sure he can handle what's already happened, let alone being moved to someplace like that."

Lisa waited, watching Eric closely. She knew, now, that he was becoming at least a little apprehensive of Peter too.

"What's wrong, Eric?" she asked, touching his shoulder. "Why didn't you disagree when I said I didn't think Mike's death was an accident? What happened?"

He took a deep breath.

"I don't know. Peter doesn't know. But he . . ."

"What, Eric? What is it?"

Eric turned and stared into Lisa's face.

"I'm not positive it was just an accident either anymore."

Lisa felt her stomach sink. She realized as soon as

he said it that she would much rather have had Eric argue her out of it then agree with her.

"I'm not saying I think Peter tried to kill Mike. I'm not saying it wasn't an accident. Not really. I told you the chief admitted he thought it highly unlikely a kid Mike's size could have broken the railings, or even two kids his size. I just mean that Peter seems to feel some responsibility for Mike's death. But he has that same hidden guilt about his grandmother too, and he didn't have anything to do with her accident. The boy went through a lot today. He tried hard to face what he could. He was very brave about it. I guess I'm worried that it may be too overwhelming for him. That pushing him into facing too much at once will hurt him. I think I should go slower. I don't want him to end up like . . ."

"Like Carol?"

Eric nodded quietly.

"But you are admitting he's dangerous?"

Lisa sat forward to put her drink down, then leaning back, rested her hand on Eric's knee.

"I'm not admitting that he is. Not at all. I still think he's really only dangerous to himself. But I won't exclude the possibility that, at some point, he could be. That does exist."

They were silent together, sitting close, as the rain splattered hard against the glass behind them. Lisa was confused.

"Eric?" She leaned her head on his shoulder. "Let's leave Hapsburg. I'm scared. I know you think it's silly, but something is going to happen to you. Something terrible. I just feel it."

Eric pulled her head up. "I can't, Lisa. Not yet. Peter needs me more than ever. If I abandoned him now, there would be no one left. He'd never pull through. I don't even know if he'll get through it with my help, but I have to try. It's my job. My profession. I have to stay."

"But—"

"Lisa, it's my responsibility. I won't run away from that. I couldn't live with myself. And you couldn't live with it either. I think you know that."

Lisa felt the tightness in her throat and couldn't stop the tears from rolling down her cheeks. Eric tried to smile as he wiped them away.

"Hey, come on. No crying now. We'll be fine. You've blown this whole thing way out of proportion. I'm a big boy, remember? I can take care of myself."

Lisa reached for a tissue and dried her eyes.

"I know that, but . . ." Then she shrugged. She could not think of how to finish it.

"No buts. How about a smile? A little one?"

The corners of her mouth turned up slightly and Eric kissed her.

"Let's forget about it, okay? Let's have another drink, then I'll make dinner. It's Friday night and we've got two whole days together. Let's not talk shop anymore."

Lisa nodded, sniffling, then wiped her nose with the tissue. She wished she could forget about it, but something inside kept telling her that the man she loved was in trouble. She just couldn't rationalize that away.

They did not speak about it again all weekend. They stayed in bed almost the whole time, talking and making love as if they had never made love before. It was quiet and wonderful and, slowly, it reassured Lisa. By Monday, her fears had been pushed far away.

She thought about that as they drove to the hospital. It was like waking up from a nightmare in the middle of the night and being scared to death of the dark and of the dream, and then waking up again with the sun filtering in brightly through the curtains and wondering what it was that could have been so terribly frightening.

Dr. Jones approached Eric as soon as they walked into the hospital. "Can I speak to you?" he said, then glancing at Lisa, "Alone."

Eric smiled at Lisa. She squeezed his hand, then left.

"What is it? Sherry?"

Dr. Jones nodded.

"I took her home Thursday. I've been keeping her mildly sedated, but she's not herself. She's taking it real hard. I think the house reminds her too much of Mike and maybe her husband too. She's not eating and she's taking the sedatives twice as often as I prescribed. The maid says she hasn't left her room in four days. She just lies in bed and talks to herself."

Eric shook his head sadly.

"I think it would be best at this point if she stayed here in the hospital. All her friends are here. Besides, she needs constant attention right now."

"It might be best."

"I tried to tell her that, but she wouldn't listen. Maybe she'd listen to you. She's taken a liking to you."

"You want me to go over there?"

"See if you can convince her to come to the hospital for a few days. I think the change of atmosphere, having a lot of people around that she knows and works with, it would be just what she needs. You know, she won't be able to stay here for long without getting up and making sure her hospital is running smoothly."

"All right, I'll talk to her."

Eric started to walk away and Dr. Jones grabbed his arm.

"One other thing. She's scared. Real scared. She feels like she's lost everything and she's decided to blame it all on Peter Delmont. She says she won't come to the hospital as long as he's here. To tell you the truth . . . I don't really blame her."

Eric stared at him angrily. The doctor decided to qualify his statement.

"I know the boy has had a tough time. I know he means a lot to you. I've watched you work with him. You're a good doctor. But I should tell you . . ." Dr. Jones looked down the hall nervously, then ran his hand up over his balding head. "Sherry wants the boy sent to Chelliston State Mental Institute."

Eric had wondered if that might happen, and although he wasn't surprised, it still cut into him sharply. A move like that would only make it harder for Peter. Too much had already happened, too many quick changes and unpleasant—even devastating—surprises. One more could send him over the edge.

"And you? Do you think that's a good idea? Put a ten-year-old boy—who's been abused all his life by his mother, a mother he wanted so much to love, who just killed herself, a boy whose grandmother, as well as his only friend, just died—in a state mental institution? Do you?"

For a moment Dr. Jones could not look at him. "I'm not sure." Then he looked Eric straight in the eyes. "Maybe it is. I'm sorry."

The Mellany mansion spread out in sections over a small hill. It was big and old, and it still put Eric in awe as he drove in, although he had sneaked over to look at it many times when he was young.

The long driveway was lined with oak trees with red-and-gold colored leaves, hanging together to form a tunnel. Eric parked and walked up to the door. Then he turned and peered out over the vast rolling lawn toward the cross-shaped rose garden. He wondered what it was like to be that rich. He thought about Sherry, alone and frightened, with no one left to love. How could her money fix that?

Eric rang the doorbell and a stately older woman, the housekeeper, answered. He introduced himself and she seemed relieved as well as nervous. Chattering nervously about Mike, she led him to Sherry's room. The house was even bigger inside than it appeared from the driveway, with high ceilings and beautiful Louis XIV furniture, the walls full of landscapes and old portrait paintings. Eric felt more as if he were in a museum than in someone's home.

The housekeeper, who ran the staff and had been like a mother to Mrs. Mellany and to Mike, she explained on the way up the huge stairway, finally stopped talking when they reached the big double doors with carved brass hinges. She knocked and ushered Eric into the room.

Sherry's bedroom opened onto a stone porch through sliding glass doors opposite the bed. It was two rooms really and bigger than the whole apartment Eric had lived in for three years in Philadelphia.

Sherry was propped up on satin pillows and waved at him to sit by her when he approached.

"Nice little house you have here," Eric said as he sat on the hand-carved white-and-gold wood armchair.

"It keeps the rain out."

Even pale and drawn, her face was still lovely. Eric was startled how beautiful she looked even after what she had been through. Then he realized a lot of it had to do with the dim lighting and the heavy makeup.

"How are you?

Eric reached out to take the hand she offered. It was cold and dry, like plastic.

"Did you send Peter Delmont to the state hospital?"

Eric felt himself tense. He was not ready for her bluntness.

"I don't think that's necessary."

"Not necessary?" Sherry yanked her hand away. "He killed my son. You're letting a murderer walk around free in my hospital!"

"He's no murderer. He's just a ten-year-old kid. He's sick, that's all. It was an accident."

Sherry shook her head as if that would keep her from hearing what he said. Eric waited until she stopped. He knew he would not be able to change her mind at this point. She needed to blame someone for her son's death.

"Dr. Jones said you wouldn't come to your own hospital. I really think you should, for some rest. Everyone is asking about you. We're all worried."

"Let them worry. They don't care. No one cares."

"You know that's not true."

Slowly she gazed up at the ceiling. Then she was crying.

"You lost someone you loved. Go ahead, cry. It'll help. It's good for you," Eric said soothingly.

Sherry gulped air and looked at Eric. There was something in his face that she had always liked and trusted, and it reassured her to look at him now. She did not, however, want to break down. She had been taught to control her emotions, and it was too frightening to her to let herself go. She felt like she would go insane if she ever let all the hurt out. The walls she'd built were just too high.

"I should never have let him move in with that boy," Sherry said, having regained her composure.

"It was a good idea."

"I should have taken him home after the operation. But I wanted him there so I could be near him for a few days while he was recuperating. I don't get to see him much with my work at the hospital and . . ." Tears streamed down her cheeks, but she ignored them and went on. "I should have taken a few days off to be with him while he recovered. I shouldn't have left him in the hospital."

Eric knew then why she fought so hard to blame Peter. She could not face the fact that she really blamed herself, not just for Mike's death, but for years of letting the housekeeper raise her son while she did other, "more important" things.

"It's not your fault. It was no one's fault. Just a horrible accident."

"Accident? Goddamn it, that boy killed my son!"

"Sherry, don't blame it on Peter. Or yourself."

"He did it."

"No."

"Yes!" she screamed, bolting off the pillows. "Yes, he did."

Then she flung herself back down on the bed, pounding her fists and sobbing.

"Sherry, I want you to come with me to the hospital for a few days. Please? As a favor to me?"

"He's still there."

"Peter's sick. I have to take care of him. He has to be there. You know that. That's why you built that hospital."

"No." She shook her head violently. "He doesn't belong there. He doesn't have an illness we can cure!"

Eric held her shoulders until she opened her eyes and looked at him.

"You need the rest. You're not getting it here. This house has too many memories right now. There's too much old guilt here. It's not good for you."

"Send Peter to Chelliston, do you hear me? *I'll* send him there. One phone call. That's all it takes."

Eric decided to try for a compromise.

"Sherry?" His voice was soft now and she felt it sink warmly into her. "Sherry. I'll move Peter in- to . . ." Eric took a slow breath. "To the security room. He'll be locked there." Eric had thought about it before, after talking with Lisa, but hearing himself say it made him shudder. He knew the boy might be dangerous, he had to admit that. Finally he realized, in that moment's decision, that it was his duty to the other patients to put Peter under some kind of re- straint until he could say positively the boy was not dangerous.

"I want him out."

"He'll be safe there. I can't just throw him away. I'm his doctor. I could be the only hope he has left. I'm the only one he trusts. I took the job you offered to try to help people, not cast them aside when it got tough. And neither did you. You care about people too much to be so cold and vengeful. I know you better than that. You just can't do that."

Sherry's eyes narrowed as she weighed the alterna- tives.

"All right. You put Peter in the security room and I'll come with you to the hospital. I disagree, but he's your patient. You have to make the final decision."

Eric forced a smile and sat back in the chair. He knew he had had to do it, but he felt terrible, having made the compromise. He wondered how he would tell Peter without driving him farther into those dark, shadowy places already so strong in his mind.

Eric helped Sherry pack a few things, then drove her to the hospital. She did not want to see the staff, so they sneaked in the side door and up the stairs to the room on the third floor that Dr. Jones had held in reserve for her. Eric got her settled into bed, then left her with the nurse she had asked for.

On his way to see Peter, Dr. Jones stopped him.

"I don't know how you did it, but I'm glad you got her to come," he said shaking Eric's hand. "And I thank you."

Eric could not feel good about the compliment. He stared down at the floor. When the hand-shaking was done, he peered up at Dr. Jones.

"I could never be a general," he said. It startled Jones, who waited for an explanation of the strange statement. "I'm no good at sacrificing a platoon to win a battle. It may be necessary, but it makes me . . ." Eric shook his head. "Ah, forget it."

Eric paused outside Peter's room before he went in. He had to think it out one more time. He was trying hard to convince himself that he was doing the right thing. He knew it was for the best, but in his heart, the logic did not matter. He forced himself to relax and tried to push the deep aching sadness away so it would not show. He knew how easily children could see through the false pretending of adults. He wondered if he could get away with the smile that felt so foolish to him then.

He opened the door quickly.

"Hello, Peter."

Eric felt the masked smile already beginning to break.

"Hi, Dr. Loman."

Peter was standing by the window. He had been having a hard time with the staff since Mike's death, Eric knew. He had had a talk with the nurses on the second floor to keep them from being obvious about their opinions, asking them to at least do their jobs politely, but he could tell Peter had seen through their pretending and was upset by it.

"So how was your weekend?"

Peter walked over to his bed and sat on it.

"All right."

Eric sat on the other bed. The smile had worn off and he was watching Peter closely.

"Are the nurses still treating you okay?"

"They try not to act scared."

"Why? Do you think you scare them?"

Peter's mouth opened and he glanced up at the ceiling contemplatively.

"Not me. David. Everyone's scared of him now because he's different." Then Peter looked over at Eric. "Except you."

"And you?"

"What?"

Peter shimmied to the edge of the bed and dangled his feet.

"Are you scared of David?"

Peter inhaled slowly.

"Sometimes."

Peter started to watch Eric the way Eric watched him. He knew Eric was uncomfortable by the way he rubbed his hands.

"What's the matter?" Peter asked, staring wide-eyed, up at Eric.

"Well, doctor, I'm not so sure."

Peter laughed and Eric smiled more easily.

"How about you?"

Peter's laughter sank into a sigh.

"I don't want to be here anymore. I'm scared. Everything keeps going around and around and I can't remember things and suddenly I'm just standing somewhere and I don't know how I got there or why and . . ." Peter sucked in air. "It's always bad now, what I see when David goes away. There was Mike and my . . . my . . ."

Peter jumped off the bed and ran headlong into Eric's arms. Eric hugged him, wishing then that he had not compromised with Sherry. But he knew it had been the only thing to do. It was time to tell him then. He had stalled long enough.

"Peter?"

Peter gazed up and Eric felt the jarring sadness and helplessness reach out to grip his throat. He coughed and sat straight, both hands tightly curled under his legs.

"If you don't want to be here anymore, how about we move you today? To another room anyway. It's on the first floor. It's got soft walls, a nice bed. I think you'll . . ."

Eric could not finish when he saw that Peter understood what padded walls meant.

"You're not scared of David too, are you?"

"No, Peter. I'm not, but . . ." Eric took a quick breath. "Well, it'll be better all around. You'll see."

"If you say so."

Peter hung his head down and began kicking his feet against the side of the bed.

"You're a brave boy."

Eric stood up. He knew he was going to break down if he stayed any longer. He ruffled Peter's hair.

"Two aides will come help you move."

Peter did not look up as Eric walked to the door.

"Peter?" He slowly gazed up at Eric. "You'll be all right. Believe that. We'll put David back in his place. You don't have to be scared."

Peter faked a smile and looked back down at the floor.

Lisa was in the big supply closet on the first floor taking inventory when she heard an angry voice echo down the hall. She walked out to see two aides hauling Peter between them.

"You'll be sorry about this," she heard the child say. His voice was deep and ominous. Lisa could see that even the aides were afraid of him. When they tried to lead him, the boy kicked and tried to bite one of them. Both of them backed away.

"I'll get you," the boy growled.

One aide opened the door to the security room and the other stood well behind the boy, letting him go in by himself. Seeing him in the pale white, almost empty room, Lisa felt a sudden surge of pity for him. It quickly snapped when she heard his voice again.

"Bastards!" he barked.

The aide closed the door and locked it. Lisa shook her head sadly.

"I don't care what they say," mumbled the one who locked the door. "It still makes me sick to lock up a ten-year-old boy."

Lisa watched the two aides until they disappeared around the corner. Then she looked nervously at the locked door.

"I want to go home." The small, frightened voice
came from behind the door.

Lisa stepped closer to the security room to listen.

*"We'll get them. They wanted to hurt you too.
They all want to hurt you."*

"Not Dr. Loman. He likes me."

"Him too. He's the worst."

"No. He likes me. He does. You can't hurt him!"

Then there was a deep, chilling laugh. It turned
Lisa's skin to gooseflesh. She inched closer to the door
and peaked in through the small, wire-mesh window.

The boy was pacing the room, talking to himself.
His arms banged stiffly against his body and he was
shaking his head constantly. Again Lisa felt that slow,
aching pity.

*"They won't keep us here. We'll get out. The others
will help. They will."*

"I don't want them." Peter stamped his foot on the
ground. "Leave me alone!"

Peter hugged himself tight around the chest.

"Please! Leave him alone. Leave me alone. It's not
fun anymore and I'm scared! Please!"

Then his head reared back and he grabbed himself
by the hair and yanked it. He cried out in pain and
Lisa gasped.

The boy's eyes darted toward the window. Lisa felt
them dig into her as she stood, frozen, watching helplessly.

"I hate you," he screamed. He charged the door and
clawed at the window. Lisa jumped back. Two small
fingers poked through the wire. They pushed and
curled frantically. The boy tried to squeeze them
through the mesh until they bled.

Then she saw his face close to hers, glaring. It was

ugly, old, not like Peter's at all. She stepped farther back in the hall.

"I'll get you. And him too."

Lisa knew he meant Eric. That made the fear turn into anger and she walked up to the door defiantly.

"You leave us alone. You won't win. You won't get anyone. You won't! You're locked in."

The boy cackled and banged on the door.

"No one can stop us. No one. *No one.*"

Lisa felt nauseous. She was going to answer him again, but caught herself. She was a nurse. She was not there to torment a mentally unbalanced boy, even if he was threatening her. She turned and walked unsteadily back into the closet to finish her job.

The boy's eyes watched her through the window, his little fingers dangling from the wire-mesh, dripping bright red blood.

Inside the closet, Lisa picked up her clipboard. In her mind, she could still hear that evil laughter. She tried to concentrate on her work to force the sound away. But suddenly she felt a cold breeze sweep down around her legs. She swung her head around to see the closet door slam closed. She stifled a scream, dropping the clipboard. Her hands were shaking as she grabbed the doorknob and twisted.

It was locked.

Lisa banged on the door, frantically calling out for help. Then she held her breath and listened for footsteps or voices. All she heard was that laughter again, echoing behind the locked door. Lisa covered her ears and yelled out again.

Then came a crash and the sound of breaking glass. She spun around to look to see that one of the shelves had collapsed and bottles were strewn across the far corner of the closet. The chemicals spilled into a puddle together. A fizzing sound began as gray curling smoke bubbled up from the chemicals. The odor assaulted her, choking her and stinging her eyes.

Chlorine gas.

She stumbled toward the spill, covering her mouth with a handkerchief. Chlorine from the bottles of hydrochloric acid was being released in a chemical reaction. She knew how toxic that could be. The room was already spinning with flashing stars and she felt her legs begin to weaken. Dizziness increased quickly. There was no air. She held the side shelves to help herself inch back toward the door.

"Help me," she cried. Her voice was barely audible and she began to cough. Words became harder to form. Her legs were like rubber. She banged against the door with her fists as she slowly slid down onto the floor.

Eric's guilt grew quickly as he sat in the lounge. He had let Peter down. He'd given him the bad news and then walked out when the kid needed him most. And it was all because he'd let his own feelings become more important than Peter's. He had given in to his own fears, to pity—and now guilt. So make up for it, he told himself. Feeling sorry for yourself won't do anyone any good.

Eric marched down the stairs to the first floor. When he entered the hallway to Peter's new room, he heard a faint, distant cry and pounding. He stopped by the security room door and listened.

He heard it again. But it wasn't coming from Peter's room. He backed down the corridor until the sounds became louder, in front of the medical supply closet. He checked the door. It was locked.

"Anyone in there?"

"Help. Quick."

The words sounded far away, but he recognized the voice immediately. Eric grabbed the door and yanked.

"Lisa?"

Then he heard coughing, but no more words.

"Lisa!" He punched at the door. "Unlock it."

Eric glanced frantically up and down the hall. Then he ran to the maintenance closet and found a heavy, foot-long screwdriver. He dashed back, jammed it into the edge of the closet door near the lock, and pulled. The wood splintered, but the door held. He jammed it again, then again, working it deeper. Finally he put his foot against the wall and tugged with his whole body.

The door broke open and the smell of chlorine gas rushed into the hall. Eric coughed and squinted his stinging eyes. He saw Lisa on the floor and quickly dragged her out.

She was gasping and coughing.

"Eric, it locked on me."

She turned her face toward the security room and pointed weakly.

"He did it. He threatened to and he did it."

She coughed again and Eric felt the spasms tear up through her chest. He held her still.

"I'm all right," she said.

She tried to stand, but her legs would not support her yet. Eric caught her, holding her against him until her legs regained their strength.

"He did it," she said again.

"How could he? He's locked in his room."

"I don't know how, but he did it. He tried to kill me. I know he did."

Eric sank down with her onto the floor. She was trembling and . . .

Above him, through the wire-meshing, two small eyes watched intently, never blinking.

CHAPTER XI

Eric drove Lisa home immediately after Dr. Jones examined her. When he put her to bed, he gave her a strong sedative and waited, holding her hand and agreeing with whatever she said, even about Peter, until she fell asleep. Then he sat and watched her and stroked her hair gently as her breathing became regular and the coughing subsided.

He knew she would be out for hours, so he decided to drive back to the hospital. He wanted to see Peter. But as he was walking out the kitchen door, the telephone rang. It was Dr. Jones.

"I wanted you to know," he told Eric.

"Know what?"

"That Sherry is still planning to have Peter sent to the hospital in Chelliston. I was there when she called them from her room."

"She can't do that. She agreed to let him—"

"She said she didn't agree to anything. She's still not—"

"But she can't."

"I'm afraid she can. She's still the director. If she says he goes, he goes."

"But . . ." Eric was squeezing the phone as he paced back and forth. Then he stopped and tried to think it out without the anger or the disgust.

"What about Peter's father? Can he stop her?"

"She can discharge any patient she wants to, especially a patient with no physical injuries. And anyway, you know as well as I do that Mr. Delmont can't cope. He might be the first one to agree to placing him in an institution."

"There must be *some* way to stop her, for Chrissake!"

"You could prepare a psychiatric presentation to take before the Board of Directors. If you can convince them Sherry's wrong, you could stop her."

"When do they meet?"

"Tuesday afternoon. But I don't think you could sway them. They listen to her. There's not much chance you could change their minds if she says otherwise."

Eric slowly let the phone down and stared at it. He felt his stomach quiver as he hung it up. Sinking into the chair, he put his head in his hands. He didn't know how much more of this he could take.

But then he thought about Peter and what he had been through—and about what he would go through soon if he were sent to the state institution. He gathered up his strength with short, quick breaths.

Behind his eyelids he saw Carol's face again, cut and bloody and festering with boils.

"Shit," he muttered. The anger and the helplessness seemed to overwhelm him. He stood up, turned toward the wall, and punched it as hard as he could. Pain shot up his arm as he pulled his fist out of the hole in the plaster.

He was glad it hurt.

Eric got the key to Peter's room from the orderly on duty. He hated to think of the boy locked in that padded cell. If he is dangerous, and there is evidence that points to that, it must be done, he told himself again, but his logic did not take away the guilt. It only made it worse. The state hospital weighed heavily on his mind now. Eric tried to push that thought away before he opened the door. He had made up his mind to give the boy one good afternoon.

"Hello, Peter," Eric said, walking in.

Peter was sitting on his bed. He was dressed, his hospital gown thrown in a heap in the corner opposite the bed.

"Would you like to go on a picnic with me? I've got permission. It's a nice afternoon. A little cold, but sunny. It's the beginning of the end of fall, I'm afraid."

Peter did not answer.

"Are you all right?" Eric asked, gently putting his arm around Peter's shoulders.

He shook his head no. Eric could see him bite his lower lip because it was trembling.

"It'll be fun to get out for a while. A little fresh air? Play a little Frisbee?" Eric leaned closer. "You know how to play with a Frisbee?"

Peter nodded.

"Come on, Peter. There's nothing wrong. Come on now. It's okay."

"I hate this room." he said, choking. His arms slipped around Eric's chest and he buried his face in Eric's shoulder. Eric squeezed him softly and stroked his head, and neither of them spoke for a long time.

Finally Eric leaned away from Peter and, holding his chin up as they looked eye to eye, he winked and said, "Among friends, huh?"

"Yeah," Peter agreed and smiled slightly. "Among friends."

Eric stood up.

"Shall we go?"

"Sure," Peter answered and pushed himself up off the bed.

They drove in silence up the curved road of the small mountain northwest of town, and then back down again into a river valley. The river was wide and shallow where it ran through the park, flanked by the open grassy fields. There were big rocks in the river that were close enough together to form a bridge from bank to bank.

Eric grabbed the ice chest packed with food and soft drinks, and Peter picked up the blue Frisbee.

"I'll put this stuff under that big tree. Think that's a good place?"

"As good as any," Peter said.

Eric put the chest under the shade of the tree and turned to get a Frisbee in the stomach. He grunted loudly and Peter laughed. Eric was relieved to hear it. The silence in the car had been hard on him and he had almost cried thinking about where Peter would be going soon. A state mental institution with facilities for the criminally insane. It's not a place for kids. Hell, it's not a place for anyone. Eric could picture the huge old buildings, the well-cut lawn, and the wire fences. Oh, damn, he sighed. He looked out at the wide river with the sun sparkling across it and the clean smooth white rocks and tried to block out everything else.

Eric picked up the Frisbee.

"Nice shot. Right in the old bread-basket."

Peter skipped away across the field and Eric flipped the Frisbee toward him. Peter caught it with one hand and threw it back, all in the same motion.

"Looks like I got a pro here," Eric called as he caught it.

Peter grinned.

They threw the Frisbee for a long time. Then the wind picked up and made it harder to control and they stopped.

"Let's go down to the river," Peter suggested.

Eric nodded and they both ran down the small hill to the rocky embankment. Eric wondered how long he could keep up his joyful facade.

"It's not so high now. In the spring all those rocks would be under water," Eric told him.

Peter knelt and picked through the small stones until he found a flat one that fit his hand. He threw it and it skipped eight times, the first three a long ways apart, and then short quick bounces until it cut into the river and sank.

"Nice one," Eric said. He picked out a rock and threw it. It only skipped twice.

"Want to see if we can get across the river on those big rocks?" Eric asked.

Peter had picked up another smooth, flat rock, but then he looked up at Eric sadly and dropped it back on the ground.

"Dad and I did that once. I waved to him from the other side."

Eric's throat tightened and he flipped the rock he had just found over his shoulder.

"I didn't do it," Peter said suddenly, staring out across the river.

"Do what?"

Eric sat down and Peter sat next to him.

"Any of it," he answered. "I didn't."

"You mean David did, not you?"

"No, I mean I didn't. David is just . . ." Peter shrugged.

"Just what?"

"I don't know." Peter kicked a few small pebbles into the quick-swirling pool. "It's all different now. David was my friend. He wasn't just make-believe. He was me too. We were both always together. Friends, you know, like you said you were with Teddy when you were a kid."

Eric had decided not to mention David or the hospital today, but he could see that Peter wanted to talk now. He knew it was best if Peter picked the time and place he was most comfortable in to talk, so Eric went with it.

"I don't think it is exactly the same, Peter." Eric shifted his weight and lifted one knee up to wrap his arms around. "David is more than just make-believe. He seems to have a will of his own." Eric was startled to realize Peter had spoken about David in the past tense. He felt that nervous apprehension flutter in his chest.

"Why did you say 'was' and not 'is' when you just talked about David?"

"It's all different now. Now that I'm out of the hospital, I don't know why, but . . . but he's not so strong here. He wasn't so strong before either."

"Before you came to the hospital?"

"Yeah." Peter picked up two large pebbles and rolled them in his palms. "Someone else takes . . ." He tossed the pebbles far out into the river.

Eric could see the confusion wrinkle Peter's face as he strained to understand what he was trying to say.

"Takes what?"

Peter shrugged again. "I don't know what." Then

he stared up at Eric and his eyes were pleading. "I'm scared. I don't understand. I'm just scared."

Eric got up off the rock.

"Come on," he said.

They walked together arm in arm to the oak tree, then sat down under its shade on the soft, cool grass.

"You'll think I'm crazy," Peter said.

"Why?"

"I had this dream. It keeps coming back. It's always the same. It scares me something awful."

"Tell me about it. It might help make it go away if we talk about it."

"You really think so?"

"Maybe." Eric watched Peter decide, then waited in silence for him to begin. He was surprised to see that David did not surface when Peter was frightened now. He could not decide if that was good or bad.

"There's this castle. I'm there inside it. It's always at night." Peter leaned back against the tree and stared up at the mountain with the steep rock cliff across the road. "It's a huge castle with thick brick walls and big rooms with real high ceilings."

"Does the castle scare you?"

Peter glanced quickly at Eric, and Eric realized he shouldn't have interrupted.

"Yeah, it sure does. It's dark and there's all shadows in it. I know there's things, people, something, in the shadows. They're always watching me. I can hear them whispering and then . . ." Peter slowly drew a breath. "I don't know. I don't remember all of it exactly but . . . I'm locked up in this tower and it's cold and damp and I can hear rats running around in the corners. I'm screaming for someone to let me out. Then I hear them again. They're calling my name.

The door opens, a thick wood door, and I see they're waiting down in a huge court with colored flags and big tables, and I'm up on the balcony and they're calling to me to jump." Peter pulled his knees up to his chest and folded his arms around them. "Then I see a lady and she's calling my name and she looks like Grandma, but not really. But that's what I see and her face keeps changing like that and then . . ." Peter let go of his knees and sat up straight against the trees.

"And then what?" Eric could almost see the dream too. He felt the cold sweat dripping down across his ribs. He began to tap the ground nervously with the hand Peter couldn't see.

"I don't know. Suddenly I'm down there with them and I'm leading them and then the castle starts to break apart. Huge bricks are falling all around and a wall collapses and they're all calling to me for help. I lead them to the tower, but I can't open the big door and the stairs behind us are collapsing. The people behind me start screaming and falling and I keep pointing at the door. Then I hear someone inside. I look through the small window in the door and I see . . ." Peter waited until he could breathe easily again, then continued. "I used to see my mother in the tower, but not anymore. Not the last few times."

"Who do you see?" Eric did not understand why, but he was afraid of the answer.

"You," Peter said, looking up at him.

Eric felt his skin crawl.

"Is that the end?"

"No. Then we break into the tower and . . ." Peter wiped his eyes and took another gulp of air. "They throw you out into the stairs and you fall, screaming, reaching up at me and . . ." Peter sighed. "And then the castle tumbles down on top of you, burying you till only your hand is sticking out of the bricks."

"For not remembering all the details, you certainly remember a lot," Eric said. Then he reached into the ice chest and took out some ham and cheese and two cans of root beer. He did not know what to say about the dream, but he knew he should say something.

"You hungry?"

"A little. Not too much," Peter said.

"Maybe, Peter, the castle is the hospital. It scares you. There's people in it you don't know. Things happen that you don't understand. At first you felt it was your mother's fault that you had to be there and couldn't go home. Then maybe you put that blame on me and you felt I was making you stay in the hospital. Does that make sense? It's just your unconscious trying to escape the place your conscious mind doesn't want to be. By unconscious, I mean, like when you're asleep. Your imagination, sort of. Does any of that make sense to you?

"Not really," Peter confessed.

"That's all right. I don't understand it myself." Eric took the bread, napkins, and a knife for the mustard and mayonnaise out of the grocery bag. He felt uneasy, threatened by the dream, but he didn't want to frighten Peter. The more he tried to decipher the dream, the less he understood it and the more it bothered him. He decided the best thing to do now was to eat and change the subject. He made the sandwiches quickly.

"Did you ever go fishing?" Eric asked, handing Peter a ham and cheese on rye.

"Once."

"I got two rods in the trunk of my car. Want to try later?"

"Sure."

Peter stopped chewing and stared at Eric. Eric felt his gaze and turned to face him.

"Sometimes it was David before it was you."

Eric put his sandwich down on the top of the ice chest.

"How did you feel, seeing him there on the other side of the door to the tower? Did that frighten you?"

Peter pondered for a few seconds.

"No. I wanted him there. Only you and . . ."

"And?"

"And Mom. Only you two really scared me."

Eric exhaled loudly and leaned against the tree. Peter sprawled back to rest on his arm. They sat together, looking at the trees and the grass and the river and ate their sandwiches. Neither wanted the other to see that he was uneasy. Then Peter glanced up and smiled.

"He doesn't bother me here," he said proudly. He thought that would make Eric feel better, seeing how sad Eric looked.

"David?"

"Yeah. He was my friend, but then . . . he wasn't nice anymore."

"After you got to the hospital?"

"Yeah."

"Do you remember what David did now? I mean in the hospital? What he did that you didn't like?"

Peter shook his head.

"No. But sometimes I just feel it. I get sort of pictures in my head too, but they don't make sense. I don't know. I just feel it."

Eric watched Peter's hands tremble as he played with a twig. Maybe he was going too far.

"Don't worry about it," Eric said. "Let's go fishing now, okay? We've talked enough for now."

"I'd like that." Peter snapped the twig and stood up. Eric could see how relieved he was.

"Good. Let's go."

As they walked toward the car, Eric thought about Peter and his dream and the strange transition he had made with David now. He was totally confused. It seemed like a breakthrough but it worried Eric more than relieved him. It was too quick, too easy. It just didn't fit together. It was like trying to jam the wrong piece of a jigsaw puzzle into place. But his suspicions went deeper than that. They went beyond analysis or logic or other professional deductions. Somehow Eric almost felt that Peter's dream and the way David kept changing so radically in such short periods of time was a warning. A warning directed at him.

The rest of the afternoon went well, and they never talked again about David or the hospital or his mother. They just had a good time fishing. Peter caught a small rainbow trout.

Eric took Peter back to the security room before dark and locked him in. Then he took the keys back to the aide on duty. He couldn't stand how they had jingled in his hand, reminding him of what he had just done. He quickly went to the lounge and called home. Lisa did not answer, so he assumed she was still under sedation.

Eric put a piece of paper in the lounge typewriter and began to outline his presentation to the board. He stopped and thought about Lisa and about Mike, then about his father and his grandfather and Mrs.

Delmont. Suddenly he felt a chilling breeze sweep over him. He buttoned his jacket and kept on typing, trying hard to ignore the strange coldness that seemed to grow all around him.

Mr. Gibbs kicked the crate full of spare parts and tools as he grumbled to himself. He was still angry at Dr. Jones. The doctor had reprimanded him a few minutes before.

For some reason, the heating on the third floor near Sherry Mellany's room had gone on the blink, and the temperature had risen to ninety-five degrees. Jones blamed Mr. Gibbs for the mishap and after a stern lecture sent the maintenance man down into the basement.

Grumbling to himself, he began checking the gauges. He adjusted the third-story pipe outlet and the heat slowly declined.

"Goddamn place, anyway," he mumbled. "Ain't worth a shit."

He grumbled all the way upstairs. He had had it with the hospital and the know-it-all doctors.

Then he saw Eric walking about the first-floor hall.

"What the hell do they want from me?" Mr. Gibbs asked loudly.

Eric stopped and waited for the old man.

"What's wrong?"

"The whole place is falling apart. Heating's screwed up. But them boilers, you should see them. Worthless pieces of scrap. I could swear they're used. Rusted inside. And they always blame it all on me. Ain't my fault this place was put together with junk."

Eric smiled. He liked Mr. Gibbs and his rough ways.

"What happened now?"

"Damn heat went way up on the third floor near

what's-her-name's room. The thermostat in the basement was stuck. Had to pound it to get it to move on the adjusting valve of the pipe."

"But you fixed it. That's the point. That's why you're so important to this hospital."

Mr. Gibbs looked at Eric and shook his head. "Don't patronize me. I'm too old for a kid like you to do that."

"Sorry."

"Don't matter. The whole building should be condemned. Them boilers, though, they should be replaced right away. They're dangerous. Real dangerous."

"You sure you're not exaggerating? What happened? Did one of the doctor's get on your case?"

"Dr. Jones. What does he know? I don't care what any of 'em think! To hell with all of you. This place is nuts. You hear me? Nuts! I quit."

Eric had never seen Mr. Gibbs so upset before.

"You can't quit. We need you. How would we keep this place running without you? Dr. Jones was just overly concerned about Mrs. Mellany. I'm sure he didn't mean anything."

Mr. Gibbs grumbled to himself and stomped away. Eric decided it was best not to follow him. He would only make things worse at that point. Then Mr. Gibbs halted and turned.

"This building ain't right. You can't fix nothin'. When you do fix somethin', it don't stay fixed. It's crazy. I ain't stepping foot in here again. Never. You hear me? Never."

CHAPTER XII

Eric Loman sat in the study typing his presentation to the Board of Directors. He had brought Lisa dinner in bed and she was sleeping again now. It was early evening. He had not told her about the presentation. He didn't want to upset her any more than she already was.

Eric was having a difficult time finishing the presentation and, reading it over, he realized it was as much an argument for sending the boy to Chelliston as for keeping him out. That startled him. He reread the therapeutic considerations as well as the awkward coincidences, then leaned back in the swivel chair and tried to put himself in the Board's position. He was seeing the problem from both sides now, and there was just no black-and-white conclusion to be drawn.

He could feel the wind blowing through the partially open window. It was cold and damp. He closed it and stared out into the coming darkness. There were no stars yet. Another storm was moving in from the northwest and the distant thunder was low and rumbling and growing louder. He watched the black clouds drift down over the mountains into the valley and wondered what was truly the right thing to do. He could not find a specific, or even reasonable, answer. Then the rain began to pound on the roof and spill in quick waves down the glass of the window.

When he turned from the storm, he saw Lisa in her nightgown, standing over his typewriter and reading his presentation. She looked at him angrily.

"Quiet as a cat tonight," he said, forcing a smile. "Couldn't sleep?"

"What are you doing?"

Lisa was not ready for polite chatter or half smiles. She had read enough to know what it was. It did not just anger her now, it offended her.

"He tried to kill me and you're still defending him!"

Eric put his hands out, palms up, and sighed. He had not wanted to go through this. He knew he had no arguments left to combat her fear. He had used them all.

"He was locked in the security room while you were in the closet. How could he do anything?"

"I don't give a damn. I heard him. That disgusting laugh." She could hear it again in her head and she shook it to keep the sound away as she walked across the room.

Eric hurried to her and touched her arm. She backed away quickly.

"He wants you dead, Eric. He tried to kill me to get at you. Can't you understand? There's more to this than you think."

"He's sick. His second personality has gotten stronger. He's scared to death of himself. He's being torn apart inside."

Lisa pushed her arms out to keep Eric away, then stomped her foot.

"So am I, goddamn it. So am I. I'm so scared I could scream."

Eric approached her again.

"Stay away from me. You won't listen, will you? I know it isn't scientific. I know it sounds like a grade-B horror movie. But it's true, Eric. That boy is evil. That hospital is evil. The goddamn land itself is evil." Lisa was crying now as she waved her arms in desperation. "Evil, Eric! It's going to kill you. I know it. Can't you just believe me even if you don't understand? Can't you?"

"How can he hurt anyone now? He's locked away. He's as good as in Chelliston already."

"No. He's more than you think. He told me before the incident in the closet that he was going to kill you. And he meant it. I don't know how, but I saw his eyes and I know he meant it."

"I just can't believe that."

"*Eric*," Lisa screamed, slamming her fists on the table. "I can't take it anymore! Not the logic. Not the poor, sick kid crap. None of it! Don't you understand?" She was staring up at him, her eyes wide with hysteria.

Eric walked past her into the living room and poured a drink.

"Want one?" he called.

"No."

She pulled her nightgown tight against her body as she stomped into the living room after him.

"It's cold," she said, sitting on the sofa.

"Might snow soon. Probably be down in the thirties tonight."

The change of subject was awkward and felt ridiculous to both of them. Eric sat across from her on the sofa and put his glass on the coffee table.

"Am I still the most important thing in the world to you, Eric?"

He looked at her seriously to reassure her that what he was going to say was sincere.

"You are always the most important thing in my life. Always."

Lisa reached out and took his hand. Hers was cold and wet and Eric could feel it trembling.

"I can't take it anymore. I'm not kidding. Even if you think I'm being ridiculous or childish or superstitious or whatever. I don't want you to work at that hospital, not with Peter there."

Eric tensed up and tried to object, but Lisa put her finger against his lips. Finally looking deep in her eyes and trying to feel what she felt, he saw just how much it meant to her.

"For me, Eric. To keep me sane."

"The boy only threatened you in his David personality because that's his protector. David strikes out at anyone who he thinks wants to hurt Peter."

"And he doesn't think you do?"

"I think he does. Not consciously. But unconsciously he blames me for keeping him in the hospital, away from his mother. He has a deep need to convince himself that he loves her, even if he really hates her. David is the only one who can hate. It is his prime emotion. He threatens me or you for the same reason a dog barks. To keep you away. To frighten you when actually he's more scared than you are."

"I understand that. But it doesn't matter. If a dog is cornered, it will attack. If it's David that wants to get you, fine. Then it's David."

"So what do you want me to do?"

"Quit. We'll leave this place. Start fresh."

"Give up just like that?" He snapped his fingers to emphasize the sarcasm.

"Yes. Just like that."

"Let the only hope Peter has left vanish? To hell with the boy?"

"Yes."

Eric stared, then shook his head. "It's my job. My life "

"And what am I?"

He felt himself backed tight into a corner. Lisa moved to take him in her arms and as she did, Eric could feel his defenses dissolving. He tried to regroup them.

"Lisa. How can I respect myself, what I do, if I just give up when it gets tough?"

"How? Because I need you more than Peter does. I need you for the rest of my life. I need you to do this for me. Eric, I know what kind of sacrifice I'm asking." Her lips were so close to his that he could feel the warmth of her breath. "I'll never ask anything like this from you again. But it's that important to me. It is. Call Bob, tell him you'll take the job at his clinic. God, Eric, I need you so much. I couldn't stand to lose you—and I feel like I'm losing you already. I love you so much. Please. Do it for me."

Her eyes were riveted on Eric's, forcing him to listen and to understand.

"All right. But it hurts me that you could ask it of me."

"I know. God, I know. And I'm sorry."

Then they were hugging and there was a terrible sadness. Eric held her and caressed her as she slid down to rest on his lap, her body curled tight against his thigh.

They sat like that, the rain splattering against the house, the thunder booming loud now and close, the quick-snapping lightning flashing outside the bay window, illuminating the lawn and the big hanging trees.

Eric could feel Lisa slowly relax. He smoothed her hair and they clung to each other without talking.

In the silence Eric's mind wandered. He thought about Peter's dream and felt a strange apprehension in his belly. If he closed his eyes he could see his hand, white and bloody, stretching up out of the rubble, just the way Peter had described it. He kept stroking Lisa and going over the dream until she fell asleep. Then he picked her up and carried her upstairs to bed. She was half awake as he tucked her in, and he smiled when she looked up at him.

"I love you more than anything in the world," he whispered. Then he kissed her gently and she closed her eyes. He felt badly that he had just promised her something he was not sure he could do.

The storm bellowed, crashing down hard out of the mountains. The wind gusted fiercely and the trees bent and shook. The weaker limbs cracked and fell, spilling their thickly leafed branches across the woods and lawns of Hapsburg.

The huge oaks next to the hospital creaked like the hulls of old wooden sailing ships. The branches of the biggest one stretched out to the hospital's wall and clawed frantically at the building, like huge, dying hands trying to scratch through the bricks. Lightning split the sky in a jagged white line, striking the enormous oak and hurtling its big overhanging limb down onto the grass.

Sherry was lightly sedated and sleeping as the storm whirled around her outside the hospital. She had kicked the blankets off the bed as she constantly flipped from one side to the other and moaned. Then the door to her room cracked open and a small shadowed figure stood outlined in the light from the hallway. The wind scratched against the window and suddenly Sherry was lying as still as death. Seconds passed. Minutes. A finger twitched. Then the hand. She moaned almost silently as her head jerked slightly to one side.

When her head snapped off the pillow, she opened her eyes, terrified. Her body was soaked in sweat and she was shivering. For a moment, in the darkness, she wondered if she were dead. The blackness grew thick and heavy around her. She tried to get out of bed but could not move. The room felt like an oven and her body was too weak to respond. She had had a nightmare. It came back to her now, swallowing her, filling her with dread. She tried to cry out, but the horror, the piercing, inescapable horror overpowered her.

She knew it was coming. There was no way to stop it. She waited, paralyzed, trying to gather enough strength to rise up out of the bed. But her feet, her arms, would not move. Slowly her eyes closed.

She heard a distant, haunting laughter and behind it the screaming of the nightmare. She smelled the smoke and the sickening stench of burning flesh. She could see the dark walls and how the gray-black smoke curled down from the ceiling. The screaming grew louder and then came the cackling again. It was hard for Sherry to breathe now. Her throat and lungs were burning.

With her last burst of strength, Sherry opened her eyes and tried to stand. She couldn't. She peered down across her bed and saw flames creeping up the blankets, and suddenly a searing pain ripped through her legs. She tried to scream, but only a tiny gasp choked out of her throat. Then she saw the faces in the dream, burning, smiling. She tried to cover her eyes, but her arms were too heavy.

The fire ate into her flesh. For a second she wanted to die—quickly, mercifully—but she knew it was too late for that. Desperately she screamed.

The nurse was sitting by the window in the middle of the hall overlooking the drive when she heard it. It sent chills down her spine. She began to run when she saw the heavy smoke coming from Sherry Mellany's room.

She flicked on the light and gasped, covering her mouth with her hand. Sherry turned her eyes, screaming now in agony, toward the nurse as she lay helplessly burning in her bed.

The nurse ran to the next room for a blanket and hurried back to pull Sherry out of bed. She rolled her in the blanket until she had smothered the burning nightgown. Then she pounded the bed with the blanket.

Working frantically, she was startled to hear a chuckling sound. Her head jerked back over her shoulder but she only saw a fleeting shadow before the door to the room slammed shut.

Quickly she extinguished the last of the flames and ran to open the door. She glanced up and down the hall. It was empty. The door to the stairway slowly closed. She dashed over to open it and peered down the steps. She thought she heard footsteps and held her breath to listen, but her heart was pounding in her ears. She couldn't hear anything. She concentrated harder. Then she heard footsteps running behind her and she spun around.

"What happened?" the aide on duty asked.

"Fire," was all she could say as she tugged him toward Sherry's room.

* * *

It was hailing and the cold wind blew hard against the windshield of Eric's car as he drove to the hospital. He was trying to sort out what he had been told a few minutes earlier over the phone.

Sherry was dead. Burned to death.

He had not awakened Lisa to tell her. It was two in the morning.

Eric pulled the car into a parking space. Then he sat, holding his hands over the steering wheel, squeezing until his knuckles turned white. A few minutes passed before he noticed the flashing red lights of the police cars all around him. He turned off the ignition and ran through the rain into the building.

"What happened?"

"She's dead," the nurse on duty said, clutching him as he walked in. "Her bed caught on fire. She was burned, but died of shock."

Eric felt the beads of sweat break out on his brow. His vision blurred and he clutched his hands tightly behind his back to steady himself. He inhaled slowly, deeply, until he regained his composure.

"They think it was murder," said the nurse.

"Murder?" He shook her. "Who would have done that?"

As soon as he had said it he knew he did not want to hear her answer.

The nurse shrugged. She put one hand over her eyes and shook her head slowly. Eric let go of her and hurried toward Police Chief Haggar, who was coming down the hall.

"Peter Delmont was seen running from her room," the chief said.

Eric ran both hands through his hair and tried to listen. He hated the smug accusation and the way the chief enjoyed his discomfort. He tensed the muscles in his legs and shoved his hands into his pockets to keep them from shaking.

"He was the only one near Mike Mellany when he had his accident." The chief glanced up at Eric. "Are you listening, Loman?"

Eric clenched his teeth, closed his eyes, then opened them and looked at Haggar.

"What?"

"Did you hear what I was saying?"

"Sure."

"You don't look too good."

The policeman was watching Eric suspiciously.

"I had a bad night."

"So did Sherry Mellany."

"You were talking about Peter," Eric said coldly.

"The nurse on duty said that someone had been in the room with Sherry. She saw him run out."

"Who was it?"

The chief glanced around, then put one hand in his pocket.

"She didn't actually see who it was. She said a child ran out and slammed the door while she was trying to save Mrs. Mellany."

"I thought you said she saw Peter. Did she or didn't she?"

"Well, she said she saw something . . . a child."

Eric let his anger build, using it as a prop to regain his balance. He unclenched his fists and stared at Haggar who looked up at him sternly.

"There's no doubt that it was murder."

Eric lowered his eyes and nodded. The anger dissolved as quickly as it erupted. Eric felt his stomach quiver and his Adam's apple pushed drily to swallow his fear.

"And you think Peter had something to do with it?"

"I'd like to talk to him."

"I don't know."

"Two people have died."

Eric looked up and could see the chief was not gloating anymore. The sadness in his voice surprised Eric. He wondered if Haggar was really as unfeeling as he had thought earlier.

"Is he your patient?" the chief asked.

"Yes."

"And you are the psychiatrist?"

"We've been through this before."

Eric knew where he was being led, but he could understand the suspicion now. He felt it, too, as much as it hurt him to admit it. He thought about Peter and in a desperate way, it gave him the distance he needed. Then he remembered the boy's obvious defense.

"I'll take you to him. He's locked in the security room. There's no way he could have done anything. You'll have to search somewhere else for your scapegoat."

"I hope you're right," Haggar said.

Eric got the key from the aide on duty, then led the chief to the security room. Before he could unlock it, the chief tried the door.

It opened.

Eric felt his heart clench under his ribs and the sweat eased down his arms. The chief glanced at him almost apologetically. Then they walked in.

"Peter, this is our police chief. He wants to ask you a few questions."

Peter smiled cautiously and sat up in bed. The chief approached him slowly. Looking at the handsome child, the chief had a hard time believing what he did. What did you expect him to be, foaming at the mouth? he thought. In a way, he realized, he had. It would have made it all so much easier if the kid at least looked crazy.

"What were you and Mike doing upstairs before he . . ." The chief glanced at Eric.

Peter looked at both men, letting his eyes rest on Eric.

"Just tell him what you can remember," Eric said. He was standing behind Haggar but stepped toward the bed now to reassure Peter.

"I don't know," Peter said. "I . . . I wasn't there."

"We know you—"

Eric grabbed the chief's arm and he stopped mid-sentence. Eric had already warned him that Peter couldn't remember things, and that it scared him not to be able to. The chief smiled again. He felt sorry for the kid, knowing what he'd had to live through at home. There was clear medical evidence that he had been beaten for years. It was no wonder if Peter was, well, unstable. But Haggar was much more comfortable interrogating people he didn't like. It was tough to get down on a pitiful little kid.

"Did you leave your room at all tonight?" The chief glanced at Eric to see if the question was all right. Eric nodded. Peter still watched them both.

"I . . . I couldn't sleep." Peter thought back. Pieces of his memory returned. "I walked for a minute. I got bored just lying here."

"Where did you go?"

The chief wished that he had given this assignment to the sergeant.

"I went . . ." Peter looked up helplessly at Eric who winked and put his hand on Peter's arm.

"I was in the hall and . . ." The chief saw the strain on Peter's face. "I don't know. I really don't. I just walked a little. That's all, I guess."

"Is that the hospital gown you've been wearing?"

"Sure. I didn't change it."

"Do you mind if I look at it?"

Peter shrugged. "Okay."

The chief pulled the covers back and checked the gown. It was clean and had no smoke residue. Too clean, the chief thought. It's hardly been worn.

"How long have you had this on?"

"A few days. Off and on. At night mostly."

The chief smiled again. Eric could see his growing concern. Then Haggar began to look around. There was really nowhere to hide anything in the padded room, except . . . The chief went to the toilet and opened up the tank behind it.

"Don't worry," Eric said to Peter, gently rubbing his shoulders. "Policemen always snoop around trying to make you feel like you've done something wrong. It's their job."

"Maybe I did," Peter said quietly.

"What do you mean?"

"You know." Peter squirmed uncomfortably. "I told you."

"David?"

"Not David," Peter said, slightly annoyed. Then the chief turned around with a wet pair of pants in his hands. He was stern now and his voice was harsh.

"I found this in the back of the toilet." He walked up to the bed and looked at Peter. "Did you hide this in there?"

"I don't . . . I . . ." Peter felt the horrible accusation and fought to hold the tears. "No, I . . . didn't . . . I didn't put that there."

"And you didn't go up to Sherry Mellany's room tonight? How did you get the door unlocked? Was it ever locked?"

The chief was raising his voice with each word.

"I locked it myself," Eric snapped. "I think you've said enough."

"I don't," the chief said angrily.

"You'll have to go now."

Eric ushered Haggar out of the room.

"I'm taking this to the lab in Janesville," the chief told Eric in the hall.

"You have to understand about Peter," Eric said.

"I understand he may have killed someone. Maybe two."

"But he's not responsible, even if you do find traces of smoke, or whatever it is you're looking for . . ."

Eric stopped himself as he watched the police chief march down the hall to the stairs. He realized, then, that he would never understand. Hell, Eric thought, *I* don't even understand.

Eric walked back into the security room and sat on the bed. He knew Peter had been trying to tell him something earlier, something frightening, but also something that was important. That was why Eric had wanted the chief out of there. But he wasn't looking forward to finding out what Peter had to say. He wished he could just go back home to Lisa, but he had a job to do. Peter needed him now, as much as he needed Lisa.

"David wants to hurt you now, doesn't he?"

It was blunt, but there was no other way to ask the question.

"Yes," he replied.

"Sit up, Peter."

Peter was surprised by the command right after the quick biting question. He sat up.

"Do you know about the fire?"

Peter slowly nodded his head.

"David?"

"I don't know. It's not clear, but I think so. I saw her . . . burning." Peter turned his head, seeing it in his mind.

"Were you there too?"

"I can't stop . . ." Peter tried to finish it. His neck tightened and his face flushed pink. He was trying to control the flashes of memory. Eric leaned over and held his hand.

Suddenly, the boy laughed. Eric saw a cold, shameless challenge develop in his eyes. He pulled his hand away.

"You're not going to let Peter get you, huh?" Eric was surprised at how easily he could deal with the change now, especially after what had just happened. He leaned back, then stood up, towering over the bed.

"Leave me alone," the boy said.

"Are you David?"

"Yes."

"I don't believe you."

"So?"

Eric had to readjust his plan quickly. He decided to be brutal, to battle for Peter. He knew there was not much time. He could tell Peter was weakening, losing control. He also knew that he could no longer keep Peter at the hospital. He could never stop them from taking him away now.

But there was something else nagging at Eric's thoughts. Somehow he had the feeling that Peter was being allowed to remember too much. It was as if—

Eric hated what he thought—as if David wanted to get rid of Peter.

Maybe David was going to let Peter drive himself crazy. Eric could tell that David did not "belong" to Peter now. But it didn't make sense. What did David want? Eric realized that he felt as threatened as Peter did.

"You locked him in," the boy said, intruding on his thoughts. "It will be on you now."

"What will be on me?"

The boy sat up tall and cackled loudly. It reminded Eric of Carol's laughter and how it had changed that last week before the exorcism.

"What will be on me?" he asked again when the cackling had subsided.

"All of it."

Eric turned angrily.

"Don't play word games. They don't suit you, David."

Slowly, silently, a grin spread across the boy's face. It was a nasty, taunting sneer.

"That's enough!" Eric yelled. He grabbed the boy by the shoulders and flung him backward onto the bed.

Peter threw both arms up in front of his face and let out a desperate cry. The sound seemed to rip through Eric's heart.

Slowly Peter let his arms down. A tear dropped to his cheek and his eyes were bright with fear. He was a frightened little boy again.

"He's no use to you anymore, is he, Peter?" Eric asked gently.

Peter nodded and began to sob.

"He always used to protect me," Peter cried.

"He wants you to be scared now. He wants to get rid of you."

Peter shook his head and let the tears stream down his face.

"Doesn't he? Peter, David can't hurt you. He's a part of you. You control him. You do."

"No," he whimpered. He flipped over and buried his face in the pillows. His body heaved as he cried. "I can't stop him."

"Yes, you can. It's all up to you."

Peter turned over slowly and looked at Eric. His face was wet and lined with desperation and a horrible confusion that Eric shared.

"He hates me now. He's gonna get me," Peter struggled to say.

Eric sat next to him. Peter reached out and put his small hand in Eric's.

"We can beat him," Eric said, putting his other hand on Peter's.

The child shrugged.

"We can. Together. We will."

Peter tried to smile but couldn't. Eric nodded at him and touched his cheek gently.

"It'll be tough, but you're a tough kid. We're both tough."

Peter smiled faintly.

Then he threw his arms around Eric and hugged him. Eric held him close, glad that Peter couldn't see that he was crying too.

CHAPTER XIII

The nightmare had engulfed him. Peter kicked the covers off the bed and groaned. He was sweating heavily.

There was a mob after him now and they had him cornered in the huge red-bricked room. Their skins were taut, yellow-white. The flames behind them began to leap up the curtains toward the cathedrallike ceiling. As they surrounded him in the corner, the pale skin on their screaming faces began to melt off like wax.

"Peter . . . Peter . . . Peter . . ."

He could not stop their horrible hollow chanting. He closed his eyes, covered his ears and let out a howl. He screamed for a long time, like a person falling to his death from a great height.

He screamed himself awake.

It was dark in the security cell. Only the light that filtered in from the hall through the small square window broke the thick-hanging blackness.

Peter was trembling. His hospital gown was soaked through with sweat. For a moment, sitting up, shaking, trying to adjust his bloodshot eyes to the dark, he could still hear the horrible breathing and the chanting as the mob encircled him.

Slowly, Peter realized where he was, but that cold,

choking fear did not subside. He reached down to the end of his bed, pulled the sheet up, and wiped his face and neck with it.

Then he heard a creaking noise. Chills ran over his wet body and, looking across the room, he watched the door slowly open. The light from the hall edged across the wall until it spot-lighted Peter. He yanked the sheet and blanket up around himself tightly.

Then he heard it again.

"Peter . . . Peter."

The eerie chanting drifted into the room, beckoning him, so distant and cold, just the way it was in his dream. Peter tried to swallow, but his throat was parched and he couldn't.

"Peter . . . Peter."

He curled up into a ball, his knees against his chest as he pushed himself against the wall, the blanket held up around his face so only his dark eyes peered out at the light.

The door slammed closed. Blackness swept over him and he screamed, terrified. The small square window slid shut. There was no light at all.

Peter could hear heavy, shuffling footsteps dragging toward him. He shook so violently that the blanket fell down off his head and shoulders. He clutched it against his chest, too horrified to move.

"Peter."

It was a single voice now and it was close. Peter could almost feel the hot breath on his face. With his last, frantic bit of courage, the child stood up and reached out, poking the darkness like a blind man.

"Go away. Please."

Only the darkness and the silence answered him.

"Please," he repeated quietly. "Leave me alone."

Then suddenly he felt a hand on his belly, slowly crawling up his chest. Peter gasped and leaped back onto the bed. The hand still clutched his hospital gown. Peter pushed himself into the corner, but there was nowhere to go.

The moist, cold hand reached up around his neck and began to squeeze.

"David?" Peter begged. "Let me go, David. Please. Please, David!"

The answering laughter seemed to echo in the tiny cell. The hand began to squeeze tighter.

Peter grabbed it, trying to pry it off his neck. In the instant that the fingers touched, a shock ran through him and he screamed for his life.

The hand choking him was his own!

Falling to the floor, Peter broke the grip on his neck.

"David, stop them! Please!" he cried, holding both hands tight between his legs.

"You cannot escape, Peter."

"David?"

Peter searched the darkness with darting eyes.

"It is time, Peter."

"David, help me. We're together, David."

"We've been waiting so long."

"No!" He stood up and banged his foot against the floor. "No. No. No."

"You have served your purpose, Peter."

"Go away."

Peter shook his head hard as he mumbled incoherently to himself.

"Peter?"

The boy froze and stared wide-eyed into the darkness, still holding his one hand at the wrist.

"I'm here, Peter."

"No, you're with me. You can't hurt me. We're together, David. Quit scaring me."

Loud rumbling laughter filled the room. Peter tried to cover his ears, but only one hand responded to his command.

The other curled quickly around his small neck.

Peter fought the hand, banging its forearm with his fist. It did not bulge. The floor began to spin beneath him. He could not inhale. He fell backward against the door and slid slowly down to the floor.

"Lie still, Peter. It will be over soon. Lie still."

Peter felt his life being squeezed out of him. His lungs ached. White stars were blinking all around him in the blackness. With his last spurt of energy, Peter ripped the hand from his throat and rolled over, pinning it with his chest against the cold floor.

"Peter. There's no escape. I'm stronger than you. I protect you."

"No!" Peter yelled. "I am who I . . . you . . . I . . . Please! Go away!"

"There is no place to go, Peter. You cannot stop it now."

"I can stop you."

A terrible growling erupted in the room. Peter wanted to roll over to see where it was coming from, but he stopped himself and kept his hand pinned to the floor. Then the door swung open, banging hard against Peter's head and sending him sprawling across the room. He tried desperately to get up and run, but his knees buckled as he spun around, and he crumbled back onto the floor.

"Please, David. Stop it. Please."

Peter felt the hand crawling up his chest again. He grabbed it by the wrist and tried to hold it down.

His strength was ebbing fast. Both arms shook as they battled each other. Then the hand pressed downward instead of fighting its way up and Peter lost his grip on it. The fingers quickly grabbed a shock of Peter's hair and began to bang his skull against the outside edge of the open door.

Blood trickled down Peter's forehead. He could hardly think now; everything was spinning.

"No more," he begged, padding his head with his other hand. His knuckles smashed against the edge of the door. Pain shot up his arm. For a second he thought—prayed—that he would black out. But the torture continued.

The fingers dug deep into Peter's face. He was trying to pry them loose when the thumb slipped over the bridge of his nose and dug into his right eye. Peter fought to pull it out, twisting and rolling as he struggled. Then the hand yanked away from his face and grabbed the loose bed sheet.

"David!" Peter wailed. When he did, the hand stuffed the end of the sheet down his throat.

He tried to gasp for air, but there was none. The hand held the sheet tight against his tongue. Each time Peter tried to breathe, the cloth was stuffed farther down his throat.

Peter began to gag. He wanted desperately to gnaw off his fingers pushing at his mouth, but the sheet padded them and he couldn't bite down.

Darkness engulfed him.

In a few minutes his struggle was over.

The orderly, while making his morning rounds, discovered Peter's body. He phoned Dr. Crane, who was on call that night, and Dr. Crane called Eric at home. Lisa was with him when he was told that Peter was dead. The doctor did not want to go into detail, but just said the boy apparently had committed suicide by suffocation.

Eric sat in bed a long time, just staring blankly at the wall. Lisa left him alone to contend with it in his own way. But when she heard him crying, she hurried to him. He held her tightly and sobbed against her chest.

She caressed his head and waited. There were no words that could soothe him and she knew it. She held him close for a long time.

Afterward, she tried to make him eat, but he couldn't. Then she suggested going for a drive in the country, far away from Hapsburg. Eric immediately grabbed his coat and headed for the door, and Lisa scurried after him.

"It wasn't your fault," she said. They had driven a long time without speaking and now they came down out of the mountains into the Amish countryside. A horse-drawn buggy passed them on the other side of the street but neither of them noticed.

"Maybe it's for the best," he said, glancing out at the farms. He didn't want to talk or think about it anymore.

"Maybe."

Eric shrugged and drove around a big hay wagon pulled by two horses. Then he turned off the highway.

"Let's get a room for the night." Eric looked over at Lisa. "I know a pretty hotel," he said. "They give you a great homemade dinner. Fresh bread, vegetables."

She knew what he really meant. She slid across the seat and put her arm around his shoulders.

"I don't want to go back yet either," she admitted. They drove along a narrow road with farms on both sides, then past a blacksmith shop and a hardware store with leather collars and harnesses hanging on the porch. The road led up a steep hill to a big white house with a porch supported by hand-carved white wood pillars.

"It's beautiful," Lisa said.

"They even serve drinks." Eric parked the car in the small lot in front. "They're not supposed to, but if you know them, they will," he explained. "I stayed here a few times with my parents when I was a kid. My father knew the owner, Mr. Green. They got along real well. That always surprised me. I could never figure out why they were such good friends. But I think I understand now. My father used to take my mother here a lot for weekends."

Eric got out of the car.

"We don't even have luggage." Lisa said.

"So?" he asked. "He always has extra toothbrushes."

Lisa looked up from the foot of the stairs to the big porch. From a distance the designs on the white porch roof looked like fine lace. "I love it already."

Mr. Green came out the screen door.

"Eric? Is that you?"

"Sure is, Mr. Green."

"Been a long time," he said.

The two men shook hands. Lisa smiled to herself. This was a part of Eric she had not known before, a part of his past, and she was happy that he would share it with her.

"This is Lisa Mitchell."

Lisa hurried up the stairs and put out her hand. Mr. Green stepped by it and gave her a big hug.

"Where's Mrs. Green?" Eric asked. He was beaming. It made Lisa tingle to watch him. He was like a little boy going to his grandparents' house. She knew how necessary it was to him to have this and to forget Peter, at least for the night. Sometimes, she thought, avoiding reality is a healthy thing.

Mr. Green sighed. "She died last winter."

Lisa watched Eric's face fall.

"I'm sorry," he said. That phrase had always sounded trite to him, but it was the only thing he could think of to say. He was shocked.

"She was with me for more than thirty-five years. That's long enough for any man, Besides, she never really left. She's all around here. All the things she made. All the times she laughed . . . or cried. They're still here. In me. In this house. And in the land we worked together." He turned and looked at the young couple as he opened the screen door. "She never left."

Eric smiled and looked at Lisa. She was thinking the same thing. They searched out each other's hands and held them tight to be sure.

The dinner was wonderful. Lisa listened to Mr. Green's stories about the Amish people and his guests and about Eric as a boy with his father and mother. Then the older man showed them to their room. Being a weekday, they were the only guests. It was not the "in" season anyway.

Eric took off his jacket and shirt and walked over to the long window with the thick flowing blue curtains roped back from it.

"It keeps changing," Eric said.

Lisa was sitting up on the bed. She unbuttoned her blouse and took it off.

"What do you mean?"

"I mean it just keeps changing. Nothing stays the same. Like this place. I always thought it would never change, I guess. It was supposed to be unaffected by time." He walked to the bed and sat facing Lisa. "But it is. Everything is. It's all too quick. Too unpredictable. It almost scares me to think about that sometimes."

Lisa reached out and stroked his arm and shoulder lightly. Then Eric leaned back to look at her.

"Let's get married." He rolled across the bed and laid his head in her lap. "I don't want to wait. Tomorrow, or sooner."

Lisa bent down and kissed him.

"We'll have to give it at least a week." She slipped her hand through his hair. "My mother would be upset if she couldn't plan it—at least part of it. It's important to her."

"All right. Next weekend then. Saturday."

Lisa couldn't help laughing. "We'll have to give my mother a couple of weeks. Just for the shock to wear off."

Eric sat up and looked at Lisa seriously. She smiled and waited.

"It's so different here," he said. He glanced around the high-ceilinged room with its gently sloping handmade dresser and the beautifully carved headboard and night tables. It all seemed so solid, so real.

"I'll sell the house. We can move out of Hapsburg if you want," he offered.

Lisa was waiting for that. She had already made up her mind.

"I'll give up being crazy and superstitious," Lisa said and grinned. Eric laughed and kissed her. The idea of marriage began to sink in. They hugged and Eric squeezed her breath away. Lisa pushed back and giggled.

"You don't have to break my ribs."

Eric felt good inside. He hadn't felt this happy in

. . . He realized that he had *never* been quite this happy before.

"I'll call Bob Thompson," he said. "He'll be the best man. I can quit my job now that Peter's . . ." He felt that fast-swelling sadness again, but forced it away. He took a deep breath. "There's nothing left at the hospital for me anyway. Bob said he'd always have an opening for me." Then Eric saw how Lisa was watching him. "Let's forget about that now. I'm here and you're going to marry me two weeks from Saturday."

"Shh," Lisa whispered.

She pulled Eric to her gently.

"It's all so . . ."

"Shh."

She raised his head and kissed him deeply. Then she reached to turn out the light, letting darkness surround them.

CHAPTER XIV

Lisa and Eric put in their two-week notices. Bob Thompson had found openings for both of them in his new clinic. He was overjoyed that Eric wanted to work with him and expressed that repeatedly in the phone calls over the last two days, in between discussions of Eric's approaching wedding.

The hospital was not frightening to Lisa now that Peter was no longer there, and she felt confident again. She did not, however, tell Eric that. Peter was a subject she did not want to bring up unless Eric did, and he hadn't once since they returned to Hapsburg.

On Thursday Eric left work early to prepare a special dinner for the two of them. He had not allowed himself to dwell on the past. He needed to think about the future now that he was going to be married. Finally he felt as if he had found a niche for himself, and each day he realized even more how glad he was to be leaving Hapsburg.

When the sadness came back and he imagined Peter's face, he took a slow, easy breath and forced himself to think of something else. It was becoming easier each time now.

Lisa arrived home early. Eric greeted her at the door and kissed her warmly and sensuously.

"Something smells good," she said, sniffing.

"I'm trying to perfect that Veal Oscar."

Lisa frowned.

"What's the matter?" he asked.

"That damn flu. Three nurses are down with it. Since I only have a week left, I . . ."

"You thought you'd be nice and agree to work tonight."

"Yeah."

"Sometimes you're just too nice," he said, pretending to scold her. "You've got to learn to say no to people."

Lisa glanced up at him and smiled. "Oh, really?"

"Well, to some people," Eric amended.

They hugged each other and Lisa squeezed him as hard as she could.

"When do you have to be there?" he asked.

"Ten minutes."

Lisa walked into the dining room. The oak table was covered with a linen tablecloth. There were candles and a large bouquet of colorful flowers.

"You made everything so nice, too," she sighed.

"There's almost no one in the hospital," Eric hinted.

"I'll be the only nurse on the floor. I guess it's the flu." Lisa grinned. "Everyone's too sick to go to the hospital."

"Then I'll bring the dinner to you," he said.

"What?"

"I'll bring the dinner to the staff lounge on the third floor around nine or nine thirty."

"But—"

"No buts about it. It's a private room. Nice view. And it's free, too."

Lisa laughed. "You're crazy," she said as she hugged him.

"I'm a psychiatrist," he told her. "It's part of my job."

The temperature had dropped ten degrees in the last two hours and the wind blew hard and cold through the bare trees as Eric drove up to the hospital. As he stepped out of the car, he thought for a second that it felt like snow, but even the threat of a storm couldn't dampen his spirits.

Lisa was at the desk when he pushed through the door on the third floor and bounded into the hall. She waved to him, then put her finger to her lips to remind him to be quiet as he passed the three elderly patients in their rooms. Eric backed through the door to the staff lounge, holding the bag of food with both hands. He flicked on the light switch with his elbow, then set the bag down on the table next to the coffee maker.

He heard Lisa opening the door.

"Don't come in," he said. "Not till it's ready."

"I just wanted to—"

"Out." He pushed the door back lightly. "Out, I said. Don't come back till I call you."

A few minutes later, Eric peeked out.

"Your table is ready, madam," he announced with a mock-English accent.

She pulled at her uniform, then pushed her hair up and back. "Just a second," she said. She hurried into an empty room to check herself in the mirror. Then she added just a touch of lipstick.

"What are you doing?" Eric called softly, still holding the door.

Lisa walked out of the room.

"Getting dressed for dinner," she said.

"Oh."

He bowed as she entered the lounge.

"Eric, it's really pretty."

He switched off the light, and the candles twinkled over the bright bouquet of flowers. The wine glasses reflected the warm yellow glow.

Eric led Lisa to her chair and seated her. Then he leaned down and kissed the soft slope of her neck. She turned her cheek against his.

"It's lovely," she said.

"This is for you." Eric handed her an orchid and helped her pin it above her breast. Then he kissed her gently.

"Some wine?" He poured each of them a glass.

"Beautiful room. It must have cost a fortune to get it for tonight. I hear this is the best restaurant in the city."

"It was nothing." Eric picked up his glass and raised it toward her. "All I had to do was mention your name. They said, for a lady as beautiful as you, nothing was too good."

Lisa smiled and raised her glass too.

"To our new life together," she toasted. "May it last a thousand years."

Eric felt his stomach flutter and he smiled and clinked his glass against hers.

"To us," he said.

"Forever," she added and they drank the toast.

The dinner was warm and romantic. Lisa left only once to check her patients, who were sound asleep. She had already done her paper work, so the rest of the dinner was uninterrupted.

"Very quiet restaurant," Eric said, pouring the last of the wine into their glasses.

"It was delicious." Lisa reached across the table and took Eric's hand.

"Good music, too," he teased, glancing at the transistor radio he had brought. "A little too much static maybe."

Lisa pushed out of her chair and walked over to the window.

"Look," she cried. "It's snowing."

The snow flickered silver in the lights from the windows of the hospital. Eric walked up behind her and put his arms around her waist.

Lisa turned and, standing on her toes, kissed him deeply. Eric pulled her tightly against him, lifting her off her feet. He held her in the air against his chest with one arm while the other reached down to stroke her. He pulled her tight to his hips.

"I don't think we . . ."

"No one's here. Who cares? We should. Just once. To say good-bye to this place."

"But I'm on duty."

"So do your duty. We're almost married, you know."

"None too soon, I think."

Eric let go of her.

"What do you mean?"

"I'm not positive yet, but I . . . I think I'm . . ."

"You're what?"

"Pregnant."

She was looking up at him apprehensively, but when she saw him grin, she smiled.

"That's wonderful," he said.

Eric carried her to the sofa and laid her down gently.

"But I—"

He stopped her with a kiss, as his hand unbuttoned her uniform.

"Eric, I don't—"

He kissed her again, hard, and his hand reached under the thin white material that covered her thighs.

"Oh Eric," she said. "I'm glad you're happy about it."

They made love slowly and it was gentle and good. They rested in each other's arms for a long time afterward, then Lisa sat up.

"We'd better get dressed." She glanced at her watch. "My God, it's been over an hour."

Eric grinned lazily and made no move to get up.

"Think you're irresistible, huh?" Lisa asked him playfully.

"To you. That's all that matters."

She leaned down and brushed his lips lightly with her own, then began to dress. He sat up and reached for his pants and shirt.

"It stopped snowing," she said, looking over at the window.

"Good. It's still too early for snow. I'm not ready for that yet. That's the trouble with living up in the mountains. Should be another month before it snows."

Eric tucked his shirt in and zipped up his pants. Lisa tied her white shoes quickly, then walked over to the window. Eric heard her gasp before she cried out to him.

"Eric," she cried. "Look!"

He dashed to the window. Black clouds of smoke were rising from the first-floor windows and the basement gratings. For a moment he froze in horror.

"The patients," she said, grabbing Eric's arm. All her old fears came tearing back through her mind.

"Let's see how bad it is first," he said. He was trying to be calm and think.

"I'll call the fire department," Lisa said.

"They should have gotten an alarm on it already."

Eric grabbed Lisa's hand as they rushed to the door. Suddenly an explosion ripped through the building, the shock throwing them against the wall. Smoke came steaming out through a crack in the floor of the lounge.

"Eric!" He grabbed her around the waist and opened the door.

There was another explosion and a thin gray smoke began to fill the hall.

"Come on. Quick," Eric ordered.

Lisa was pulling Eric back away from the stairs to the rooms where the patients were.

"We've got to get them out," she cried.

"We've got to see where, first. I'll check the stairs."

Eric had already seen smoke pouring out from the elevator doors and knew they couldn't get out that way. Lisa watched him run to the stairs. He opened the door quickly and started down. Then there was another explosion. Smoke puffed up thick and black through the stairway door.

"*Eric!*" Lisa screamed and ran toward the door.

He slammed the door back as he fell into the hall. His face was blackened by the smoke and he was coughing badly.

Lisa knelt and pulled him up into her arms.

"Smoke's too thick. Can't get down." Eric tried to stand up but fell back against Lisa's chest.

"Did you hear them?"

"Hear who?" Lisa asked.

"The screaming. It was awful."

"I didn't hear any screaming," she said.

Eric shook his head hard.

"Call the fire department," he said. "They should

have been here already. The alarm must not have gone off."

Lisa ran to the desk and picked up the phone, but there was no dial tone.

"It's dead," she yelled, running back. Eric pushed himself up against the wall, his eyes wide and horrified. His head was spinning and then he heard the strange, distant screams again.

"Eric?"

Lisa shook his arm.

"We'll have to get the patients on this floor up onto the roof. I don't know what we can do about the others. There's no way down," Eric said, finally. "I think we can still make it up the stairs."

Lisa helped the elderly patients out of their rooms as quickly as possible. Two of them could walk and were already up because of the explosions, but Lisa had to find a wheelchair for the third.

"Are you all right?" she asked Eric, having assembled the patients by the stairs. Eric was still wobbly from the explosion on the stairs. He took a few quick breaths to help himself think straight.

"Yeah," he lied. "Let's go."

Lisa led the way and two patients followed. Eric pulled the third up the stairs on the wheelchair.

"Stay low, below the smoke," Eric yelled. "Crawl up if you have to."

He picked up the withered old man and caught up to the others at the top of the stairs.

"It's locked," Lisa yelled, pulling frantically at the door to the roof.

"I'll get something to open it."

Eric put the old man on the stairs and stumbled back down to the third floor. The smoke was getting thicker across the ceiling and now flames shot out of the elevator shaft.

Eric broke the glass to reach the fire extinguisher and hurried back up the stairs. He felt dizzy and fought for air, but he forced himself to keep going.

"Out of the way," he ordered.

He smashed the extinguisher against the bolt on the door. It cracked. The two women were screaming now. He smashed it again and the door flew open. Lisa helped the two patients out onto the roof and Eric went down to carry up the third.

"Hurry, Eric!"

A blast of hot air rushed up the stairs. Eric held the old man close to his chest and raced through the door. He put him down by the edge of the roof where Lisa had taken the others.

"God," he muttered, feeling the back of his head. The hair was singed badly and his scalp was tender. Part of the back of his shirt was burned and stuck to his skin. Then he heard the screaming again. He ran back to the stairs. Eric could hear his name being called over and over again.

"What are you doing?" Lisa asked frantically.

"I've got to go back," he cried. "They're screaming for me."

"Who?" Lisa cried. Eric was frightening her as much as the fire now. She grabbed his shirt to keep him from leaving.

Then they heard the fire engines blaring up the drive.

"They're coming," Lisa yelled, pointing.

Eric dashed to the edge of the roof and waved at them as they parked the first truck. The driver saw him and backed up the ladder truck close to the building. The ladder extended quickly and stuck up over the edge of the roof beside them.

"We've got three patients up here," Eric screamed. "The rest are still inside."

Lisa huddled the old people close together behind the short wall at the edge of the building to keep them out of the wind. It was cold and the wind seemed to circle down, blowing hard against them. Behind them, part of the roof exploded and bricks hurled out into the night. Lisa pushed the patients even closer together.

Then a fireman climbed up the ladder and Eric helped him strap the old woman, the strongest of the three, onto his back. As he went down, another fireman came up, swung around under the ladder to let the first pass with the woman, then scurried up to the roof. Eric helped strap the two other patients onto the backs of the two fireman.

"Lisa. It's our turn. Can you make it? Do you need help?"

"I can make it," she said. She climbed out onto the ladder above another waiting fireman and started down. Eric went after her.

They had climbed down almost to the first floor when Eric felt the dizziness again. His head began to spin and, looking at the hospital, the wall began pulling, sucking at him like a whirlpool. He saw faces looking at him through the windows, screaming, calling his name, beckoning him. Eric wrapped his arms through the ladder just before his feet slipped off the rungs.

"Eric!" Lisa's cry pierced the night. She scrambled back up and helped him fit his feet back onto the ladder. "Hurry. We're almost down."

"I can't," he said. "I can't leave them."

"Please, Eric. Try." Lisa held his ankles and pulled, making him step down another rung.

They had almost reached the ground when another explosion shook the building. It blew out the wall above Lisa, blasting Eric high into the air.

Lisa was knocked from the ladder, but the firemen below were able to save her. Eric was killed instantly.

EPILOGUE

Lisa Mitchell left Hapsburg the day after Eric's funeral. She took a nursing job in Doylestown, Pennsylvania. Eight and a half months later, she gave birth to a son, Samuel Mitchell. In the next twenty-two years, she never married. Neither did she socialize much with anyone in Doylestown. Instead, she saved her money and sent Samuel to a good private prep school, then to Duke University, where he earned a master's degree in child psychology.

After he graduated, Lisa Mitchell died. The family doctor told Sam that it seemed like "she just gave up." Sam did not question what he meant. In the last few years, he had noticed more and more that his mother dwelled in her own little dream world, a world from deep in her past. Even when Sam asked about it, she would not discuss it with him. In all other things, Sam had always gotten his way with her, but not in that. He did not even know his father's name, only that he had died before Sam was born. The rest of Lisa's past remained a mystery which now he would never solve.

Samuel Mitchell was thinking about that as he drove down out of the Pennsylvania mountains into a beautiful valley on a clear, crisp, colorful fall afternoon. He had been offered an assistant director's job at an orphanage that was just about to open. It was exactly what Sam had been hoping for and, as he drove through the small, clean town with the towering oaks along its streets, Sam knew he wanted to live there. It seemed like a place he could call home.

He drove up a small hill after passing the shopping mall and the park, and pulled up in front of the orphanage. It was a four-story, red-brick building that stood proudly on the crest of the hill, backed by mountains and surrounded by sloping green lawns. There was still scaffolding on both side walls.

A bent old man with a three-day growth on his chin hobbled down from the building and stood in Sam's path.

"What do you want here?" the old man asked, cocking his head to carefully inspect the intruder.

"I came about the assistant director's job. My name's Sam Mitchell."

"I'm Mr. Gibbs."

They shook hands. The old man kept eyeing him suspiciously.

"You look familiar. Can't seem to place you, though," Mr. Gibbs said.

"I've never been to . . . ah . . ." Sam snapped his fingers, trying to remember.

"Hapsburg," Mr. Gibbs filled in.

"Right. Never been here before. I doubt you know me."

"Probably right," Gibbs agreed, pushing his way back toward the leaf pile he had been raking under the scaffolding.

Sam went into the building, found the director whom he liked instantly, and in twenty minutes had agreed to take the job. On his way back to the parking lot, he saw Mr. Gibbs still raking leaves. The old man waved him over and Sam jogged up to him.

"Get the job?"

Sam nodded, smiling, as he leaned his shoulder on the scaffolding.

"I start tomorrow."

"People need to work. It's good for the heart. Got me into my eighty-seventh year."

Sam grinned and turned to leave when the third-story scaffolding above him shook. A metal crossbar snapped.

"Look out!" Mr. Gibbs yelled.

Sam leaped to his left. The metal bar stuck six inches into the ground like a sharpened spike, only inches from Sam's feet.

"That was close," said Mr. Gibbs.

"Sure was. Bad sign, huh?"

Samuel Mitchell smiled and waved it off, then walked briskly back to the parking lot. Mr. Gibbs watched the tall, thin, dark-eyed man get into his car, then glanced back at the jutting metal bar.

Suddenly he realized who the young man reminded him of. He quickly hailed Sam's car.

"What was your mother's name?" he yelled from up the hill.

Eric looked at him oddly.

"Mitchell. Lisa Mitchell. Why? Did you know her?"

The old man shook his head. Sam watched him hobble away and, assuming he didn't, drove off.

Mr. Gibbs stared up at the big red-brick building for a long time afterward, then glanced down at his rake.

"Couldn't be," he mumbled. He peered at the building again. The windows seemed like a hundred eyes, staring back at him.

"Ah, hell." He threw down his rake and walked off the job for good.

When the head maintenance man called and asked why he quit, Mr. Gibbs just mumbled something about bad blood and hung up.